E.R. PUN:
THE HOUSE OF GODWINSSON

ERNEST ROBERTSON PUNSHON was born in London in 1872.

At the age of fourteen he started life in an office. His employers soon informed him that he would never make a really satisfactory clerk, and he, agreeing, spent the next few years wandering about Canada and the United States, endeavouring without great success to earn a living in any occupation that offered. Returning home by way of working a passage on a cattle boat, he began to write. He contributed to many magazines and periodicals, wrote plays, and published nearly fifty novels, among which his detective stories proved the most popular and enduring.

He died in 1956.

The Bobby Owen Mysteries

E.R. PUNSHON

THE HOUSE OF GODWINSSON

With an introduction
by Curtis Evans

DEAN STREET PRESS

Published by Dean Street Press 2016

Copyright © 1948 E.R. Punshon

Introduction copyright © 2016 Curtis Evans

Published by licence, issued under the
UK Orphan Works Licensing Scheme.

First published in 1948 by Victor Gollancz

Cover by DSP

ISBN 978 1 911413 49 3

www.deanstreetpress.co.uk

INTRODUCTION

IN 1933 CRIME WRITER and critical authority Dorothy L. Sayers gave a terrific boost to E.R. Punshon's mystery writing career with her "What is distinction?" *Sunday Times* review of *Information Received*, Punshon's first Bobby Owen detective novel. From the glowing review Victor Gollancz, Punshon's English publisher, copiously extracted Sayers's brightly affirmative words, emblazoning them on the covers of Punshon mysteries for more than two decades, right up until the author's death in 1956. That Sayers's publicly expressed admiration for the detective fiction of E.R. Punshon, a fellow member of the Detection Club, was both genuinely felt and of considerable duration is indicated by a private letter she wrote Punshon over fifteen years later, on 6 January 1949, in which she noted that she was enjoying reading the author's 25th and latest Bobby Owen mystery, *The House of Godwinsson* (1948). Sayers lauded a particular exchange in the novel with clear feminist implication that took place between Bobby Owen and his wife Olive, resoundingly declaring that this passage "should be written in letters of gold on tablets of iron and circulated to the entire male population of this country":

> Olive wasn't listening. She said:
> "That's the week's meat ration I got to-day. Will you have it all now, or shall we save some for to-morrow?"
> "Let us eat to-day and be merry," Bobby answered, "for to-morrow there may be fish."
> "Dreamer," said Olive.
> "Well, anyhow," Bobby said, "to-day is here and now, and let to-morrow look after itself."
> So he spoke, but what he really meant in his carefree, masculine way was that not itself but the woman should look after it. However, on second thoughts he left enough of the dish for the next day.

Over the course of the Bobby Owen series the police detective's spouse, the former Olive Farrar, had gone from being a chic career woman (*Suspects–Nine*, 1939) and no less than a political revolutionary (*Dictator's Way*, 1938) to a housewife intensely preoccupied, as British housewives in the 1940s admittedly had ample reason to be, with matters of domestic help and goods rationing. Although during the war years Olive occasionally participated more actively in Bobby's cases (*Diabolic Candelabra*, 1942), even to the point of obtaining valuable information (*Secrets Can't Be Kept*, 1944) and putting her own life at risk (*Night's Cloak*, 1944), by the late 1940s she seems much more to have withdrawn within the confines of her own household. Though some critics over the years have expressed disappointment with this development, it was one which reflected contemporary trends not only in crime fiction but in the real world, as women who had patriotically taken jobs in service of their country during the war were urged after the end of the conflict to leave the public sphere to marry and make families. (In this latter respect Olive diverged from cultural expectations, for she and Bobby, like Punshon and his wife Sarah, would never have any children during the recorded years of their marriage.) Yet Olive continued to serve as Bobby's most important confidant concerning the course of his criminal investigations, and often Punshon would spice these exchanges between the two spouses, as in *The House of Godwinsson*, with the sort of feminist commentary that had so appealed to Dorothy L. Sayers when she was reading the novel. (Given her strong religious faith, Sayers doubtlessly also noted that Bobby's cavalier comments to Olive--"Let us eat to-day and be merry, for to-morrow there may be fish" and "To-day is here and now, and let to-morrow look after itself"--paraphrased passages from the Bible.) By this time Olive may be very much a policeman's wife, but she remains a more interesting policeman's wife than earlier incarnations of such women, like Emily French, bland helpmate to Freeman Wills Crofts's archetypal dauntless striver, Inspector French.

The House of Godwinsson reflects another important contemporary social development in the United Kingdom in its focus on the rise of postwar crime and violence which so concerned the British public at the time. In Punshon's immediately previous Bobby Owen detective novel, *Music Tells All* (1948), the author had included in the plot of what was in most ways a classic village mystery a smash-and-grab gang of jewelry shop robbers. In *Godwinsson* Punshon went several steps farther, producing a suspenseful London crime story wherein the violent criminal activities of urban toughs and outright gangsters take center stage (though the murder puzzle element demanded by fans of classic crime fiction is retained). More realistic portrayal of crime was a preoccupation in both books and films of this time, both in the United States, where the hard-boiled, noir and police procedural subgenres had gained great popularity, and in the United Kingdom, where gang activity was being portrayed not only on the screen in such groundbreaking acclaimed cinema as *Brighton Rock* (1947) and *Night and the City* (1950), but in novels by Punshon's own Detection Club colleagues, notable examples of the latter being Michael Gilbert's *They Never Looked Inside* (1947) and *Fear to Tread* (1953), Henry Wade's *Be Kind to the Killer* (1952) and, no doubt most familiar to modern readers, Margery Allingham's much lauded *The Tiger in the Smoke* (1952).

The greater level of criminal carnage in *The House of Godwinsson*--book reviewer and future poet laureate John Betjeman praised the novel's "tense horror"—quickly becomes apparent to the reader. During the first few chapters of *Godwinsson* we see Bobby examining the gunned-down corpse of a "spiv" (British slang for fast talking, flashily dressed petty criminals of the day who illicitly dealt in rationed goods on the black market), then getting violently set upon, along with a strapping police constable, by a trio of murderous hoodlums led by the notorious knifeman Cyrus "Cy" King. When Divisional Detective Inspector Ulyett, whom Punshon devotees may recall from *Mystery of Mr. Jessop* (1937), shows up on the scene, classically shouting "Now, then; what's all this about?", he is promptly stunned by a hurled brick and falls back bleeding, "into the arms of his attendant sergeant." Later, after Bobby has emerged, seemingly rather a tough bloke indeed, from the melee with Cy King and his thuggish henchmen, he confides to Ulyett, "it was a good clean turn-up on both sides while it lasted. ... I don't think I've ever known better," which produces this ironic exchange:

"Sounds," grunted the Superintendent—"sounds as if you rather enjoyed it."

Bobby looked alarmed.

"For the lord's sake," he exclaimed, "don't let my wife hear you say that, or I shall never hear the last of it—never."

E. R. Punshon, who for part of the 1890s had lived a vagabond life in the still frontier-like North American West and had published a novel, *Old Fighting Days* (1921), about bare knuckle brawling in Georgian England, handles the roughhousing sections of *Godwinsson* with an aplomb that American pulp fiction writers might have envied; yet he does not neglect the novel's fine formal puzzle, which classically involves a missing London socialite of dubious morals, a duchess's priceless lost jewels and an elite family, the Godwinssons, of most distinguished lineage. (The family traditionally claims descent from Earl Godwin, father of King Harold, famously slain in 1066 at the Battle of Hastings, and considers the royal descendants of William the Conqueror mere upstarts.) Between plots and counterplots by ancient aristocrats and modern-day gangsters, Bobby has his hands full in *The House of Godwinsson*, much to the reader's enjoyment.

Curtis Evans

CHAPTER I

IDENTIFICATION PARADE

BOBBY OWEN stood for a time in silence, looking down thoughtfully at the dead man's face. A small, insignificant face, lacking even that touch of repose and dignity which death, even violent death, so often gives, and one that Bobby had never seen before. Of that at least he was sure.

"Age about forty or a little under," said the doctor. Then he added: "Well nourished. Took care of himself. First-class condition. Not like most of those we get about here. Hard muscles and all that."

The speaker was the house physician in this small London hospital in whose mortuary they were standing. On hearing of Bobby's arrival, and because he was still young and believed that the life of a highly placed official at Scotland Yard must be full of the colour and variety so sadly lacking, in his opinion, in that of a house physician, he had himself conducted Bobby to the mortuary, instead of leaving it to the attendant. He had been hoping to hear strange tales of crime and mystery, but he had not found Bobby very responsive. In fact, he had already classified Bobby as a rather dull, routine-ridden official. Nearly as much so, he considered, as his own seniors at the hospital.

In happy ignorance of this unfavourable verdict, Bobby was still staring at the quiet, dead face, wondering what answer those silent lips would have given to the questions that could never now be asked. A typical 'little man', to all appearance, insignificant and ordinary, one of those whom cartoonists to-day delight to depict, complete with bowler hat, umbrella, dispatch-case, for the gratification and delight of other 'little men', who do not so see themselves, since they are so well aware—and rightly—of their own immense significance. But about this man there was nothing in his outward appearance to distinguish him from any of those many millions who go daily to and fro about their business in the great cities of the world.

Yet there had been found in his pockets a careful, accurate, and detailed plan, correct to the last item, showing even the position of each piece of furniture, of Bobby's own flat in a West-End

London square, now less fashionable than once it had been. This flat had recently been obtained for him under what is at present called 'top priority' when his tenancy of the country cottage where he and Olive, his wife, had hoped to settle down had been terminated by untoward circumstances. Olive still at times lamented that lost country garden from which she had hoped to obtain fruit galore—rare and refreshing fruit, as fruit is in very truth in these days. Bobby's own regrets, however, were less poignant. He had found reason to fear that he suffered from a weak back, one that much bending, as for instance, when planting out cabbages, might injure permanently. Olive had been less sympathetic than good, kind wives should be, nor had her suggestion of a mustard plaster and plenty of them been received with any favour. But she admitted that a flat in town had its advantages, and of course to obtain possession of one did mark them out as among fortune's favourites. Fallen human nature always finds it pleasant to be conducted to the head of the queue.

It was the report of the discovery of this plan that had made Bobby leave his work at Scotland Yard—and there was plenty of it, for a fresh crime wave was in full vigour, with a new, and important jewel robbery reported almost every week—to see if he could identify the dead man in whose possession the plan had been found. He had already seen and examined it, and he was puzzled. Great trouble and much care and thought must have been involved in its preparation. But generally speaking plans of that sort are prepared only when there is some specially valuable loot in sight—such as for example the jewels of the Duchess of Wharton, whose famous diamonds and rubies had recently vanished without trace. Nor had either duke or duchess been slow in expressing their opinion of a police unable either to prevent such a robbery or recover the lost jewellery. Yet very certainly in Bobby's flat there was nothing of any outstanding value. Nothing to tempt the experts who had given the Wharton duke and duchess such a display of skill in planning and knowledge of jewellery, even though that demonstration had been received with small gratitude.

It might just possibly be bravado, Bobby supposed. The idea of burgling the home of a prominent Scotland Yard man might have been found amusing. It might have seemed a bit of fun. But crime is too serious a business for the idea of fun to enter into it. Too healthy an idea, perhaps, for the twisted mind of the criminal. Or again the idea might have been to discredit Bobby, whose appointment to the Yard was comparatively recent. But that seemed too far-fetched to be taken seriously. Or defiance? A challenge? But who could associate defiance or bravado with that insignificant, commonplace looking little man to whom even death had failed so entirely to lend dignity or meaning?

There had been nothing else on the body of much interest. An identity card made out in the name of Joseph Parsons and already known to have been lost by the genuine Mr Parsons some time previously, a small sum in notes and change—about £10 in all—keys, a pen-knife, and so on. Some of these things had been sent to experts for further examination. It had been noticed, too, that while the outer clothing was old, shabby, and as inconspicuous as its wearer, the under-garments were new and of fine quality, silk and wool; most certainly not what might have been expected.

Nothing, however, to give any clue to identity. No laundry marks, for example. A hanger-on of the underworld, Bobby supposed, a dabbler on the fringe of criminality. A 'spiv', to use the new word momentarily popular. Possibly this time one who had dabbled a little too deeply and had paid the penalty. It might be that his possession of a plan so clearly the work of an expert hand meant that he had been acting as a messenger between the expert and the expert's employer, and had tried to double-cross one or other.

The house physician was growing a trifle bored by Bobby's silence. He said now:

"Common little East-End type, except that he took care of himself. Most of them are riddled through and through with drink and disease. This chap had good teeth, even. Cleaned them, evidently. Quite rare."

"He never recovered consciousness, did he?" Bobby asked.

"No. Whoever shot him knew where to put the bullet. Passed out within ten minutes of admittance. Only thing was that while the nurse was trying to dress his wound he opened his eyes and said: 'Don't do that, dad,' and next moment he was dead. Like that. Unusual. I mean dying chaps do sometimes talk about their mothers, call the nurse 'mum'—that sort of thing. But not about their fathers. I expect he was an orphan and his dad brought him up—and gave him a good thrashing at times. Eh?"

Obviously the house physician was a trifle pleased with this exercise in deduction. He looked at Bobby to see what the Scotland Yard man thought of it. Bobby said very likely that was how it was. The house physician glanced at his wrist watch and said he must be off. Matron would be on his track if he didn't look out. He departed accordingly, confiding to the sister who had been searching for him everywhere that he didn't think much of the Scotland Yard johnny, who didn't seem to have anything to say for himself. Nor had he been gone more than a minute or two, and Bobby was on the point of following his example, when the door opened and there appeared the mortuary attendant, accompanied by a big, burly man of middle age.

"Beg pardon, sir. I didn't know any one was here," the attendant said. "Gentleman for identification," he explained.

Bobby was looking at the attendant's companion.

"Stokes, isn't it?" Bobby said. "Tim Stokes, I think?"

"That's right, Mr Owen," the other answered, looking a little uncomfortable.

For he and Bobby knew each other well. One of the very first duties Bobby had been called upon to perform after his acceptance of the Scotland Yard appointment had been to sit on a disciplinary board before which had appeared Mr Stokes, then a station sergeant in the double X division. Sergeant Stokes had clearly been guilty of gross neglect of duty; but there was little to substantiate the more serious suspicion that for some time he had been working with a criminal gang, giving them information of police procedure and plans. This he had strenuously denied, and all that could be done was to dismiss him from the Force for his proved negligence. Since then little had been heard of him, but Bobby had seen one report to the effect that ex-Sergeant Stokes had been noticed on several occasions loitering near the Canon Square car park, whence rather too many cars had vanished, even though nearly all had been quickly recovered. It had almost begun to seem that this car park was being made use of as a handy spot where to find a car when any rogue happened to have need of one. Finally the car attendant had been changed, and as a result cars appeared now to be more inclined to stay put. Nothing to implicate Mr Stokes, though.

The attendant drew back the sheet Bobby had replaced to cover the dead man's face. Stokes said slowly:

"That's him right enough. Poor old Joey. Never thought he would end up that way."

"Known him long?" Bobby asked.

Still speaking slowly, even too slowly, Stokes answered:

"I don't know as you could rightly call it knowing him. I used to see him at 'The Green Dragon'. That's the house I use pretty regular, and so did he. We got chatting. About the dogs generally. He was interested, and so was I. He knew a lot. Tipped me off on a good thing more than once. That's all."

"I think not," Bobby said, and Stokes looked hurt. Bobby went on: "Any idea who did this? Or why?"

"I wish I had," Stokes answered; and this time not slowly at all but with an emphasis and vigour that at least sounded genuine, sounded, indeed, as if inspired by real feeling. "Joey was always straight with you, always ready to do you a good turn." He looked again at Bobby and spoke with the same emphasis as before: "If I knew anything to help you spot who did him in, I would tell you quick as you like. And so would others, too. One of the best. But I don't, Mr Owen, sir, and that's gospel."

Bobby was not sure whether to believe this or not. Stokes seemed really moved. But, then, that made it all the more difficult to believe that his acquaintance with the dead man had been as casual as he pretended. Strange, too, that he had heard so quickly of what had happened and come so promptly, to identify the victim. But for the accident of Bobby's presence, would that identification have been made, or would Stokes have slipped away, satisfying himself, but saying nothing? Stokes was speaking again. He said:

"It's a bad business. I don't hold with murder. So I don't. You can believe me, Mr Owen. If I get to know anything, I'll pass it on O.K." Again there seemed real feeling in his voice. "Poor old Joe," he said once more.

"If you feel like that," Bobby asked quietly, "why not tell us all you really know?"

"So I have," Stokes asserted, and, as if to avoid saying more went to help the attendant rearrange the sheet covering the dead man. "Narrow squeak that first time," he remarked. "Must have meant it all right to shoot again. Wonder why any one had it in for him so bad as that?"

"How do you mean—narrow squeak the first time?" Bobby asked.

"Well, it looks like it, don't it?" Stokes said, and pointed to a small abrasion just above the top of the left ear where certainly, now it was pointed out, it seemed as if a bullet had grazed the head.

Bobby stooped to look, frowning and puzzled. When he looked up again Stokes had slipped away. The attendant said:

"If you ask me, guv., that bloke knows more'n he wants to say."

Bobby nodded an absent-minded agreement and departed. He did not feel over-confident that the help Stokes promised would ever be received. The contrary, perhaps. But he decided that he would 'phone the D.D.I.—the Divisional Detective Inspector—and suggest that Mr Stokes should be kept under observation.

CHAPTER II
MISFITS

An odd, somewhat disturbing lack of conformity seemed to be shown in all this, or so Bobby thought in a worried way as he went slowly back to his waiting car. Too much that didn't fit, he thought. That odd difference between the under and the outer clothing of the dead man, for example. A difference, too, between his physical condition and that usually found in the spiv: the 'living-by-your-wits' type to which he seemed to belong. And why did Stokes seem so genuinely moved by the death of a man whom yet he claimed to be no more than a public-house acquaintance, and why had he come so quickly to identify him? How, indeed, had he come to hear so soon? Not all the morning papers had even troubled to report the death of an unknown man in the East End.

Troubled by such thoughts, Bobby drove to the nearest police station, and there obtained the address where the murder had been committed.

"Angel Alley, cul de sac, off Emmett Street," the station sergeant told him. "Tough district, sir. They copped it about there pretty bad in the first blitz. Nos. 5 and 6 at the top aren't there any more. Blast did them in. No. 4 is unoccupied. Dangerous condition. No. 3 the same. No. 2 is let off to three families—all Irish, and they all take lodgers. Casual labourers mostly. Not a steady job to the whole boiling. Rowdy on a Saturday night and fight among themselves, but that's all. We don't interfere more than we can help, and they never lodge complaints. They would call that 'snooping' or 'in-forming'. No. 1 is a low-class fancy house, let off in single rooms to women and no questions asked. We get complaints sometimes, but how can you prove that a drunken sailor didn't lose his wallet or have his watch stolen somewhere else? Besides, they generally know better than to bring a charge. If they do, they are liable to get a brick heaved at them from round the corner, or something worse for that matter. The women all have their bullies."

Bobby knew that well enough. It is an unhappy feature of all big ports, though one that is diminishing with the improved status and pay of the merchant seaman. Bobby said he thought he would go and have a look for himself. He couldn't understand that business of the plan of his flat found in the dead man's possession. And would the station sergeant inform Divisional Detective Inspector Ulyett that ex-Sergeant Stokes had identified the dead man, but claimed he had known him merely as a casual public-house acquaintance with whom his only tie had been a common interest in greyhound racing.

"Smells a bit, sir, don't you think?" commented the station sergeant. "Sticks out a mile there's more to it than that."

Bobby agreed. He said he wondered if Mr Ulyett would think it as well to keep an eye on Stokes, or even take a statement from him. Having dropped this gentle and tactful hint he saw the station sergeant understood, Bobby departed. It was in fact fairly well understood in the Force that Ulyett, though an energetic, trustworthy officer of long and meritorious service, was a trifle lacking in imagination and initiative. Probably it was to the scarcity of suitable candidates during the war that he owed his promotion to the important post he now held.

From here Bobby drove to Angel Alley, or rather to the Canon Square car park. There he left his car, for he thought it better not to go in it to Angel Alley, where private cars were not often seen and where indeed it might receive undesirable attentions if left standing too long. He completed the journey on foot, and found Angel Alley to be a long, narrow court with four small three-story houses on one side and the tall blank wall of a warehouse on the other. The farther end, where two more houses had once stood, closing it, was now open to a waste of ruin and rubble that stretched to a main thoroughfare behind, parallel with Emmett Street.

From the health point of view this was a considerable improvement, since the wind could now blow freely down the narrow court, but Bobby could not help reflecting that it was no longer a 'cul de sac', since access was easy from the main thoroughfare behind, across the still-uncleared mass of rubble and ruin that once had been occupied by two or three streets of small and humble homes. Convenient, Bobby reflected, for those who might wish to come and go unnoticed. Possibly examination might show signs of any such regular use. Not very likely, though, and then it was sure to be a favourite playground for children, who would probably leave their own tracks and destroy those of others. A point to keep in mind.

At first sight, Nos. 3 and 4 looked no more damaged than did Nos. 1 and 2, where occupation was apparently still permitted by the authorities. True, the windows of these latter houses had been repaired, though with glass through which vision was almost impossible, and No. 2 had been provided with a new door, while the windows of Nos. 3 and 4 were still gaping and shattered and their doors still hung drunkenly on broken hinges. But a glance within No. 3 showed no stairs standing, and a back wall sagging so dangerously that only beams shoring it up saved it from collapse. No. 4 was in slightly better condition. The stairs at any rate were still there and could still be used.

But now it began to occur to Bobby that the whole place was oddly silent and deserted. Even in Emmett Street, from which Angel Alley opened, there had not been many people about, and here there was no one. He would have expected to find gossiping groups on each doorstep, loiterers standing staring at 'the scene of the crime', excited children running about, a general air of bustle and interest in so sensational an event as murder breaking in unexpectedly on the ordinary routine of life. Yet he might have come to an uninhabited place, so still, so silent it was—not even an onlooker at a window, no one anywhere visible. Curious, he thought, but perhaps they had all adjourned to the public-house at the corner, opposite the warehouse. Or the light rain now beginning to fall might account for it. Indeed, when he looked round he saw a head poked out from the door of the public-house and turned his way. It was withdrawn swiftly. Bobby remained with an impression that there had been a kind of uneasy expectation about that brief appearance, an excitement or fear over something that it was thought might be about to happen.

Telling himself it would be as well to be on the alert, Bobby entered No. 4. A uniformed policeman at the head of the stairs got to his feet and peered down at him. Evidently the man had been sitting on the top stair, and Bobby thought he detected a smell of tobacco in the air. Very wrong, of course, for this was a tour of duty, and on duty smoking is strictly forbidden, especially so where Mr Ulyett reigned, for he was a strict disciplinarian. But Bobby belonged to that class of senior official who know well when it is best not to know. He gave his name, and the constable said he knew Mr Owen, he had attended one or two of Mr. Owen's lectures—those being given to new recruits and men rejoining after long years of war service. So Bobby said he hoped they had been found helpful and interesting, and went on to remark that it all seemed very quiet and deserted outside. No one about, no staring and gaping spectators; he didn't understand it. The constable, who had given his name as Dawson, said in a worried voice that he didn't understand it either. And he didn't much like it.

"There was plenty hanging about at first," he said, "same as always when it's murder, and then they all began to slip away till there was no one left. It was same as if they had got the word to go and knew it was best to do as told."

"Did you notice any one giving orders or directing in any way?" Bobby asked.

"No, sir, nothing like that. They just began to slip off one by one till no one was left. Even the children were quiet and went off all silent like. It seemed unnatural, somehow."

Bobby rubbed hard the end of his nose, a gesture indicating extreme perplexity and some uneasiness. He thought it very unnatural indeed. Dawson was plainly worried, and Bobby was inclined to think he had reason.

"The calm before the storm," said Dawson unexpectedly.

"Yes, but what storm?" Bobby asked, and to that Dawson had no answer. Nor Bobby either, for that matter.

"There can't be anything else in the house, can there?" Bobby asked. "I take it it's been searched?"

"Well, sir," Dawson answered, "I don't know as you can call it searched. Dabs took, of course, and photos and all that before the body was moved, and a general look round to make sure there was nobody hiding and for the murder weapon. Mr Ulyett is coming himself for another look as soon as he can, but you know yourself, sir, how busy he is with other cases and about the Duchess of Wharton's jewellery being heard of in these parts."

Bobby nodded. He was inclined to suspect that Ulyett would think it more important to trace the Wharton jewellery, if possible, than to find the murderers of an unknown man who was probably one of a gang himself, no loss to the community, and certainly without the power the Whartons possessed to make themselves a nuisance to an overworked and worried D.D.I.

"Nothing else you've noticed?" Bobby asked.

"No, sir," Dawson answered. "Nothing—except ..."

"Yes. Well?" Bobby encouraged him when he hesitated.

"Except just before they all slipped off the way I said, there was a young lady came. I was on the front door then, and I noticed her because of her being different—a real lady, sir; you could see at once. A sort of a way with her. You couldn't miss it and how she looked out of place, and yet as if she were quite at home, too, because of being so sure of herself."

"The governing-class touch," Bobby commented with a faint smile—for now that is a trifle out of date—but keenly interested all the same, for what was a girl like that doing in Angel Alley in the East End of London? "Did she speak to you?" he asked.

"No, sir. When I saw her first she was talking to one of the women, and then she went away. I asked if they knew the young lady. I thought it might be some one from the church. They all said they had never seen her before and she was only asking what had happened because of the way every one was standing about and staring. When they said a man called Joey Parsons had been murdered at No. 4 she looked very upset and went off in a great hurry. 'Looked like death, they said."

"Pity you didn't get her name and address," Bobby remarked. "It looks as if she knew something and ought to be questioned. Oh, I'm not blaming you, Dawson," he added. "You did very well to notice her at all. But we must try to get hold of her if we can. She may turn up again somewhere, I suppose. There's reason to think these jewel-thieves get inside information, and it may come from some society hanger-on—a woman, possibly. Can you describe her?"

"Smart young lady," Dawson answered at once and very much as if she had made an admiring impression on him. "She had on a check coat and skirt, one of those scarf things for a hat and a swell handbag it's a wonder they let her get away with. It was her class air did it, most like. They didn't dare."

"More likely because she seemed to know something about Mr Joseph Parsons," Bobby commented. "They may have guessed she was one of the gang. Or known she was, for that matter. What about her looks?"

"Well, sir, I never saw her face plain, only just for a moment, and what I noticed mostly was how strange and startled she stared. On the small side, though—about five foot one or two. Small face, dark complexion, brunette type. I remember her nose, somehow; it seemed to stick out in a way. I'm afraid that's all I can say, sir. I only had just a glimpse. I'd know her again all right, though. She's the sort you remember. I'm sorry I can't say more, sir."

"Oh, that's quite good," Bobby told him. "Quite as much as any one could expect. We might get more from the women she spoke to."

But Dawson shook his head and spoke with emphasis.

"No, sir," he declared. "I know that Irish lot, and you won't ever get them to help police. Sort of principle with them not to."

"Agin the Government and all its works, I suppose," agreed Bobby. "Oh, well, Mr Ulyett will know how to carry on."

"Yes, sir. I heard him saying we should have to take statements from them all as soon as he could get down to it. Most likely their line will be that they don't know a thing about anything. They've said already they didn't know there was any one using this house in any way. They never saw any one going in or out, and access must have been gained across the open bombed area at the back." He added hesitatingly: "It did just cross my mind it might be the young gentleman in Emmett Street had something to do with this young lady."

"What young gentleman was that?" Bobby asked. "Does Mr Ulyett know?"

"Yes, sir. Bert Barlow was on this beat yesterday afternoon, and he reported it when he heard about the murder. But Mr Ulyett said there wasn't enough to go on and nothing to show any connection, seeing it was early afternoon and the murder was after dark, the doctor said."

"What was the report? Do you know?"

"Barlow said he noticed the young man because he didn't look as if he belonged to these parts—a real gentleman, he looked. Barlow said he seemed to be looking around as if he wasn't sure of his way, and Barlow rather expected to be asked. But instead the young gent, crossed to the other side of the street in a bit of a hurry, Barlow thought, and went into a shop. When he came out he went straight to Angel Alley. Barlow guessed he had been asking his way there and most likely he had been at the fancy house with one of the women and lost a watch or money he wanted back. Barlow thought likely that was why the young gent, had sort of tried to dodge him, because of not wanting it known where he had been, so he didn't bother any more. Only when he heard of the murder he thought it best to mention it."

"Quite right, too," Bobby said. "You never know. I think I'll have a look round now I'm here. This is the murder room, I take it. Door locked. Have you the key?"

CHAPTER III

VISITORS

THE ROOM Bobby entered as Dawson unlocked the door was the only one in the house that was "reasonably habitable" as the bureaucrats say. All others presented a variety of gaps in the walls, broken flooring, vanished ceilings, often enough all these together. One side of the house was, indeed, in such danger of collapse that it had been necessary to shore it up with two great beams. Even in this room, Bobby, as he walked across to the window, felt the floor shake, and hoped it would not suddenly collapse under his weight. Broken joists, he guessed.

A chalk outline in the middle of the room showed where the dying and unconscious man had been lying when the police arrived. The furniture was poor and scanty. A small deal table, two wooden chairs, a rubber air-mattress of the type often used in air-raid shelters, that was about all. In one corner stood a small tin trunk which had been opened but found to contain only a few odds and ends of no interest. No toilet articles, no plates or dishes, no cooking utensils, nothing of that kind. A gallon oil-can stood against the wall, and on the table there was a lamp that looked new and of good quality. Probably it had cost more than all else in the room put together. Beside it lay a small dispatch-case. Dawson saw Bobby looking at this, and said:

"Mr Ulyett left that, sir. He is coming back with Sergeant Smith as soon as they've checked up on a report that came in

about the Wharton jewels. Not likely to be anything in it, Mr Ulyett said, but it had to be seen to."

"Yes of course," agreed Bobby, "and it is a bit odd how many
hints there seem to be that all this jewellery that's vanished recently finds its way down here."

"Near the docks, sir," Dawson reminded him, "if the stuff's
being smuggled abroad."

"Yes, there's that," agreed Bobby. "Though there does seem
to be some idea that it goes to the Channel Islands first. Even the
papers have got hold of that. And if so, you would expect South-
ampton would be used."

He looked round doubtfully. It did not seem to him that even
the closest examination of the room was likely to throw much
light on the activities of the late Joseph Parsons. Not, at least, beyond what already could be guessed—that he was connected with
one of the criminal gangs infesting London since the conclusion
of the war, and that he had lost his life as a consequence of some
internal feud. Or possibly as a result of having aroused suspicion
of double dealing or treachery. Of course, one could never tell.
Closer examination might reveal significant indications and clues
of value. But Bobby did not think it very likely. The place gave
him the general impression of a hide-out where every possible
precaution had been taken against discovery. Well chosen, too,
with its double access, either from Emmett Street or across the
bombed-out area at the rear. All of which suggested a powerful
and well-organized gang. But, then, the skill with which so many
highly successful robberies of valuable jewellery had taken place
recently had already provided proof of that—proof equally convincing and unpleasant.

"What's that for?" Bobby asked, nodding towards a kind of
screen he noticed standing against the wall.

"Sort of black-out, sir," Dawson explained. "Covers the window. Wood backed with thick felt. When it's in place no one could
see there was any light in here."

"No precaution omitted," Bobby remarked. "It doesn't look as
if any one ever tried to live here. Is the water supply on?"

"No, sir; turned off at the main when the premises were marked 'dangerous'."

"Couldn't even wash or make a cup of tea," Bobby commented. "Must have been a sort of rendezvous or meeting-place—a kind of general post office, perhaps. It may be that's where your pretty brunette comes in. On her way with some message or another, and cleared out in a hurry when she heard what had happened. And it might explain, too, the young man who was looking for Angel Alley. Looks to me as if the unlucky Joey Parsons had been sent here on some pretext and found his murderer waiting for him. That same young man, perhaps."

"Yes, sir, it does look like that, doesn't it?" agreed Dawson, much impressed; secretly determining to adopt the idea as his own and to mention it to Mr Ulyett if he got the chance.

Bobby went back to the window and stood there, looking out thoughtfully. He was not too well satisfied with the theory he had just put forward. Too much unaccounted for. Besides, if a well-organized, well-led gang wished to get rid of a hanger-on suspected of treachery, why choose for the deed what was clearly a general centre of activity, well guarded and carefully selected and concealed? Why not some spot as far distant as possible from any connection with gang activities? There was that pretty brunette, too, Dawson had talked about. Bobby suspected she had made a deeper impression on Dawson than Dawson was prepared to admit. But where did she come in? And the well-dressed, tall young man whose appearance had also been noticed. His mind played fancifully with the idea that there might be some connection between them. Both young, both well dressed, both strangers to the district, both apparently of a higher social class than most of its denizens. And was there not a theory that a tall man was often attracted by a small woman, and a tall girl by a small man? A case of extremes meeting. He said over his shoulder as he stood there by the window.

"Looks like some one coming this way across that bombed-out space."

"Short cut, sir, from the High Street," Dawson explained. "It's often used. All right by day, but tricky at night. There've been one or two accidents."

"Three or four of them," Bobby said after a minute or two. It seemed to him that there was a certain furtiveness in the manner of their approach, an apparent desire to avoid attracting attention. He said, "Do you know, I think it might be as well to prepare to receive visitors."

"Shall I go downstairs and let 'em see we're still here?" Dawson asked.

"Oh, Lord, no!" Bobby exclaimed. "All visitors welcome. What we want, and the more the better." He moved away from the window. "If I'm right, and they are coming here," he remarked, "we mustn't let them see us too soon." He walked slowly away, across the room, noticing uneasily how the flooring shook again beneath his weight. He looked at the chalk lines which showed where Joey Parsons had been found, unconscious and dying. Taking a direction from it, he went to examine the wall opposite, and soon found what he was searching for.

"Looks like a bullet-hole," he remarked. "See? When Mr Ulyett gets here, you had better show him and see what he thinks."

"That's a bullet-hole all right enough," declared Dawson, confirming with excitement what was in fact sufficiently plain, though Bobby had thought it tactful to appear to rely on Ulyett's opinion, "I don't know how they came to miss that," he said, shaking his head gravely and ignoring the fact that he had missed it himself.

"No reason to look for it," Bobby remarked. "Doesn't mean much, anyhow—unless it turns out to be a different calibre from the one found in the body, and that's not likely. I expect the bullet will be too flattened by impact on the brick to be much good for identification purposes. Still, don't forget to tell Mr Ulyett."

"No, sir," answered Dawson, wondering now if he could manage to let it be thought that the discovery was all his own. Might do him a bit of good if he could put that one over. Mr Owen must have sharp eyes, though; and odd the way he had gone straight to that part of the wall where the bullet had struck. Nor did Bobby explain he had acted on the hint given him when in the mortuary Stokes pointed out where a bullet seemed to have grazed the dead man's head just above one ear. In Bobby's experience, explanations were not only tedious but very apt to give rise to more misunderstandings than they cleared up. Dawson turned sharply from his close examination of the bullet-hole. Both he and Bobby had heard sounds below.

"Some one there, sir," Dawson said.

Bobby nodded, at the same time lifting a warning finger for silence. Some one there beyond a doubt. He listened intently. Visitors certainly. Who and for what purpose? Nothing apparent in here that could interest any one. Or was there? Bobby glanced at that tin trunk standing in one corner. Was that the objective? Could it contain incriminating papers, or possibly some of the recently stolen jewellery—not only the Wharton jewellery, but the product perhaps of some or all of the other successful robberies that had lately occupied so much space in the press, and worried so much the police all over the country? True, the tin trunk had been searched and its contents examined. But there are, for example, such things as false bottoms and other devices that might escape any but careful and expert examination.

All these thoughts flashed rapidly through Bobby's mind, and then he thought that it might well be that he was letting his imagination run away with him. It was still raining, and now more heavily. Perhaps people innocently making use of the short cut across the bombed-out area were merely taking shelter in the entrance passage below. But he didn't much believe it. There was something ominous about the quiet and cautious sounds coming from below, as there had been something furtive and secret in the manner of approach.

He wondered what they were waiting for. Laying plans? Did they know or suspect there was a police constable on duty? Well, they would have a surprise when they found not one, but two. Two men are much more than twice as difficult to deal with than is one by himself. Bobby glanced at Dawson, and was not altogether satisfied. Dawson was looking rather too nervous and excited, and Bobby felt that if a rough house did develop, he would prefer a companion in better physical condition. All recruits, of course, pass a medical test, but recently the standard has been drastically lowered. Bobby told himself that Dawson must have scraped through by the narrowest of margins and the favour of a doctor who knew how badly the Force needed men. Not of course that you can always judge strength by appearance. Strength is largely a matter of a muscular interaction, which it is not always possible to estimate accurately. Who could have guessed, for example, that the little wisp of a man known as Jimmy Wilde could hit with such devastating effect?

Down below all sounds had ceased. Bobby began to wonder if whoever had been there had slipped away again, unheard. He fancied the same idea had occurred to Dawson, whose air of tension had been succeeded by a certain manner of relief. But now there came the sound of careful, cautious steps upon the stairs. Bobby stepped across to stand near the door where he would not be seen at once. He signed to Dawson to have his truncheon ready. The steps on the stairs ceased. There must be three or four of them out there on the landing, Bobby thought, and if there were four—well, two to one are long odds all the world over. But prestige counts, and all the underworld knows well that injury to one of the Force does add very considerable zest and vigour to the subsequent hunt.

What were they waiting for, Bobby wondered, huddled there outside the door? He was waiting himself, every muscle tense, every nerve a coiled spring quivering with the expectation of release. He gave Dawson a reassuring nod and smile. He felt that Dawson looked very much as if he might lose his head if trouble developed, and in a fight it is often the use of the head rather than of either fist or weapon that gives the victory.

CHAPTER IV

MASKED MEN

EVEN AT THIS moment, as he stood close back by the wall near the door, a part of Bobby's mind was busy with the puzzle of what this incursion meant and what was behind it. As a rule the merest glimpse of a policeman's helmet is enough to make every rogue depart at speed elsewhere. Not so apparently with these men, now, as it seemed, whispering and consulting on the other side of the door. Something here there must be, or so Bobby was thinking, of such desperate and urgent import, of such great value, that every risk was to be run in order to secure possession. Yet what could be in this bare room to have escaped the search already made? Was it perhaps something that implicated these men in the murder of the dead Joey Parsons? If so, was it not uncomfortably probable that they might be ready to commit a second to cover up the first?

Such were the thoughts that raced through Bobby's mind as he stood there, back against the wall, listening.

The door was opening now, slowly at first, as it were reluctantly, for since the bombing it moved but uneasily upon its hinges, then violently, as greater force was applied. A masked face appeared. An arm was thrust forward. It held a small automatic, small and deadly, of the kind that can be carried comfortably in a coat pocket. A voice said: "Hands up." Dawson gaped, taken by surprise, for this was a command he had read about but had never expected to hear, and he felt bewildered and at a loss. The masked intruder had concentrated all his attention on Dawson, the man in uniform, whom alone he had expected to find here, and Bobby was as yet unseen and unnoticed. Bobby lifted his right hand and brought it down, forcefully, edgeways, like an axe, upon the outheld wrist of the hand grasping the automatic. The weapon clattered to the floor. Its former holder yelped in surprise and pain. With the extreme, startling rapidity he could and did show when need was, Bobby swooped on the fallen automatic, seized it, and with almost the same movement snatched the mask from its wearer's face.

"Well, well," Bobby said amiably, "if it isn't Pitcher Barnes. Who would have thought we should meet again so soon?" This was a reference to a recent interview when it had been Bobby's task to interrogate Pitcher about certain jewel robberies, though nothing much had resulted, beyond the fact that Pitcher had received a note or communication of some sort outside a fashionable restaurant from a smartly dressed woman who had then entered the restaurant but had not been identified. Pitcher's own version was that the lady had done no more than give him a shilling for opening her car door, that he had no previous knowledge of her, and not even the remotest idea of her identity. Nor had the note been found in his possession. In the end it had been necessary to release him. But Bobby's interrogation had been searching and prolonged, and now, as Bobby beamed upon him in the friendliest manner possible, Pitcher looked back steadily and sullenly. "Who are your friends, Pitcher?" Bobby asked; and still Pitcher did not answer, nor did any of his companions, crowding in the door behind him, either move or speak.

Pitcher himself was a man of middle age and height, powerfully built, a deep chest, long arms ending in enormous hands, broad shoulders. The makings of a magnificent athlete, but now one somewhat run to seed. At one time he had been a professional boxer, and it had seemed likely he might develop into a really first-class man—a potential middle-weight world champion even. But the flattery of admiring friends, a fundamental lack of self-control and unwillingness to submit to the severe discipline of training, had before very long relegated him to the 'has-been' class. Finally he had drifted into criminal courses, and he had served more than one term of imprisonment. A truculent ruffian, in short; and now he stood and stared at Bobby and at the mask Bobby had taken and thrown down upon the floor.

From behind, one of Pitcher's companions coughed softly. As though this were a signal, Pitcher stretched out a foot and pushed softly at the mask where it lay. In almost a meditative, oddly reluctant voice, he said:

"You didn't ought to have gone for to do that, Mr Owen, sir. So you didn't."

Bobby was standing now in the middle of the room, drawing back a little from where he had stooped to pick up the automatic he held, not without finding it a comfortable thing to have in hand. For he was beginning to scent danger in the air. As he stepped back Pitcher lurched forward. Behind his great lumbering body three other men filed silently and softly into the room. They were all masked. It was probably in order to adjust their masks that they had lingered so long on the other side of the door.

About two of them there was nothing remarkable. They were of average height and size. The third man—he sidled in after the other two—was small and wiry and bald, and there was something purposeful about his air and movements that made Bobby look at him more closely, so as to notice that his rather prominent ears showed the peculiarity of a lobe attached to the flesh of the cheek. That, Bobby remembered, was a peculiarity of a man named Cyrus King. King had the reputation of being dangerous, intelligent, and reckless, with a readiness to use a knife not characteristic of the ordinary criminal in this country. He was known to have boasted more than once that he would kill any cop any day rather than run any chance of being 'sent up'—a fate he had so far managed to avoid. He was beginning now to sidle along the wall, slowly, unobtrusively. Bobby noticed the movement. He said sharply:

"You there, stop that."

The other obeyed. He and Bobby looked at each other, the gangster's eyes sharp and intent through the holes in the mask. He was still silent. Every one was watching him, as if all realized that in him lay the crisis. Lifting the automatic he had picked up, Bobby said:

"My turn now, I think, to say 'hands up'."

"It isn't loaded," Pitcher mumbled. "I never hold with them things. They go off when you don't mean it. Noisy. And miss as often as not. A straight left don't."

"A knife doesn't either," said the man Bobby thought might be Cyrus King. "Three inches where it'll do most good. That's enough." He spoke in a high cracked voice, obviously disguised, and now a knife gleamed in his hand, thin and fierce. "Sure and silent," he said. "That's this."

Bobby pulled the trigger of the automatic, pointing the weapon out of the window as he did so. There was no response. He moved back the slide. The magazine was empty. He sent the useless weapon flying through the window to fall with a tinkle of broken glass in the roadway outside.

"Very sensible, Pitcher," he said approvingly. "Any judge would be sure to take that into consideration. Might get you off a year or two. Well, perhaps you would like to explain what you and your anonymous friends want. A man was murdered here yesterday. I expect you've heard. Name of Joey Parsons. Any of you know him?"

They did not answer. The man with the knife was beginning again his slow and crab-like progress along the wall. Bobby said to him:

"Stop that—you."

The fellow turned slowly at Bobby's summons. He was staring at Bobby, from whom, indeed, he had hardly ever removed those eyes that glittered and shone like pin-points through the slits in his mask. He said now:

"You think you know me, don't you?" When Bobby made no reply, he went on: "I saw the way you looked at me."

"You didn't ought never to have done it," Pitcher mumbled again. He had picked up from the floor the mask he had been wearing and was holding it in one hand. "Now you've made it so it has to be," he complained.

One of the two other men spoke for the first time. He was the taller of the two, and he held in one hand a short iron crowbar. He said:

"What's that dispatch-case on the table? Looks as if they had got it."

"Not them," said the man with the knife. "Or they wouldn't be hanging about still." He changed his voice suddenly. It became soft and silken, very different from the high, cracked tone he had been using before. He said: "O.K., Mr Owen. I know you, too, and I know you think I'm Cy King. That's right, isn't it? Very clever of you to spot it. You're a bit of a nuisance, Mr Owen. We expected only one of you bogeys here, and we reckoned to fix him and no bother. Tie him up and be done with it. Pitcher's job to out him if he tried to give trouble. You've messed things up, Mr Owen, messing and meddling and snooping around. It don't make sense. But no harm done, and we'll call it square if you'll step downstairs, you and the other bogey, and let us have this room to ourselves, private like, for a bit of a talk between ourselves, for half an hour or thereabouts. Then we quit and you come back and everything nice and cosy all round. Call it a deal?"

"What's the big idea?" Bobby asked. He was playing for time now, for he felt more than ever that there was danger in the air, and he hoped Ulyett would soon make an appearance. The man who had called himself Cy King was still fingering and stroking that knife of his as though it were a living thing he had difficulty in controlling. When no one spoke to answer Bobby's question, Bobby said again: "Well, what's the big idea? I take it none of you four had anything to do with the murder, or you wouldn't be likely to come back here. Why not tell us what you know? You might find it useful some day if I could put it on record that you helped. What about it?"

"We know nothing about any murder," King answered. "Not our affair. Whoever did it can swing for all we care." He had edged back towards the door now, apparently convinced that his efforts to slip behind Bobby unnoticed were not going to succeed. He said: "Better go while you can."

"Why not begin," Bobby suggested, "by throwing that knife of yours away? Can't talk comfortably while you're playing about with a thing like that."

"I'll give you another chance," was all Cy said, still fingering his weapon.

"They mean murder, sir," Dawson muttered in Bobby's ear. "He'll knife us as we go out."

Bobby nodded. He was of the same opinion. He waited. "Rush 'em," Cy yelled suddenly, and in a moment it had begun.

CHAPTER V
ROUGH HOUSE

THE PLAN of action had evidently been settled in advance. To Pitcher Barnes had clearly been allotted the task of 'liquidating' Bobby, 'liquidating' being the word that had actually been used, as Bobby learned later. The other two members of the gang had as clearly been instructed to deal with Dawson. Cy King had assigned to himself the position of strategic reserve; and now hovered in the background, his knife-blade flickering in the dull afternoon light, his dry and protruded tongue passing ceaselessly over his dry lips, as in an attempt to moisten them.

But though so carefully and well planned, this first attack did not go well. Dawson, less nervous in time of action than during moments of suspense, adopted the policeman's traditional method of defence against a rush attack, using his drawn truncheon, not to strike with, but to thrust. Unexpectedly and very hard he drove it into the stomach of the first of his two assailants. The man gasped, doubled up, bending forward, and Dawson flung up his knee, smashing that bony bit of himself violently against the other's face. The victim went reeling back with the loss of a few teeth and collapsed on the floor, his mouth and nose bleeding profusely, his tongue badly bitten; and Dawson had time to use his truncheon, both to ward off the blow the second man—the one with the crowbar—aimed at him, and to return it, though without great effect. Crowbar against truncheon, the two men faced each other, alert and cautious; while the first gangster swore and cursed, trying to raise himself from the floor and spitting out blood and teeth, and Cy King began again his crab-like progress, sidling along the wall of the room.

Nor had the attack launched by Pitcher Barnes against Bobby met with greater success. Carelessly sure of himself, over-confident in his knowledge that his fame as a professional boxer who had fought in famous contests generally, assured him of victory without the trouble of having to fight for it, Pitcher dashed forward at Bobby, swinging his great arms like flails and mouthing fearful threats. Least of all did he expect not a hesitant, half-frightened defence, but swift attack.

Bobby, however, had no attention of passively awaiting the big man's rush. He leaped, he struck. With two tremendous blows, right and left, delivered in such swift succession as to be almost simultaneous, he sent Pitcher reeling back, astonished and dazed—so much so, indeed, that had Bobby been able to press home his attack, he might have succeeded in disposing finally of an adversary whose mind for the moment had ceased to function, whose arms dangled helplessly at his side. But Bobby had seen Cy King's tongue slipping in and out over his dry lips like the fangs of a snake ready to strike, had marked that sidling progress along the room wall as King crept nearer and nearer to work his way behind Dawson's back. Not an instant, nor the fraction of an instant, was to be lost, for the flickering knife was poised and ready. Since needs must, Pitcher had to be allowed time to recover as Bobby sprang aside to aim a blow at King—a blow that had behind it all the force and energy he could give it, all the hot anger that he felt against this crawling creature with the knife. Had it landed, it would, as Bobby meant it to do, have settled accounts with King for some considerable time. But King, though much the smallest of all engaged in this confused and confusing struggle, was as quick, as ready, as watchful as the weasel he so much resembled. He stooped, as it were shrank into himself. Bobby's blow only grazed the top of his head, though still with force enough to send him sprawling. His knife dropped, tinkling. Pitcher had already recovered, and was coming again. Bobby had but time to kick away the fallen knife into a dark corner of the room and leap to meet this fresh menacing advance.

This time Pitcher was better prepared, because less confident. He was remembering now, he was calling once more upon the experience and skill gained in the battles that had at one time brought him within possible reach of a world-championship contest. To Bobby it was apparent that the chance of swift victory had passed by, and now there was nothing for it but blow for blow, given and returned, in equal exchange, with superior skill and strength and endurance to decide.

If ...

If, that is, skill and strength and endurance were allowed to operate undisturbed. For the moment, indeed, Cy King was out of the fight; 'unserviceable', as they used to say in the Army. He had lost his knife—kicked away. He himself still sprawled angrily and harmlessly on the floor, yelping again as Dawson and the second gangster, truncheon against crowbar, circled each other, cautiously, alert and watchful, and as they did so kicked or trod on the recumbent Cyrus.

With no space for ring craft, for manoeuvre, Bobby and Pitcher stood toe to toe, breast to breast, and traded blow for blow.

Bobby had taken a left hook that had shaken him, and two very heavy body-blows that might well have been decisive, so heavy and well placed were they, had his physical condition been less sound than it was. Pitcher had many advantages. His reach was longer, his skill greater, he possessed those heavy bony ridges guarding small, deep-set eyes, which are such an advantage to the boxer, which, indeed, had already prevented a right swing Bobby had got in from closing one eye. There was swelling, but that was all; and Pitcher had only grunted and shaken his great head when Bobby landed another on the side of the temple with such clear force as would have sent most men to the floor.

Yet if in these respects Bobby was inferior, he had one advantage, one likely to be decisive in the end if he could hold out long enough in this close exchange of blow for blow, when actual physical strength counted and footwork was at a discount from lack of space to move in. His physical condition was superb. Pitcher's was very much the reverse, and already he was showing himself troubled by a succession of half-arm jabs Bobby had landed over his heart. His breathing was becoming irregular, his heart was beginning to miss a beat or two and then hurrying to catch up again, his movements were growing slower as his less taut nerves responded less swiftly to the given impulse. Subconsciously he was aware that unless he could end the fight soon with some smashing and decisive blow, he must lose it for the lack of power to continue.

The table and chairs had been overturned and broken. From the lamp that had been standing on the table and been overturned with it, a pool of oil spread slowly across the floor, a floor that shook and creaked, that swayed and shuddered beneath the heavy-footed stamping of the struggling men. King, crying with pain, for Dawson, dodging a vicious swing from his adversary's crowbar, had trodden on his hand, bruising it badly, was groping for his fallen knife. The gangster Dawson had incapacitated for the time in the first rush was getting to his feet again, urged by a snarled and angry order from King. Bobby had to give back to a fiercer onslaught from Pitcher, as Pitcher, feeling his strength beginning to ebb, called up all his resources to make an end before it was too late. Now Bobby had his back to the wall and could go no further. Now Dawson, seeing his chance, struck with his truncheon and all his strength, but as he did so his foot slipped in the spreading oil from the overturned lamp. His blow missed, he lost his balance. Before he could recover, his opponent, seizing the opportunity, hit back with his crowbar. The blow landed full on Dawson's helmet, smashing it in and sending its wearer senseless to the floor.

Bobby, taking a heavy blow from Pitcher on his forearm, smashed his own right against the side of Pitcher's head. It had no apparent effect. One might almost as well have smacked a brick wall. King had recovered his knife and was slipping towards them. As he passed the prostrate and unconscious Dawson he paused to kick him viciously in the face. It was an act of senseless brutality that had an unexpected and unforeseen result. It gave Bobby just the second or two of respite he needed in which to recover from so fierce an exchange of blows, given and received, as to leave him for the moment almost defenceless, as it had also caused Pitcher to go reeling back, exhausted, too. King said softly:

"Leave him to me, I'll finish," and he poised his recovered knife on the palm of his hand, ready to throw.

"No, leave him to me," Pitcher gasped; and, whether by accident or not, trod heavily on King's foot as he lurched forward.

King, no stoic when it came to enduring pain, gave a loud yell, and once more dropped his knife, that once more Bobby, recovered from his momentary exhaustion, kicked away as he sprang to grapple again with Pitcher before King came back. Unprepared for this renewed and desperate assault on which Bobby knew hung his hope of life, Pitcher went crashing to the floor, and Bobby with him, but uppermost, and with his mind made up to end it somehow, then and there, within or without the rules, since now it seemed so certain there was murder in the air.

But for this there was no time nor chance. The impact of their heavy fall was too much for the already shaken, weakened floor. It gaped, gave way. With a rending scream of breaking wood, in a cloud of dust and dirt, they were all, in a confused, struggling mass, precipitated into the room beneath, just as a police car drew up at the entrance outside and Divisional Detective Inspector Ulyett came leaping out with the traditional inquiry:

"Now, then; what's all this about?"

CHAPTER VI
TECHNICAL DISCUSSION

ULYETT'S INQUIRY through the shattered window of the downstairs room, through the dense and baffling cloud of dust and dirt rising within, received the prompt reply of a heavy fragment of broken brick, hurled with force and precision. It took him between the eyes and sent him back, stunned and bleeding, into the arms of his attendant sergeant.

When the floor above gave way, Bobby and Pitcher, closely entwined, had been the first precipitated into the room below. Fortunately for Bobby, he was uppermost and so remained, escaping injury, as Pitcher's large body provided a very efficient cushion. In his capacity as cushion, however, Pitcher himself suffered somewhat severely. He was bruised all over, had a broken rib or two, a badly damaged knee, and was so shaken as to be for the moment entirely uninterested in his surroundings. After him had come tumbling first Dawson, still unconscious from the injuries he had received, and then the two other gangsters, both with longer warning of what was happening and more time to protect themselves. Neither had been much hurt. Last of all arrived Cy King, lowering himself quite comfortably and alighting on his feet. When the floor collapsed he had been in a corner of the room near the door, trying to recover his knife Bobby had kicked away. He had still not found it when, the floor giving way under him, he had been forced to make his more careful, restrained descent into the room beneath.

He it was who had answered Ulyett with that well-aimed halfbrick. He shouted a command to his companions to make their escape. Bobby, a little dazed himself, not quite certain what was happening, was scrambling to his feet. Through the door burst Ulyett's constable-chauffeur, trying to distinguish objects through the blinding, choking clouds of dust that still hung in the air.

"There's one of them," he yelled, seeing Bobby, now upon his feet and in his turn trying to make out his surroundings. The chauffeur dashed forward, tripped over the debris, nearly fell. Bobby caught him and held him up. He gasped out: "Good Lord, it's Mr Owen."

"So it is," agreed Bobby. "They've got away. No one left. Through the back and across that bombed area. What about Mr Ulyett?"

"Knocked out," called a sergeant, Ulyett's assistant, through the window. He also had recognized Bobby. He came scrambling into the room. "You hurt, Mr Owen?" he asked. "There's one of them," he said, pointing to Pitcher, now more clearly visible as the clouds of dust began to settle and making himself heard by a loud groaning, a result not so much of returning consciousness as of his many and competing aches and pains. Then the sergeant saw Dawson and bent over him. "Looks bad," he said with concern.

"Get an ambulance," Bobby said. "Your wireless working? Good. Get busy. Dawson wants attention. Report to the Yard, but the ambulance and a doctor first."

"What about the crooks?" asked the chauffeur as the sergeant vanished.

"We'll have to pass them up for the time," Bobby said. "Ten to one they had a car waiting. The flying squad can have a try, but most likely by now they're having a comfortable cup of coffee in a cafe somewhere with a proprietor ready to swear they have been there the last hour or two. Only one of them marked as far as I know, and they'll hide him."

"There's this one," the chauffeur said, bending over the prostrate and still-groaning Pitcher. "We've got him, anyhow. Why, it's Pitcher Barnes," he exclaimed. "Knocked out all right," he said. He looked at Bobby, and began to take more notice of Bobby's appearance. "Things been happening, Mr Owen, sir?" he asked with much interest.

"Quite a lot of them," Bobby agreed. He had been trying to make sure none of his bones were broken and to get rid of some of the dirt and plaster with which he was covered. Now he was examining with some distress the condition of the unfortunate

Dawson. He told the chauffeur to get water, clean towels, brandy, from the public-house at the corner. "One of the brutes kicked him when he was unconscious and couldn't protect himself," Bobby said. "It was Cy King, I think."

The sergeant had returned from sending off his message, and heard the name. He said with some excitement:

"Cy King? Was he one? Are you sure, sir? Can I send out a call?"

"I don't think so. Not yet, anyhow," Bobby answered. "I'm sure enough myself, but not to swear to, though he didn't deny it. I never saw his face. It was masked. I think he meant murder."

"But if he admitted it?" the sergeant protested.

"No proof," Bobby answered. "It could have been some one else just saying it to put us off. Unfounded claim. I'm sure myself, but that's not good enough." He went to look at Pitcher, who by now had managed to get into a sitting position and was still groaning loudly. "Don't make that row," Bobby said unsympathetically. "No bones broken, I think. Looks like that knee dislocated, though." He turned away and asked the sergeant: "How about Mr Ulyett?"

"I'm all right," said Ulyett himself, making a somewhat unsteady entrance and looking anything but 'all right'. He was bleeding badly from a cut over the right temple, he could hardly see, and was still much shaken. The chauffeur returned with a basin of warm water and some brandy. Bobby began to wash and clean Ulyett's injuries, but Ulyett, a strict teetotaller, refused to touch the brandy. "Don't like the stuff," he said and added, looking at Bobby: "Been through it yourself, haven't you?"

"We've got one of them," the chauffeur said with satisfaction. "Pitcher Barnes."

"I never had nothing to do with it," Pitcher protested, trying to sound injured and indignant. "It was Mr Owen there as set about me something cruel. Innocent as the babe unborn, so I am. Some blokes I don't know from Adam stood me a drink and said to come along and meet some pals of theirs, because of me being famous like and proud to meet me. As often happens, and me suspecting nothing; and why should I? They said to come upstairs, and I did; same as dropping in anywheres for a friendly chat, and next thing there was Mr Owen going for me like a bagful of wild cats, and me defending myself, though taken unexpected, same as any one would."

Bobby began to laugh at this version, which he thought admirable in its sheer impudence, but stopped at once, for he found laughing painful. He sat down on a broken box, and began to feel himself all over, trying to discover which parts hurt the most. Ulyett said:

"All right, Pitcher. You can tell that yarn in court." To Bobby, Ulyett said: "What's the charge?"

"Well, I'm not sure," Bobby answered slowly. He had not forgotten that timely foot Pitcher had placed on Cy King's toes with an emphasis sufficient to distract his attention from the use he had seemed to be contemplating of the knife whereof Bobby had all the time been so acutely conscious. Then, too, Bobby was not displeased with the way in which he had found himself able to stand up to Pitcher, whose reputation was still formidable. The story would, as Bobby knew, soon be told, probably with many embellishments, all through the underworld, and through his own comrades of the police as well. His prestige would be increased considerably, and prestige is always useful. Then, too, for some inexplicable reason, one is apt to have friendly feelings towards the man with whom one has had a brisk exchange of lefts and rights. Probably there results a mutual heightening of masculine self-respect. Anyhow, Bobby had no wish to prefer any charge at present. He said, as Ulyett, looking faintly surprised at this hesitation, waited for a reply: "It was fair enough while it lasted, as far as Pitcher was concerned. The rest of them played dirty, but not Pitcher. We had it to ourselves, and I think Pitcher got as good as he gave."

"More," groaned Pitcher. "Me being all unsuspecting like and knocked about cruel before I knew where I was, in a manner of speaking."

"Now, Pitcher," Bobby warned him, "don't start telling too many lies, or I may change my mind. At the moment I'm not thinking of making any charge, and when the ambulance comes you can go along and get patched up, no questions asked—at present. But don't think you've heard the last of this, because you haven't. And remember—what begins with murder may end in hanging."

"Mr Owen, sir," began Pitcher earnestly, but Bobby stopped him.

"That's enough from you just now," he said. "Put in a little quiet thinking, though—hard thinking."

Pitcher subsided, looking very disturbed. Bobby began to occupy himself feeling his bruises again.

"Anyone got a bit of a looking-glass?" he asked. "I want to see my face."

"I wouldn't try, sir, not if I were you," the sergeant advised him earnestly, though producing a small mirror he sometimes found useful for observing people and things without attracting attention. "No, sir, I wouldn't," the sergeant repeated. "You wouldn't know it again."

Bobby took the mirror, but not the advice. He looked sadly at it and sighed. He said in a depressed voice:

"I'm going to get into an awful row at home. What my wife is going to say—" and for lack of suitable words he left the sentence unfinished.

"That's women all over," observed Pitcher sympathetically. "No understanding, no feeling. Nag, nag, nag, all the time they're doing you up."

"It was fair enough while it lasted," Bobby said reminiscently. "That left hook of yours, Pitcher ... !"

"A fair sleeping-draught if it gets there," Pitcher agreed with satisfaction. "Only it never did same as it ought. It was that straight left of yours kept me off—seemed to run into it every time, so I did."

The conversation became technical—abstruse and technical, for experts only, as it might be Messrs Whitehead and Russell on actual entities. Ulyett contributed some criticism, hotly contested by his sergeant, who had once won an inter-divisional boxing championship. The chauffeur put the point that a boxer wins more often and more easily with his feet than with his fists.

Bobby conceded this, but observed that as regards recent events the remark was irrelevant, since, in the room upstairs with a good deal else going on, there had been no room for footwork. By the time the ambulance appeared they had got to the stage of cigarettes all round. Other police presently arrived, and with them the superintendent of the division, at first inclined to smack his lips over Pitcher Barnes, and then disappointed when informed that no charge was being made. After the departure of the ambulance with the damaged men requiring attention, Bobby had to tell his story again and to explain why he wished Pitcher to be left at liberty, for the time at least.

"He ought to be more useful at large than doing six weeks in gaol," Bobby said. "We can keep him under observation, and then he did happen to tread on the toe of a man who was playing about with a knife in a way I didn't much like. Besides," Bobby added with what might have been a smile had his face been in any condition to produce such an effect, "it was a good clean turn-up on both sides while it lasted." He said reflectively: "I don't think I've ever known a better."

"Sounds," grunted the superintendent—"sounds as if you had rather enjoyed it."

Bobby looked alarmed.

"For the lord's sake," he exclaimed, "don't let my wife hear you say that, or I shall never hear the last of it—never."

"Bad conscience," said the superintendent severely.

CHAPTER VII
"THE LINE"

THE NEXT DAY Bobby spent in bed. This was not his own wish, but *force majeure*, for Olive had arisen, terrible in wrath, and he had quailed and obeyed under threat that if he didn't, he would have to stop there another week, most likely. And in fact, when he was allowed to get up, he not only felt a great deal better, but also looked almost respectable—almost, but not quite.

He was due that morning to preside at a conference on steps to be taken to deal with the current outburst of armed banditry. There had been too many cases, almost unknown before the war, of armed and masked men breaking into houses and flats and using violence towards their occupants. But he had no formal engagements in the afternoon. He made inquiries about the progress of the Angel Alley case, and found little or none had been made. Ulyett's injuries had proved more serious than appeared at first, and he had gone on sick leave. There was evidently a tendency to regard the murder of the man known as Joey Parsons as the result of a gang feud and a good riddance to bad though unimportant rubbish. The visit of the other gangsters to the scene of the crime was, it was being said, due to mere curiosity. There are always crowds to stare and gape at any spot where murder has been committed. As for the scrimmage that had taken place— well, imagine Bobby's horror, indignation and surprise when he found it was also being said that every one knew Mr Owen would rather scrap than eat any day, and most likely he simply hadn't been able to resist the chance of a bit of a turn-up with Pitcher Barnes. Never in all his life had Bobby's feelings been more deeply wounded.

Still all ablaze with inner indignation, determined to prove, as indeed he was convinced, that there were strange and hidden motives for the desperation of the attack made on Dawson and himself; certain again, as he was in his own mind, that all these happenings hovered on the outskirts of something that reached very far into the dark London underworld, he set out to make a few inquiries on his own account. He knew from the reports he had called for and studied over luncheon that the attendant at the car park in Canon Square, whence cars had at one time so frequently vanished, was emphatic in declaring that none had been taken recently. Another report pointed out that that part of the High Street bordering on the bombed area behind Angel Alley was busy, congested, and extremely narrow. No car could have been left there or lingered, or even returned at short intervals, without being noticed. Nor could the presence be traced of any car in any of the poverty-stricken side streets, where cars were sufficiently rare to attract notice. As a result not much attention had been paid to Canon Square, and Bobby decided he would begin his own inquiries there.

He found the car attendant to be an alert and intelligent man, unfitted for heavier work, as he had lost an arm and an eye in the war. He was quite clear in his testimony that no car had been removed unlawfully and that he had seen nothing in any way suspicious or unusual. Bobby had provided himself with photographs of Pitcher Barnes, of the dead Joey Parsons, and with a description of Cy King, who for his part had always been very careful never to allow himself to be photographed. The car attendant examined the photograph of Pitcher Barnes with great interest. He knew all about Pitcher's boxing record, but had never seen him, certainly never in the vicinity of Canon Square.

"Not a bloke," said the car attendant admiringly as he gazed on Pitcher's battered features, scarred by so many combats, "as you wouldn't notice—old-timer and done his bit in the boxing game, you would say at once, and most likely ask who he was."

Of Cy King he knew nothing, and he was only puzzled by Bobby's reference to the lobe of an ear that was attached to the cheek. It was not a thing he had ever heard of. But over the photograph of Joey Parsons he wrinkled a puzzled brow.

"It does look a bit like a bloke I saw with a gent, as it might be a week ago," he said, after long consideration. "But I couldn't swear to it. I noticed him because him and the gent, were talking rather intimate like, if you see what I mean—a bit as if the gent, was wanting something the other bloke wasn't agreeable to."

"Would you know the gentleman again?" Bobby asked, but the car attendant shook his head.

"He had his back to me most of the time," he said, "and I didn't notice much, except for wondering what they were talking about so interested like. Tall gentleman he was, back like a poker. Old Army officer—you could see that much and a real swell, as you could immediate tell—Spit-and-polish type, if you ask me. In the service I should have spotted him for a bit of a tartar the moment he came on parade. Lost an eye, too, I think; but of course I couldn't be sure—only an idea."

"What made you think that?"

"It was something in the way he walked. I've lost an eye myself, and it makes you notice."

There seemed no more the car attendant could say, and even Bobby wondered if so slender a clue was worth following up. He went back to his car and sat in it for a while, smoking a cigarette and thinking. A 'real swell' and an old Army officer. What had he been doing in this neighbourhood, and why had he been talking so earnestly to a man who might or might not have been the dead Joey Parsons, and what was it he had been wanting that the other had not been willing to agree to? Or was it all merely that the car attendant had been allowing his imagination to run loose? Bobby did not much think so. A 'real swell,' an old Army officer? Then possibly he might belong to one of the West End clubs. 'Spit-and-polish' type? At a guess that meant an infantry man. Infantry give more attention to 'spit and polish' than do the specialist corps, and infantry officers are often more easily recognizable as military men than are engineers and others who tend more to the normal professional type. One eye only?—not much help there; too many have suffered that loss.

All very slender grounds from which to draw any conclusion.

Bobby lighted another cigarette and was minded to go home. Still, one never knew. There were several military clubs in London—the Cavalry, the Guards, for instance. Others as well, including the 'The Line', where the men of the 'P.B.I.' do chiefly congregate. Bobby decided that on his way home he would stop at 'The Line' and ask a question or two, slender as was the hope of any useful result. Still, the most slender clues—a lost button, a dropped pin, a forgotten cigarette end—had all proved at one time or another signposts pointing the way to follow.

Interesting and a little puzzling, he told himself as he threw away what was left of his cigarette and started his car—this abrupt intrusion of a 'real swell' into the story of the death of a man hitherto thought of as a 'spiv', a 'lay-about', a hanger-on of some criminal gang or another. Of course, there was that underclothing the dead man had been wearing of such unexpectedly good quality—almost of the 'luxury' type, indeed. Surprising, but quite possibly merely the casual result of some shop theft or black-market transaction.

Outside 'The Line'—occasionally known as 'The Line-up'—
Bobby parked his car, and went in to interview the head porter,
by good luck a former member of the Metropolitan police, though
ill health had forced him to resign after only a few years' service,
and still with relatives in the Force. He was very willing to help,
but he shook his head over the photograph Bobby showed him. It
had of course, though taken from the dead man, been touched up
to make it look as much like life as possible.

"No one I've ever seen," he said. "And no one who ever
worked here."

So that seemed the end of Bobby's faint hope that if there really were any connection between any member of the club and the
dead man, he might have been noticed in the vicinity.

"It was rather a shot in the dark," Bobby admitted. "We have
some reason to believe that this man has been watching a gentleman who might belong to your club and that the gentleman
has noticed it and spoken to him—asked him what he wanted, perhaps. It's possible another of these robberies is being
planned. If we could get in touch with whoever is concerned, we
could take precautions. Our information is that he is tall, very
erect, 'back like a poker,' and is probably blind in one eye—from
war service, perhaps."

"There's more than one like that," the head porter remarked;
and agreed to Bobby's suggestion that the photograph should be
left on his desk and that any member who seemed to recognize it
should be asked to communicate with Scotland Yard.

With that, and feeling he had gone to a good deal of trouble
with very little to show for it, Bobby departed. Next morning, on
his way to the Yard, he stopped at the 'The Line', and again the
head porter shook his head as he saw Bobby come in.

"None of our gentlemen noticed it," he said. "One or two gave
it a bit of a look—sort of wondering what it was doing there, most
likely—but they didn't say anything. I saw Colonel Godwinsson
pick it up and look at it, so I told him it had been left by the police because it was thought he had been annoying people, and the
police would be glad of any information they could proceed on."

"Did Colonel Godwinsson say anything?"

"No, just 'oh, yes', and asked for his letters, so it's not him, though I did think it might be, being tall and very stiff and erect, and lost an eye at Mons in 1914, which is why they kept him at home this time. In charge of a training camp, and kept them at it all right, too, if you ask me. Very nice gentleman, and always very pleasant; but I wouldn't like to be on charge before him. Strict in his ideas."

The description interested Bobby, but he made no comment. "No use bothering him," he agreed. "He would have said so if he had recognized the photo. Does he use the club much?"

"Country member," replied the head porter, with a slight suggestion in his voice that these were of a lesser breed. "Only comes when he's in town, and that's not so often. Only when Lady Geraldine Rafe has been getting into a bit more hot water than usual and he has to try to get her out again." Bobby smiled at this, said he had heard of Lady Geraldine, who seemed a lively young lady, and he only hoped she wouldn't go a bit too far some day. Was she any relation of this Colonel Godwinsson? The porter said he didn't know. Colonel Godwinsson was her godfather. Very likely there was some relationship as well. The colonel belonged to the oldest family in the country, or so he claimed, and Lady Geraldine, though an only child and without close relatives, was connected in some way with everybody who was anybody. The title had become extinct when her father, the Earl of Sands, died. In his opinion, said the porter, a good many of the young people of the day needed a touch of discipline—the sort of discipline Colonel Godwinsson always looked as if he were ready to provide.

Bobby expressed a mild opinion that young people to-day were no worse, and probably better, than their parents and grand-parents, though no doubt at times inclined to kick over the traces. A general habit of the colt not yet broken to harness by the hard discipline of life. There was a little more desultory conversation, turning largely on the prospects for the three-thirty that afternoon. Then Bobby departed, leaving the head porter wishing he had a nice easy job like that, with nothing to do except ask a lot of footling questions that couldn't possibly lead anywhere.

CHAPTER VIII

LADY GERALDINE

BOBBY HAD BEEN interested, and a little amused, too, on hearing that Lady Geraldine was a god-daughter of Colonel Godwinsson, who seemed to give every one he met such an impression of sternness and severity. Possibly he had overdone it as regarded his god-daughter. High-spirited young women are apt to resent too heavy a hand. Though Lady Geraldine did seem inclined to let her high spirits carry her much too far. Two or three times she had appeared in the police court, escaping with a lecture and a small fine when the presiding magistrate happened to be feeling paternal, though once, from a less paternally inclined magistrate, she had narrowly escaped a prison sentence without the option of a fine.

A rowdy, irresponsible young woman, it appeared, and one whose behaviour was tending to render her less and less welcome in such aristocratic circles as still upheld Victorian traditions. But also more and more welcome elsewhere, where those enriched by the war were swiftly forcing their way into that Society of which the capital 'S' is becoming just a little worn. Nothing, though, had ever been hinted against her private life. She would flirt with any one, from a dustman to a duke, she would distribute 'darlings' and kisses with a liberality that went even beyond the genial customs of the day, but there it stopped. It was even said that she had used a champagne bottle, not without effect, on the head of one too-pressing admirer; and had chased another, who had allowed a straying hand to stray too far, into a corner where, under threat of a brandished carving-knife, he had begged forgiveness on his knees. A handful, Bobby told himself, for an old Army officer with strict, old-fashioned ideas to feel responsible for.

Advisable, Bobby decided, to pay her a call. There was a chance that Colonel Godwinsson's interview with the possible Joey Parsons might be connected with whatever new scrape the young lady had got herself into. She might be able to give some information about a personality already beginning to seem strangely enigmatic. Bobby got her address from the telephone directory. It was that of a large and expensive block of flats in the north-west district of London. But first he drove to the police station nearest to the flats—a convenient place to leave his car—and there he asked a few questions about Lady Geraldine.

"Off on the spree again," the station sergeant informed him, smiling broadly. "Been away a week, the porter told our man on the beat, and no one knows where. Doing a good old soak somewhere most likely."

"Does that happen often?" Bobby asked.

"Oh, no," answered the station sergeant tolerantly. "Now and again. In between whiles you wouldn't think butter would melt in her mouth. All prunes and prism, if you see what I mean. And then that time when it took three of them doing all they knew to get her into the cells. But afterwards she came round handsome to say how sorry she was—apologizing all round, shaking hands and wanting to kiss to make it well where she had bit one man. And I do believe," said the station sergeant, severe now, "he would have let her if I hadn't been there. And came down handsome for the police orphanage."

"When was this?" Bobby asked.

"Let me see now," said the station sergeant, trying to remember. "She came in to do her apologizing—and very pretty, too—the same week the Wharton jewels went. It was her and another young lady gave the alarm. They went upstairs, found the door of the duchess's bedroom locked, and asked one of the maids if it was all right. Which it wasn't. A 'bus conductor had just seen a man climb out of the duchess's window, and he had dialled 999, so our men were on the spot before the young ladies had finished explaining. That was a night, that was."

"I remember," said Bobby, who indeed had been called from slippers and arm-chair to take part in the hunt started by one of the most sensational of the many sensational robberies that have disgraced post-war London.

"What she wants," pronounced the station sergeant, "is a husband to put her over his knee now and again. Discipline. And plenty of it. Then she would settle down all right. But at present, no self-control. Irresponsible."

"Seems like it," agreed Bobby. "Expensive where she lives, isn't it? Wasn't the earl bankrupt when he died?"

"He was," agreed the station sergeant. "And when he lived as well. Never had a penny to bless himself with. In and out the bankruptcy court all the time. Lummy, what a life—being an earl and not a brass farthing with it! But there," said the station sergeant, tolerant as ever, "I daresay it's hard, when you're an earl, like, to roll up your sleeves and take a job like the next man."

Bobby, who had himself an impecunious and aristocratic uncle, agreed heartily. He asked how Lady Geraldine managed if her father had left nothing but debts and if she had no employment. The station sergeant said he didn't know. He supposed she had come in for some money somehow. Anyhow, she spent freely, met all her bills without delay, paid £400 or £500 rent for her flat, possessed an expensive limousine as well as a small sports car, and frequented fashionable restaurants and exclusive night clubs. No, there was no rich man in the background, or, if there were, he kept himself very much there, and very carefully. The station sergeant, still tolerant, accompanied this information with a wink; and Bobby, repressing an inclination to wink back, went on to the flats. The one Lady Geraldine occupied was on the first floor, so without troubling to wait for the lift, which was in use, Bobby walked up the stairs. When he knocked there was no answer at first; but when he knocked again the door was opened by a young man so good looking that Bobby's first impression was that he couldn't possibly be real, but must have walked straight off the screen from the latest superb film masterpiece. He had yellow curly hair, large very bright eyes—'lustrous' eyes, shadowed by long, silky lashes calculated to rouse the envy of any girl that ever lived—and nearly perfect features. Tall and well made, too, and a dazzling smile that disclosed teeth almost too good to be true. Bobby, though slightly overwhelmed by this vision not so much of a Greek god as of a Viking hero from ancient Icelandic saga, asked for Lady Geraldine, and was told that she was away. No, it was not known exactly when she would return. Any moment, but nothing certain. Bobby explained he was a police officer and had called to make a few inquiries. Did the young man live here, or was there any one else of whom he could ask a question or two?

"About Gerry?" the young man asked. "What for? I suppose if you are a cop that other bloke was, too, though he swore he wasn't."

"What other bloke?" Bobby asked, but the young man did not answer. Instead he went back into the interior of the flat, leaving Bobby standing in the doorway, and Bobby heard him calling: "Mona. Mona. Where are you? There's a bloke here says he's a cop, and he's asking about Gerry."

There appeared a small, young, pretty girl—dark, dark eyes, dark hair, dark complexion, her only unfortunate feature a nose a little too long and narrow for that small oval face. Bobby remembered the brief description Dawson had given of the fashionable-looking young lady whom he had seen in Angel Alley. He wondered if this could be the same. She asked him to come in, and led the way into a sitting-room. It was furnished in a frivolous feminine fashion, very up to date—eccentric dolls, knick-knacks, cushions, and so on—and not a single comfortable chair in the place, not one that Bobby felt he could sit down on without considerable risk of its collapsing under his weight. There was a large cocktail cabinet, and on the walls some astonishing pictures of the very latest French school. Bobby had visited a recent exhibition of the kind, and was almost certain that at least two of them were hung upside down, but he didn't suppose that mattered much. Mona—if that was the girl's name—impressed him as looking somehow slightly out of place in these exotic surroundings.

"What is it?" she was saying now. "Why? Has something happened?"

"Not that I know of," Bobby answered. "Are you the young lady who was in Angel Alley the day before yesterday?"

She looked at him steadily—too steadily and too long. She said:—

"Angel Alley? Where is that? I thought it was about Lady Geraldine?"

Bobby let the Angel Alley question drop. He was fairly sure it meant something to her, even a good deal, and he was even more sure that she did not intend to say what that something was.

"Not about Lady Geraldine exactly," he answered. "I'm told she is away and you have not heard from her for some time. Is that so? Has it made you uneasy at all?"

"Well, she didn't say anything about stopping away, and she didn't take much with her, and then there was a visit to some friends in the country she meant to make, and they haven't heard from her either," Mona explained. "That's all, only when Mr Godwinsson said some one was asking about her, I thought perhaps there had been an accident or something."

The tall young Wagner-like hero Bobby had spoken to before had now returned, and was standing in the doorway with his hands in his pockets, looking both sulky and troubled. Bobby regarded him with fresh interest. He had noticed the name used, 'Godwinsson,'—the same name as that mentioned by the porter at 'The Line'. An unusual name, so almost certainly there was some connection, and that connection might, or might not, be significant. For the time, however, he decided it would be better not to press the point. He said to the girl:

"May I ask your name? Do you live here?"

"My name is Leigh—Monica Leigh," she answered; and he had the impression that since his mention of Angel Alley she spoke with caution and restraint. "Lady Geraldine is an old friend and school-fellow, and I am staying with her till I get a job. I've just been demobbed from the Wrens," she explained, and Bobby felt she mentioned this as a kind of guarantee of respectability.

"If you wish it," he said, "we can make inquiries for you. The hospitals and so on," he explained.

"Oh, no," she exclaimed quickly. "I expect it's all right; it's sure to be. It's only your coming, and then that other man. I thought something must have happened."

"The man Mr Godwinsson spoke of? The one who said he wasn't a policeman?"

"That's right," the tall young Godwinsson said. "I suppose he was, wasn't he?"

"Not if he said he wasn't," Bobby answered. "Can you describe him?"

"Big sort of chap—about forty or so. Gone to seed a bit. Red face and smelt of beer. I didn't notice particularly."

Not much of a description, Bobby thought, but one that could very well apply to ex-Sergeant Stokes.

"I think I know who you mean," he said. "If you will let me use your 'phone, I think I might be able to get a photo I should like you to identify, if you will." The girl nodded an assent. Bobby rang up the Yard, and asked for a special messenger to be sent immediately with a photograph of Stokes. If possible, he would like one of a group in which Stokes appeared. The identification would be more sure if he could be picked out from among others. "I ought to tell you," Bobby said, turning to the two young people, who had been watching with obvious unease, "that if it is the man I think, I don't much like it. Sounds a bit like mischief—as if something may be wrong. What did he want to know?"

"He asked for Gerry," Mona answered. "Where she was. He asked a lot of questions. I couldn't understand what he meant. He said he wasn't a policeman. At last I told him to go away, and he did. That's all."

"I wish I had been here," young Godwinsson muttered. "This is what I came about," Bobby said. He produced another of the Joey Parsons photographs. "I wanted to ask if Lady Geraldine knew this man. Have either of you seen him?"

Monica gave the photograph only a casual glance and shook her head, then began to look puzzled. But young Godwinsson stiffened as if in recognition of some threat or imminent danger, and his first air of startled apprehension changed to an expression so blank, controlled and stiff that Bobby was at once convinced that he both knew and did not mean to tell—perhaps even that he dared not.

CHAPTER IX

URGENT MESSAGE

BOBBY WAITED patiently. He felt as certain that Mona knew nothing but was going to say something as he did that young Godwinsson knew something and would say nothing. When Mona did speak it was to Godwinsson. She said:

"You never met Mr Brown, Gurth, did you?"

"I don't know. Who is he?" asked the young man, who apparently owned the unusual first name of 'Gurth.'

"He's a clergyman," Mona answered. "He comes to see Gerry sometimes." She picked up the photo and looked at it again. "He has a much fuller face and a little pimple or something by the side of his nose, and it's a different shape, too, and the eyes are ever so different. Only it's funny, because somehow it reminds you of Mr Brown—almost like a sort of family resemblance."

"Could you give me Mr Brown's address?" Bobby asked.

"I've no idea," Mona answered. "He comes to see Gerry about a boys' club he runs somewhere near the docks, I think. He gets her to subscribe."

"Does he, though?" said Gurth, impressed. "One up to him."

Mona looked severe.

"Gerry's never mean," she said, "and Mr Brown is awfully impressive." She paused, flushed slightly, and then said with a little air of defiance: "Last time he was here he had us all on our knees—he just made us, Mrs Cook, too."

"Good Lord!" said Gurth. "Gerry as well."

"He's rather frightening," Mona said. "He makes it all sound so real. It would scare any one."

She looked hard at Gurth, defying him to say a word. He didn't. Bobby was still looking at the photo. An air of Joey Parsons about it? A kind of family resemblance? But fuller cheeks? Could that mean padding? A 'pimple or something' at the side of the nose, and that nose of a different shape? Yes, but much can be done with the aid of flesh-coloured wax. The eyes different? Not even the most expert and careful touching up can give life to the eyes of a dead man. Bobby said absently:

"Who is Mrs Cook?"

"She is out," Mona answered. "It's her day off. She is Gerry's cook and housekeeper and everything."

"When you see Mr Brown again, will you please ask him to get in touch with us?" Bobby asked.

"Well, he doesn't come very often," Mona said. "He was here a few days ago. I didn't see him, but Gerry told me. He touched her for five pounds for his boy's club."

"Good Lord!" said Gurth again, and he shook a disbelieving head.

A knock at the door announced the arrival of a dispatch-rider from Scotland Yard with a group photograph in which ex-Sergeant Stokes appeared. Gurth Godwinsson pointed out Stokes at once.

"That's the bloke," he said, and to Bobby he said with a slight air of 'caught you this time': "Thought you told us he wasn't a cop?"

"He was, but he isn't," Bobby answered. "His name is Stokes. He left the Force some time ago. I don't understand what he can want with Lady Geraldine. We shall have to pick him up and ask. It needs explaining. If he comes again, let us know at once—dial 999—and a flying-squad car will be here immediately. I'll warn them to be on the look-out for any call from you."

"I don't understand all this," Gurth said, "I think you ought to tell us what it's all about."

"Perhaps I ought, but I can't, because I don't know," Bobby answered. "What I want is to get information about the original of this photo I've shown you. He is under suspicion. He seems to have been annoying people, and Lady Geraldine's name got mentioned. It was possible she might be able to tell us something. Now you say this man Stokes has been here asking about her. Very likely there's nothing to it, but it is a trifle disturbing." He paused, and then said, speaking very slowly and carefully: "There's nothing much to go on, and it may all mean nothing, but there is a suggestion of rather serious complications in the background. A mare's nest, very likely. One never knows. A mare's nest has to be searched for even if it isn't there." Looking from one to the other of the two listening young people, he said: "I hope you are both telling me all you know. I hope very much you are being absolutely frank. I shall probably have to call here again. Meanwhile will you both please try very hard to remember anything at all? Even the merest trifle may help."

"Help what? How?" Gurth grumbled. "How can we, when we haven't the foggiest idea what it's all about."

"It's about," Bobby replied, "why Lady Geraldine hasn't come back? What Stokes wanted? Who is Mr Brown? Where is his boys' club?" He paused, and bestowed upon them his most amiable smile. "Why? What? Where? Who?" he said. "There ought to be a 'When', too. Shall we say 'When we three meet again'?" Once again he paused, looking from one to the other. He said very slowly: "I do most earnestly ask you to be absolutely frank."

Mona flushed slightly and looked away from Bobby towards Gurth. Gurth's eyes were hard and stubborn, his expression angry, defiant. For a minute or two they were both silent. Then Gurth mumbled: "Of course," but his eyes remained as hard, as hostile, as before.

"Thank you," Bobby said. Carefully making his voice quiet and as ordinary as possible, he continued: "I felt sure I could rely on you when it may be something serious. At least, I think it may, and I think you think so, too. Good-bye for the present."

Then he went quickly away. It was never his practice to begin by trying to press a witness or to drive him or her into a corner. If necessary, that could come later. But at first it was always the wiser course to allow time for thought. The willing witness had opportunity to remember and to reflect, so recollecting forgotten details and perceiving meanings not before understood. The hostile or guilty witness had time to grow uneasy, to see danger, to seek ways of safety that as often as not involved him in fresh difficulties, even in self-betrayals. There was of course the hostile witness who remained obstinately silent, finding in silence a sure refuge. Fortunately that is very, very rare, so great and pressing is the human urge to talk.

At the entrance to the flats Bobby spoke to the porter on duty, showing his card and explaining who he was. As it happened, by a slip, he gave his private card, with his private address and telephone number. The porter, learning Bobby's identity, was plainly impressed. He had seen a paragraph in the papers about Bobby's record and recent appointment to Scotland Yard, and he was quite willing to help. When shown the group photograph sent at Bobby's request from Scotland Yard and asked if he recognized any one, he picked out Stokes at once.

"That bloke was here yesterday," he said. "Been drinking, if you ask me. I saw him come in. I didn't take much notice. It wasn't as if he was selling anything. We clear that sort out quick when we spot them. Tenants don't like it. Then he came down again and went out, and popped back at once, scared most to death, by his looks. The way blokes looked when they saw the tanks coming and them in the open. I asked him what was up. I thought maybe he was wanted—police, I mean. I had a look, but there wasn't any one—not to notice. I asked him, and he said it wasn't cops; it was his wife. He said if she saw him she would be sure he was after a girl they knew about here and, anyway, why wasn't he at work? He said could he go out the back way? Well, me being a married man myself, I said O.K., and he did. But afterwards I began to think he was lying, and it was more than his wife made him look the way he did."

"I shouldn't wonder," agreed Bobby, who found this story disturbing. "If there are any more men frightened of being seen by their wives, or if you notice anything else in any way out of the ordinary, dial 999, no matter even if it seems the merest trifle. You know Miss Mona Leigh?"

"The young lady staying with Lady Geraldine Rafe?"

"Yes. I've been to see her. She seems a little worried about Lady Geraldine. She has been away some days, and Miss Leigh hasn't heard from her."

The porter gave a discreet smile.

"It's happened before," he said. "She'll be back and looking none the worse for it. Why, I've seen her come in hardly able to stand, and next morning as spry as you please. It's a gift, that's what it is."

"I suppose it is," agreed Bobby, and looked thoughtful. "Interesting," he said, and meant it.

Then he departed, and back at Scotland Yard found a new piece of information waiting for him. The two bullets—the one that had been discovered in the dead body and the other Bobby had pointed out in the wall of the Angel Alley room—had been subjected to expert examination. A report had now come in and declared, with some excitement showing through the formal language employed, that both bullets had been fired from a once-popular, but now obsolete, and very rare, small automatic, known as the Lege Mark 4, and long out of production. It had still been in use for a time at the beginning of the first world war, but a tendency to jam unless kept in the most meticulous order had soon proved it useless for the rough purposes of war. The report did rather seem to suggest that identification of this rare make of pistol as the weapon used was much the same as identification of the criminal—a postulate Bobby found himself unable to accept. Of course, the discovery of such a weapon in the possession of any person in any way connected with the crime would require a lot of explanation, but most likely the thing was by this time at the bottom of the Thames.

Bobby turned to other matters. First he looked up Colonel Godwinsson in *Who's Who*, obtained his country address, and rang up the county police to ask for information about him. The reply, given in a voice equally surprised and shocked, was to the effect that Colonel Godwinsson was one of the most respected and influential personalities in the county. Not popular exactly. His standards were too high and his judgments too severe for popularity. He ruled with a rod of iron, but always with justice. "A beast, but a just beast," Bobby quoted, but this was not approved. "Only riff-raff and criminals would ever call him a beast," declared the voice at the other end of the line. Not rich by any means, the voice continued. At one time the Godwinssons had been very large landowners till death duties and recurring agricultural depressions hit them very badly. But the Colonel still owned a fair amount of land, some of which was said to have been in possession of the family since before the Norman Conquest. The Godwinssons—by the way, the two Vs' were important, the Colonel didn't like it if one was forgotten—claimed to be descended from Earl Godwin, the father of King Harold slain at the Battle of Hastings. The legend was that they had never accepted the peerage offered more than once through the centuries, because they had never recognized the right of William the Conqueror or his descendants to the throne. They considered that their own title was much superior through Earl Godwin as father of King Harold. The Colonel had three sons, Harold, Gurth, and Leofric, these names being traditional in the family. Harold had been shot by the Germans during the first days of the invasion of France. Gurth was on the Stock Exchange. Leofric was interested in horse-racing and in the breeding of pedigree stock. He was assistant to a well-known racehorse trainer. The voice over the 'phone said a little anxiously that it hoped neither of the young men had been getting into trouble. This was an obvious hint that information as to the why and wherefore of these inquiries would be gratefully received; but Bobby merely said that there were some preliminary investigations on foot and it was desirable to know something of Colonel Godwinsson and his sons. That was all, and probably all quite unimportant.

Next Bobby rang up the police of the Angel Alley district. By good luck, Constable Barlow, who had reported the tall young gentleman noticed near Angel Alley, was on the spot, and soon came to the 'phone. He didn't think he would be able to recognize the young gentleman again. He had only had a passing glimpse of him. Oh, no, not in any way outstandingly good-looking. Just ordinary, in fact. Bobby thanked him and rang off. Apparently this young man was not, then, identical with Gurth Godwinsson, whom no one could possibly describe as 'just ordinary'.

One possible clue faded out, then. But that was the way of clues. They had a trick of fading out, and Bobby hardly felt even disappointed as he turned to a list of boys' clubs. Necessary, he decided, to have an inquiry made at every known boys' club in London in an effort to trace Lady Geraldine's friend.

"Not much chance, though," Bobby told himself. "Ten to one the fellow's a fake. Only what's the idea? Why the boys' club? And why Lady Geraldine?"

He was still moodily contemplating a problem that, starting with the death of an unknown man, apparently a mere hanger-on of some gang or another, seemed now to be involving curious and diversified personalities. His 'phone rang. He answered. A familiar voice—that of his wife, Olive—asked:

"Who is your girl friend?"

"You," said Bobby promptly.

"Smarty," said Olive. "A girl has just rung up. It was rather funny: She said: 'Are you there, Bobby?' I said, No, it was me, and who was speaking? She said: 'Mona speaking. Tell Bobby not to come. Tell him I'm all tied up with engagements and things and I have to go out, so it's no good his coming to-day.'"

"Good God!" Bobby exclaimed, and his face was very pale as he sprang to his feet.

CHAPTER X

RESCUE AND DENIAL

BOBBY STARED but a moment or two to be sure that instructions went out immediately to all Flying Squad cars to concentrate on the block of flats where Mona Leigh was staying with the missing Lady Geraldine. Then he fled; and in the yard outside found, by good luck, a returning dispatch-rider dismounting in leisurely fashion from his motor-cycle. There was nothing leisurely about Bobby as he grabbed the cycle, leaped into the saddle, and tore off, leaving a gaping and highly indignant dispatch-rider staring after him.

"That's our Bobby, that was," explained the uniformed man on duty; and how bitterly indignant and hurt 'our Bobby' would have been had he heard how the constable added in a meditative voice: "Most likely he's heard there's a scrap going and he's afraid he'll miss it if he doesn't hurry."

Flying Squad men in their more expansive moments, and provided no senior officer is within hearing, will sometimes tell you that when 999 is dialled they are on the spot before there has been time to hang up the receiver. Bobby, indeed, fully expected to find two or three cars already there and the crews, he hoped, in possession of Lady Geraldine's flat. Unfortunately this time it did not happen quite like that. A specially urgent call had gone out only the moment before, warning all cars in the district that there had been a smash-and-grab raid. The raiders, escaping in a stolen car, were travelling that way, and every effort must be made to intercept them. Not even the Flying Squad can carry out efficiently at the same time two mutually contradictory orders, and the general feeling was that precedence should be given to the smash-and-grab call, clear and definite, over this other call Bobby had had sent out. It specified no definite reason, and might easily be a false alarm, as was so often the case even with calls that, like this, were 'urgent'.

Of this unfortunate complication Bobby was of course quite unaware, but, as he sped through the streets, thought only, erroneously, that his luck was in, since time after time he came to the traffic lights just as they were changing to 'Go'. Dis-appointment awaited him, though, when he reached the flats, where all was quiet and normal and no police cars in sight. He ran into the building, and to the startled porter he called:

"Get a key to Lady Geraldine's flat. There's something wrong—quick, I tell you," he added, as the porter only stood and gaped. "Hurry."

This time there was that in his voice sent the porter scurrying. Nor did Bobby wait for the lift, which, as it happened, was again in use. He went up the stairs at a rush, and at once thundered insistently on the door of the flat, hammering with both fists. It was a solid door, well made and strong. Useless to try to break it down, he felt, even though, just as he arrived, before he began his loud assault, it seemed to him—or had his over-heated imagination deceived him?—that he heard come through that solid door the faint echo of the cry of one in dreadful fear. Or was it of one in still more dreadful pain?

He wished, as he hammered away, that he had brought a pistol with him. Had he done so he would have used it to try to shoot away the lock. He stopped hammering for a moment and drew back to throw all his weight against the door in the vain hope that the lock might yield. It held. He hammered at the door again, beating with ineffectual fists, and from the nearer flats startled inmates came hurrying out to see what was the matter. One elderly and indignant gentleman, whose afternoon peace had been most rudely disturbed, tried, indeed, to interfere, and got brushed aside with a vigour that nearly sent him sprawling. Fortunately he was saved by a wall against which he was somewhat abruptly brought up.

"The fellow's mad, drunk. Disgraceful," he protested at the top of his voice. "Where's the porter?" he demanded, and was returning gallantly to the charge when a uniformed figure appeared from out the lift. "Ah, the police," said the elderly gentleman with great satisfaction as he bustled forward. "Officer," he began, "this man's creating a most outrageous disturbance—"

But there he stopped, for the outrageous disturber of the peace shouted an order to the newcomer to go round to the rear of the building, make sure no one escaped that way, and then come back—'and hurry'.

The uniformed man vanished as juniors in rank do when seniors use that tone of voice. The elderly gentleman stared and thought vaguely of writing to *The Times*. The manager of the flat came hurrying, the porter with him.

"The key?" Bobby snapped, snatched it from the manager, opened the door, and ran in, flinging over his shoulder a brief order to the manager to keep every one out.

The manager passed the order to the porter and hurried after Bobby. A faint moaning sound directed them. They ran into that frivolous sitting-room with its background of knick-knacks, eccentric dolls, frilly curtains and cushions, and so on. On the floor lay Mona, her hands tied behind her, her face bruised and bleeding. One leg was bare, the shoe and stocking having been torn off. On the flesh of the calf showed the angry scar of a recent burn, and near by a lighted cigarette was burning a hole in the carpet. Bobby knelt by her side. She looked up. She said:

"You've come—I thought you might."

"You're safe now," Bobby told her, and began to free her hands. She cried out with the sharp pain as he did so and as the blood began to flow back into her numbed fingers.

"You're hurting," she said, whimpering like a hurt child. "He burnt my leg," she said.

Bobby picked her up and put her down on a bed in an adjoining room. He set the manager of the flats to chafe her numbed hands, where the returning circulation was still being painful. Also he gave her a drop or two of brandy from his pocket flask, and he did his best—he always carried a first-aid box with him—to dress the burn on her leg. She was crying quietly. The Flying Squad man came back into the room.

"There's a window open at the rear," he said, "and a stack-pipe handy. A man's been seen climbing out. No one did anything. Just thought it was funny. One lady said he wasn't climbing in, only out, so she thought it was all right. That's people," he said, with a gesture of washing his hands of the whole human race.

Bobby told him to get a doctor and an ambulance to take Mona to hospital. Mona opened her eyes and said she didn't want to go to any hospital. Bobby said 'O.K.', but to hospital she was going. She could fight it out with the hospital when she got there. Meanwhile was she strong enough to tell him what had happened? Could she manage? It was in rather a trembling and shaken voice that Mona said she would try, and she looked very grateful when the Flying Squad man appeared with a cup of tea.

"There was a knock," she began, "and when I went to answer it—I thought perhaps it was Gurth come back, he had only been gone a minute or two—a man pushed in and got hold of me. He said he would kill me if I made a sound. He had a knife and poked it at me. He had a mask on, and he looked awful—oh, and great black gloves."

"Surgical rubber gloves, to prevent leaving dabs," Bobby said. "Go on."

"He pushed me down on the floor and he tied my hands—it did hurt. He said he was going to hurt me much worse than that if I wasn't careful. He told me not to move or he would come back and cut my throat. He went into the other rooms, and then he came back, and he wanted to know where Gerry was. I said I didn't know, and he said I was lying, and he pulled me up and hit me. He kept asking, and I couldn't tell him because I don't know, but I wouldn't have if I had, only I didn't. He got one of Gerry's cigarettes and lighted it and he said he was going to burn my eyes out with it if I wouldn't talk. He pulled my stocking off and burnt my leg, and when I screamed because it hurt so awfully he put his hand over my mouth and did it again, and I think perhaps I fainted or something, but I don't know. I remember I began to scream again, and he put his hand back on my mouth, and then there was a great banging at the door and I suppose it was you. He listened, and he jumped up and went away, and then it was you. You are Mr Owen, aren't you?"

"Yes," Bobby answered. "How did you manage to get that 'phone message through?"

"That was before," Mona answered. "I told him he didn't dare do anything because my brother was coming. I said he had just rung up to say he was coming to take me out. He said I must 'phone to tell him not to come, and I said I wouldn't, so he hit me and said I must. I pretended I wouldn't because I was afraid he might get suspicious if I gave in too easily. And he hit me again and I still wouldn't, till he began to twist my ear. It did hurt, and I gave in. I said I would do what he wanted if he would stop. I knew your 'phone number because of your card you gave the porter, and he brought it up to show us and tell us who you were, and Gurth was awfully interested. He said your 'phone number was easy to remember because each number doubled the other—1 2 4 8. I thought perhaps you might understand what I meant, and it was all I could think of, but a woman's voice answered, and I was so terrified she wouldn't."

"My wife," Bobby said. "She passed it on. You really don't know where Lady Geraldine is?"

"I've no idea," Mona answered. "Do you think something's happened? Why did that man want to know?"

"I wish I could tell you," Bobby answered. "It was you in Angel Alley, wasn't it?"

Mona was silent for a moment or two. She looked straight at Bobby.

"You understood and you came at once and saved me," she said slowly, very slowly, weighing each word as it were. "You will never know how grateful I am. I feel I could lick your boots or al-most anything." She paused and, speaking still more slowly, still more deliberately, she said: "I have never heard of Angel Alley and I have never been there in my life."

CHAPTER XI

BACKGROUND

MORE POLICE began to arrive as the alarm became more wide-ly spread. The ordinary routine of an investigation took shape. Mona, near to collapse now that the first effect of the excitement of her rescue was wearing off, was dispatched to hospital. Bobby made arrangements for a married constable and his wife to come to the flat as temporary caretakers till either Lady Geraldine was heard from or till Mona was well enough to return.

He took no active part in the investigation now begun. Any trained detective officer of any experience was as well qualified as himself to follow up such obvious clues as finger-prints, or other recognizable physical trace discovered, any information any witness could supply, and so on. What he now set himself to do was to obtain some idea of the background against which these events had occurred and to trace if possible the thread that led from the unknown dead man in an East-End slum to this ex-pensive apartment in a fashionable block of flats. Fortunately there was no need to break open desks or drawers in order to ob-tain papers and letters for examination. The breaking open had been done very effectively by Mona's assailant and all contents strewn on the floor. One of the first things Bobby picked up was a cheque-book, which, though some of the counterfoils had never been filled in, showed fairly heavy payments at frequent inter-vals. At a rough guess Bobby estimated that Lady Geraldine had been living at the rate of two or three thousand a year. Nothing to show the source of her income, though, and no trace of that prolonged correspondence with the income-tax authorities most people have to endure in these days. The letters Bobby found, few in number, seemed to be all trivial: everyday notes of no im-portance, invitations, bills, and so on. Very likely, as is so often the case to-day, Lady Geraldine never wrote a letter if she could help it, making use of the telephone instead. On the face of it, the record of any young society woman enjoying herself on a basis of satisfactory private means.

Bobby put them all—papers, invitations, bills, receipts, everything—in a heap together for their owner to sort out on her return. Next he turned his attention to the two or three framed photographs he had noticed and took to be those of Lady Geraldine. He studied these with care, with absorbed interest, with an increasing feeling of doubt and even of bewilderment. He was still so engaged when the sergeant in charge came up.

"Rather a dead end, sir, I'm afraid," he reported. "No Jabs, nothing, no one noticed anything, no description of the man seen climbing down the stack-pipe that amounts to anything of any use whatever."

"I think we can be quite sure it was Cy King," Bobby remarked. "He comes in it somewhere. No proof, of course, and you'll find conclusive evidence he was filling up football-pool coupons all afternoon with highly respectable friends. What do you make of these?" he added, showing the photographs of Lady Geraldine he had been studying with such care. "She doesn't look to me like a drunk."

"No, sir; we've noticed that," the sergeant agreed. "She's young. Hasn't begun to tell yet. Now in a few years ..."

"Yes, in a few years," Bobby agreed.

But all the same that was not quite what he had meant. The sergeant went away. Bobby continued staring at the photographs. Difficult to relate them to the irresponsible and senseless folly for which Lady Geraldine seemed to have gained a reputation. They showed a tall girl, bigly made, with large hands and feet, and large, strongly marked features. Handsome rather than pretty, with a thin, long, tightly closed mouth, and an expression of indefinable pride and resolution. Not, as Bobby had meant when he remarked that Lady Geraldine did not look like a 'drunk', the face of one likely to seek an easy refuge in drink.

A formidable face, Bobby thought, and one of many possibilities. He found himself wishing that photographs could show, as neither can they nor the portrait-painter, the vivid life that lies in the most revealing feature of all—the eyes.

The sergeant came back. He said:

"There's a lady, sir. Says she lives here. Housekeeper. Mrs Cook."

"Oh, yes," Bobby said. "Just explain what's happened and then let me have a talk with her, will you?"

He resumed his study of the photographs, trying with ill success to wrest from them the secret of the personality lying behind that dark, brooding face. Capacity there, he felt, for good or ill; and which way had it turned? Pride, he thought, the 'directive'; but how had pride worked?—pride which is, by strange paradox, both one of the seven deadly sins and yet a foundation stone of courage and of virtue.

"Mrs. Cook, sir," announced the sergeant, returning.

Mrs Cook was a stout, elderly woman, now flushed with excitement. Bobby listened patiently while she told him how she had never heard of such goings on, that she didn't know what things were coming to, that it was worse than war, that she never did, never, and why had poor dear Miss Mona, as sweet a child as ever was, been sent off to hospital, where she would be no more than a number on a ticket, when she, Mrs Cook, would have taken good care of the poor lamb in her own home?

Bobby, listening carefully, dropping in an occasional question or two, came to the conclusion that Mrs Cook was an honest, kindly, trustworthy woman, though not perhaps very highly intelligent. He explained that Miss Leigh required the skilled medical attention the hospital would provide. Mrs Cook sniffed.

"Them nurses," she said, and as she said it, it was enough.

Bobby began to question her discreetly about Lady Geraldine. It seemed Mrs Cook was an old family servant. The connection had been broken during one of Lord Sands's periodic retreats to the Continent away from bills and creditors and all that. It had been resumed when Lady Geraldine took this flat and needed a housekeeper. Mrs Cook seemed to have no idea of where Lady Geraldine's income came from and had apparently never given the matter a thought. Lady Geraldine was 'quality', real quali-

ty, and it was a part of the natural order of things for 'quality'
to have money, even though temporary embarrassments might
arise at times. Mrs Cook supposed Lady Geraldine had 'come into
money', but she didn't know. Certainly she spent freely, as a real
lady should; and why not? As nice a lady as ever lived, Mrs Cook
declared heatedly, and all a pack of lies about her drinking too
much. Cocktails now and then, and nasty things, too, but that was
all, and the talk all rubbish, as who should know better than Mrs
Cook herself?

"It was the police out of spite," declared Mrs Cook defiantly.
"They had it in for her, and it ought to be seen to. Not so long ago
the police summonsed her for being drunk in charge of a car. A
little upset of course she was, with being stopped and questioned
like that, as was only natural, poor lamb, but as sober as any judge
as I could see for myself. And one time the police pretended she
was so mad drunk it took three of them to get her to the cells."

More lies, Mrs Cook protested volubly, and silly lies, too. As
if it needed three big policemen to handle one woman, and her
a lady brought up delicate like. What had really happened, Mrs
Cook explained, was that her ladyship had smacked a policeman's
face for being rude, and then they had all set about her. A fair
scandal, and it ought to have been seen to, but Lady Geraldine
hadn't wanted to make a fuss and her name in the papers and all.

Bobby shook his head, said he was sorry to hear these complaints, and he would make inquiries. Did Lady Geraldine often
go away and stay away without notice or explanation? Miss Leigh
seemed a little worried.

Mrs Cook didn't think there was anything to be worried about.
Lady Geraldine went abroad sometimes, and most likely this time
she had had to go in a hurry. Generally it was when she had to
write something for the papers. About the fashions and what they
were going to be like. She never talked about it, because it was
rather low and demeaning for real quality to write for the papers,
and Mr Owen would oblige if he didn't mention it. Bobby promised faithfully to do his best to preserve this dark secret; and Mrs
Cook, pleased, then admitted that sometimes, too, Lady Geral-

dine liked to slip away for peace and quiet, away from the racket of society, to enjoy the country where no one knew her.

"I always knew when that was it," Mrs Cook explained, "because of the flowers she brought back—primroses and violets and such like she had picked where she had been staying. What she loved more than anything else."

Bobby suppressed an inward gasp. This idyllic picture went ill, he thought, with that dark, enigmatic face of many possibilities he had studied with such care. Recovering slightly, he said, with false enthusiasm, that there was nothing he enjoyed more than a quiet day in the country among the bluebells and the cowslips. The sergeant, at this, entirely failed to suppress his inward gasp. Bobby gave him a severe look and asked him if he remembered that day when they had spent an afternoon making daisy chains with the village children. The sergeant, looking a little wild now, said he remembered it perfectly; and Mrs Cook lost all distrust of policemen who could so employ their afternoons. She went on chatting. To her—and it was clear this was a genuine belief—Lady Geraldine was of a pre-eminently shy and retiring disposition, unfortunately obliged by the exigencies of her birth, to take a prominent part in the social round, though her own wishes were for a quiet country cottage and a garden full of flowers. Above all, timid and nervous to a degree that Mrs Cook evidently thought was highly becoming. Why, she had even insisted on getting one of those ladders advertised as providing a means of escape in case of fire and on keeping it always somewhere handy in her bedroom.

Questioned about visitors, Mrs Cook became vague. It wasn't her place to notice visitors. There weren't many. Colonel Godwinsson and the two young gentlemen, and others of Lady Geraldine's friends. Some of them, Mrs Cook was afraid, not quite her class. Lady Geraldine was so friendly and trusting. Very often Mrs Cook didn't even know their names. If Lady Geraldine wanted to entertain, it was generally at a restaurant or a night club. Shown the photograph Bobby had brought of the dead man of Angel Alley, Mrs Cook failed to recognize it. Asked about Mr Brown, she looked grave. A really good man, though perhaps rather too strict in his views, but that was just as well in these days. She had heard him talk very straight to some of Lady Geraldine's friends, telling them off proper and warning them where it would end. They would laugh about it afterwards, but not while he was talking to them. He made no bones about reminding them of the fire that was never quenched and the worm that dieth not. Made them think. Other times he could talk wonderful nice and gentle, so it made you cry to hear him, yearning over you, like a mother over her babes. Bobby might laugh, she told him defiantly, but he ought to have heard Mr Brown when he was talking like that.

Bobby said he had no wish to laugh, which was quite true. He was far too interested. He tried to get some definite information from her about Mr Brown, but it seemed she had no idea of where he lived or worked. All she knew was that the world would be a better place if there were more like him. A saint, though expecting others to live same as he did, as was more than most could. Sometimes Lady Geraldine would joke about his visits being so expensive because he always went off with a cheque from her for his boys' club. Sometimes from other people as well.

Asked about Mona, Mrs Cook had little to say, except that she was a very nice young lady, though not quite of the same class as Lady Geraldine. When Bobby wondered if Miss Leigh and Gurth Godwinsson were thinking of getting engaged, Mrs Cook was frankly amused. If you asked her, Mr Gurth was head over heels in love with Lady Geraldine, but Lady Geraldine wasn't one for the men. She kept them at arm's length and boxed their ears for them if they came any nearer. Oh, yes, gentle and quiet as she was as a rule, if she were roused she could show all the spirit of her fighting ancestors, who had been soldiers since no one knew when. Not that there was any truth in that silly tale about her hitting a too-pressing admirer on the head with a champagne bottle. Just another lie. A coffeepot had been used.

On this triumphant note the interview ended; and as it was now late, and time for dinner, Bobby, wondering a little if the background he had thus so laboriously built up was really going to be much use, returned home to consider the information gathered and to decide on future action.

CHAPTER XII
27495?

THE NEXT MORNING Bobby found on his desk at the Yard, as a result of the inquiry he had set on foot, a list of all London boys' clubs in whose affairs any one of the name of Brown took part. There were several, including two or three in the Canon Square-Angel Alley district, and these Bobby decided to visit first. A long shot, of course, and a shot in the dark, but one never knew. The faintest indication sometimes proved of primary importance.

There was a good deal of desk work he had to attend to before he was free, and it was getting late in the afternoon before he drew up his car outside the police station in whose district was Angel Alley. He had rung up to say he was coming and why, and the station sergeant had ready the information required. It seemed the Mr Brown connected with one of the neighbouring clubs was a local business man, well known for his interest in social activities and for his rather more than local fame as an athlete in former days. Bobby lost interest in him at once. At the other club there was a Mr Brown, a well-to-do stockbroker, resident in the West End, who came somewhat irregularly. He was always very welcome both for his lively and invigorating personality and for his influence on the lads, and also because he was a liberal contributor to the club funds. Of Mr Brown himself the local police knew nothing, nor was there any reason why they should. Bobby took a note of the address of the club. He thought it might be worth while to pay it a visit.

"Is it well attended?" he asked.

"Very popular indeed," said the station sergeant. "For one thing, they don't overwork the religious side. It's there, but they don't push it down the boys' throats. I remember hearing that's why they got Mr Brown's help and his subscriptions. He visited one or two other clubs, but thought they were too much like Sunday schools. He says he's not a religious man himself, but he does believe in decent living."

"He doesn't think there is any connection?" Bobby asked.

The sergeant considered this, and decided to pass it over.

"The club does very good work," he said, slightly on the defensive now. "It gets called 'Angel's Home' very often, or 'Angels' for short, because some one said it was founded to turn the little devils from Angel Alley into little angels. Has a good try, anyhow. The proper name is 'Action Stations', because that is what they are always on against the bad conditions here."

"Do the boys pay any subscription?" Bobby asked.

"No. And in my humble opinion it's a mistake. 'Let 'em all come' is the idea, and it means too many black sheep get in. I've known alibis sworn to when we knew well enough the lad had been mixed up with some of these gangs. But his pals swore he was at 'Action Stations', and it sounded so good the jury gulped it down."

"I suppose," Bobby suggested, "they think if they can get hold of the black sheep in time, there may be a chance of getting some of the dye off before it's soaked in for good."

"There's that," agreed the sergeant, "but you do get some thorough young scoundrels, rotten bad through and through, and they spread the rot. We've one in the cells now—Eddy Heron. They did get round at the club to thinking about barring him altogether, but this Mr Brown begged him off. Said couldn't he have another chance? Acts tough, Mr Brown does, and that's why the boys like him, but if you ask me," said the sergeant tolerantly, "as soft as any other old woman who thinks all you have to do is to be nice to people and then they'll be nice to you."

Bobby produced his photograph of dead Joey Parsons, but the sergeant had never seen Mr Brown, and could not say if there was any resemblance. They would know at the club, suggested the sergeant. Bobby said he would go round there and make a few inquiries. He asked what the charge was against Eddy Heron. The sergeant scratched his head and said it was funny. As funny a business as he had ever known. Eddy, narrow-chested, ill-developed, suspected of incipient T.B., had walked up to a policeman and quite deliberately smacked his face. The constable, recovering with some difficulty from his astonishment, had turned Eddy round, smacked him in turn in the place kindly provided by nature for the purpose, and told him to run home to mother. But Eddy tried again, and in the end he had to be brought in.

"Can't make it out," said the sergeant. "Seems as if he wanted to be pinched, and wanted it bad. Hadn't been drinking either. Gone off his nut, in my humble opinion, or else it's been a dare."

Bobby agreed it was strange; and, because all strange things interested him, since for all such happenings there must be a cause, he said he thought he would like a word or two with Eddy. He asked if anything had been found in Eddy's pockets. The sergeant said, No, but Mr Owen could see what there was if he wished. Privately he wondered what there could possibly be about a young street rat getting himself into trouble to interest this big noise from head-quarters. Probably just another 'V.I.P.' making a fuss about nothing to show he really was a very important person. The contents of Eddy's pockets were produced. They did not seem very interesting. A dirty handkerchief; an empty cigarette-case; an old tram-ticket or two; a piece of blank paper, folded, crumpled, dirty, and with a small safety-pin sticking in it; some bits of string and a broken boot-lace; and that was about all.

"Looks to me," Bobby said thoughtfully, "as if he had cleared out his pockets in preparation. What's this?" he added, pointing to the dirty bit of paper with the safety pin attached.

"Just a bit of paper, isn't it?" the station sergeant said. "It's blank, nothing on it. I did ask him what he was taking such care of it for, and he said he wasn't. We found it pinned inside his vest pocket."

"Well, then, why, for if he wasn't taking care of it?" Bobby wondered, and the sergeant said he didn't know, and quite plainly meant that he didn't care either.

Eddy himself was brought in. An unpleasant-looking, furtive-eyed youth; to all appearance as uninteresting and deplorable an example of what bad environment and bad heredity can make of bad material as Bobby had ever seen. He offered Eddy a cigarette, which was accepted with alacrity and suspicion. There followed a little aimless chatting, and then Bobby dropped a casual inquiry as to why Eddy had wanted so badly to be 'taken inside'. Eddy denied this with great indigestion. What had happened had been that the cop had started pushing him around, and he wasn't going to stand for that, so he wasn't. He straightened his pitifully narrow little shoulders as he said this, and tried to look tough. A question or two about the 'Action Stations' club brought no response beyond a sneer. A reference to Mr Brown, however, brought a new look into the lad's sly eyes, and he hesitated a moment or two before replying.

"Oh him?" he said at last. "He tried the reform game on me. Offered me a job. Hard work and low pay. Nothing doing. Nothing soft about me. I'm tough." And again there was that pitiful attempt at a swagger.

"Soft all through, I should say," Bobby remarked.

"Me?" protested Eddy, quite taken aback.

"You," repeated Bobby. "Tough lads don't get pinched because they think they'll be safer in than out. What are you afraid of?"

But this direct assault failed. Eddy merely looked sulky and said nothing.

"Well, think it over," Bobby advised him. "I'll tell you one thing, though. If it's what I suspect, you'll need more than a week or two at Wormwood Scrubs if you don't want to be picked out of the Thames by the river police some day. You'll want to get as far away from London as you can, or even farther."

Eddy first looked frightened, then sulkier than ever, and finally brightened up as a brilliant idea struck him.

"There's Australy," he said ingratiatingly. "If I got a bit of help ... a fresh start."

"Australia wouldn't have you at any price," Bobby told him, and Eddy looked very hurt. "Put a few years hard, honest work behind you and save half what you earn. Then there might be something doing," and now Eddy looked very dismayed. "Meanwhile, what about this?" and Bobby pointed to that folded, dirty piece of paper found pinned inside one of Eddy's pockets.

"Never saw it before," Eddy declared promptly. "The cops must have picked it up themselves somewhere."

"Any time you feel like trying to tell the truth—if you know how, that is—let us know," Bobby told him. "Meanwhile, think it over. You're in a bit of a jam, aren't you?"

Therewith Eddy was returned to the cells, and the station sergeant, looking very puzzled, said:

"Is he really up against something, do you think, sir?"

"Oh, yes. He is a badly frightened boy," Bobby answered. "I wish I knew what of. Perhaps he'll talk after a time." He picked up the piece of paper of which Eddy had denied all knowledge. "Got a canteen here, haven't you?"

"A canteen?" repeated the sergeant, slightly bewildered.

"I want to do a bit of cooking," Bobby explained gravely, and was conducted to the canteen.

There in the oven he carefully heated Eddy's bit of paper. On it there presently appeared figures—27495. Bobby, both satisfied and puzzled, made a note of them, and then returned the paper to the station sergeant, telling him that he, too, had better make a note of the figures.

"But what do they mean?" the station sergeant asked. "Your guess is as good as mine," Bobby answered, "but they probably mean something important, or why the invisible-ink business and why the safety-pin to make sure the paper wasn't lost?"

"I don't see what made you think of it," the sergeant said; slightly annoyed that he hadn't himself, but suspecting, in fact sure, that Bobby had been 'tipped off' somehow.

"Eddie lied about it," Bobby explained. "I don't know what we should do without liars," he said thoughtfully. "When I showed him that bit of paper, he swore he had never seen it before. Something you had picked up here yourselves," he said. "Well, if he was taking the trouble to tell lies about it, obviously it must have its importance. A message or note of some sort, probably. But it was apparently blank, nothing visible. So I tried it for invisible ink and those numbers showed up. Question is, what do they mean?"

The station sergeant said he thought it was a bit of a teaser. He also looked as if that fact rather pleased him. Mr Acting Deputy Commissioner, or whatever he was, Bobby Owen might be very clever, but what was the use of being clever if it didn't take you any further? Give me, the station sergeant told himself, good solid routine, and none of your fancy tricks.

Bobby, if he had known these thoughts—he only guessed them—would have agreed that there was a lot to be said for such a point of view. He agreed also, and said so, that to get at the significance of those figures was going to take a lot of hard thinking. Then he asked to be informed if Eddy decided to make a statement, and drove to the 'Action Stations' club, where the resident superintendent—a Mr Fry—shook his head sadly when he heard that young Eddy Heron was in trouble again.

"A difficult boy," he said. "That's what his school report said—difficult."

"Why not say 'vicious'?" Bobby asked. "Call a kid difficult and he is rather pleased. He is just difficult—and different—and it's your job to get over difficulties, not his. Tell him he is a vicious little rat and will come to a bad end if he doesn't pull himself together, and anyhow he knows where he is."

Mr Fry looked shocked, and said modern psychiatry—Bobby interrupted to make the large, unfounded, and somewhat presumptuous claim that he knew all about modern psychiatry, the whole bag of tricks of it, and could Mr Fry tell him anything about Mr Brown?

Mr Fry brightened up. Much more agreeable to talk about Mr Brown than about Eddy Heron, too 'difficult' to reflect much credit on the club. Mr Brown was, said Mr Fry, one of the nicest gentlemen he had ever met, and a great help in every way. Very popular with the boys. He had a way with him and he took them as they were. He never preached. Just accepted them as man to man. Unfortunately he was not so frequent a visitor as Mr Fry could have wished. A busy City man. He had not visited the club for several days, but no doubt would 'breeze in', as he liked to say, sometime before long. He was a most liberal contributor to the club funds. He was always specially interested in any 'difficult' boy—Mr Fry's tone was slightly defiant as he stressed the word 'difficult'. Mr Brown often made a point of visiting such boys in their homes so as to be able to form a better judgment, and once or twice had obtained jobs for them, in the country, away from their present associates. No, Mr Brown had never given either his private or business address. In fact, he had specially asked that no attempt should be made to get in touch with him in any way. It appeared, said Mr Fry, a trifle amused, that he was a bit ashamed of taking an interest in social work. He had always laughed at it as 'pampering' and 'sentimentality', and he did not want any of his hard-boiled City friends to know what he was doing. Not at any rate till he had results to show.

"A fine character," reported Mr Fry. "A heart of gold behind an outward cynicism. He told me frankly the first time I saw him that he was a materialist and an atheist. All I can say," declared Mr Fry with emphasis, "is that I wish some of our church members were more like him, atheist though he may be and cynic though he may call himself."

Bobby said 'yes indeed', and wondered very much whether this Mr Brown, the hard-boiled, cynical but nevertheless golden-hearted Mr Brown, as known to Mr Fry, could be identical with the 'hot gospeller' of Lady Geraldine's acquaintance, and whether there could be any possible connection with the 'spiv' or 'lay about', the gangster hanger on, known as Joey Parsons. Bobby was more than ever aware of an impression that he was embarking on deep and strange waters.

Producing the photograph that had been taken of dead Joey Parsons, he asked Mr Fry if he recognized it. Mr Fry examined it with a good deal of hesitation. Not Mr Brown, he decided. Mr Brown was fuller in the face, and he had a small wart or something of the kind at the side of his nose. That did not appear in this photograph. Then Mr Brown wore spectacles—large, horn-rimmed glasses—and Mr Fry had noticed that if he took them off for a moment his eyes were very bright and quick. The eyes in the photograph were quite different—almost a dead look about them.

Bobby did not explain that they were in fact the eyes of a dead man. He thanked Mr Fry for giving him so much information, offered a contribution to the funds of the club, decided that he would only charge one half of it to his expenses account, asked to be rung up and informed if Mr Brown returned, and, as it was now late, went home for dinner.

CHAPTER XIII

THE KILBURN HOUSE

BOBBY SAT DOWN to dinner that night in one of those moods which to-day it is fashionable to call 'frustrated'.

"How are you to find out," he asked crossly—or 'frustrated-ly'—"what a number means when there's no context or anything else to suggest any connection?"

Olive wasn't listening. She said:

"That's the week's meat ration I got to-day. Will you have it all now, or shall we save some for to-morrow?"

"Let us eat to-day and be merry," Bobby answered, "for to-morrow there may be fish."

"Dreamer," said Olive.

"Well, anyhow," Bobby said, "to-day is here and now, and let to-morrow look after itself."

So he spoke, but what he really meant in his carefree, masculine way was that not itself but the woman should look after it. However, on second thoughts he left enough on the dish for next day. Then, between two thoughtful mouthfuls, he continued:

"There must be some meaning in the figures; they must mean something Eddy knew he had to remember because it was important. Or he wouldn't have lied about them. Only what? And if we did get the answer, would it come into the case?"

"Why should it?" Olive asked as, taking advantage of Bobby's worried absorption in the puzzle, she slipped back half her helping of meat on to the dish again, so making sure of a more respectable allowance for the next day. "Could it be the key to a cypher?" she asked.

"Well, you know," Bobby agreed, "that's an idea—but I don't think our criminals go in much for cyphers. Some of the spies who got rounded up during the war did, of course. But it's pretty rare in crime, though you do come across it. Only if it is, what is the good of a key if you haven't the cypher?"

"I don't know," said Olive obligingly, as Bobby seemed to expect an answer.

"It might be the number of a safe in a deposit company's vaults," he went on. "Or almost anything. But I don't know how we can find out. It is even possible Eddy doesn't know himself. Given him to keep safely or to hand on to some one else. Or even for identification purposes. He shows it, and another fellow shows the same lot, and then they click. Those," said Bobby, "are a few ideas for you to sort out."

"For me?" asked Olive, surprised.

"For you," said Bobby sternly. "What number could a little street rat like Eddy Heron want so much to remember he had to keep a note of it pinned in his pocket for safety? Any suggestions?"

"The only numbers I ever want to remember and can't," observed Olive, "are telephone numbers."

Bobby looked at her, rose from his seat, picked her up bodily, kissed her as she waved an ineffectual knife and fork in the air, put her down again, remarked that it was obvious and why the mischief hadn't she thought of it before, and went to the 'phone.

"Your dinner's going cold and you've messed my hair most awfully," said Olive.

Bobby came back to resume his meal he was no longer interested in—or at least not so much.

"I told them," he said, "to get the names of every subscriber in the country using that number, and to get 'em quick. But don't you go giving yourself airs, my girl. You may be all wet."

"What a horrid expression!" said Olive disgustedly.

"Nothing to show the exchange," Bobby remarked, "but Eddy might think he could remember that."

"I always can," observed Olive with a touch of complacence. "It's only numbers are such a bore."

Presently the 'phone rang. Bobby took pencil and pad and went to answer it. He came back with a short list of names and addresses.

"First lot," he explained. "More to follow. One's a legation—no good. Another is 'Hats and Gowns, Ltd., Bond St.' No good either. Joseph Porter, Kilburn. Um-um. Joseph Porter—Joey Parsons. Same initials. Coincidence. I think I had better slip along at once and look up Mr Porter. It's a chance."

"Oh, must you to-night?" Olive protested. "I thought we might go and see that new picture—'As Little Children'. Mrs Mills says it's lovely—every one cried and cried the whole time."

"Sounds jolly," agreed Bobby, "and I suppose we could take an umbrella." He hesitated. The picture was one the critics had all spoken of in terms usually reserved exclusively for those produced in France. He said: "Sorry, old girl. But there is just a chance this may be it, and there's more going on in the background of all this business than I like—or understand. It's not far, and I may be back in time. Anyhow, the thing's pretty sure to run a bit."

"You aren't going alone, are you?" Olive asked, a little anxiously.

Bobby said he thought on the whole he had better go by himself. The kind of preliminary chat he had in view always went better when it was kept as informal as possible. Two visitors appearing together gave a much more official air to an inquiry, and was apt at times to make people uneasy. So then they became hesitant and reserved, just when you wanted them to chat as freely as possible.

He departed then, reluctantly enough, for he had no more taste than any one else for turning out again in the evening. But there was an uneasy tagging in his mind, reminding him that he had arrived at Lady Geraldine's flat only just in time—better indeed had he been earlier. Twenty minutes drive brought him to the address given. It was a small house in a quiet Kilburn street where it seemed always Sunday afternoon—quiet, respectable, inhibited and dull. Small as were the houses, a diversity of curtains upstairs and down suggested that many of them, in the present shortage of accommodation, were occupied by two families. Almost all were badly in need of paint and general repair, as indeed are nine out of ten of the houses in this country. No. 17, the number before which Bobby drew up, had been freshly painted, however, and therefore stood out conspicuously in the generally drab extent of the street.

"Touch of black market, most likely," Bobby told himself as he alighted.

He locked the car and turned towards the house. Some one was looking at him through the front-room window. A small, white, malignant face it was; and so swiftly withdrawn Bobby had but a glimpse of it and yet was sure he recognized Cy King.

But Cy King's habitat was in the East End docks area, and from it he seldom emerged save when engaged on some criminal enterprise or another. What errand was he on, then, in this quiet, sober street where he was little likely to find either plunder or congenial companions? Bobby banged on the knocker. There was no reply. He had not much expected one. It was a terrace house with no back door or any way round to the rear. He banged on the knocker again and pressed the bell-push. He heard it ringing. Without waiting for an answer, he tried the window of the front sitting-room, the one from which he thought he had seen Cy King look out at him. It was not fastened, and he pushed it open. A maze of lace curtains and a barrage of aspidistras had to be negotiated and then he was inside, wondering a little what would happen if some indignant householder appeared, demanding explanation.

But a first glance showed him there was little likelihood of that. The room was in utter disorder. Originally it had been such a one as could be matched, almost item for item, in many thousands of houses throughout the land. The same plush suite of two fat armchairs and a settee, the spindly china cabinet, the enlarged photographs and Landseer engravings on the walls, the brass fender and fire-irons. But now the spindly china cabinet and its contents had been overturned. One of the plush armchairs was on its side. Even the enlarged photographs and the Landseer engravings either hung askew or had been thrown down, as though some one had looked behind them. The carpet was all rucked up, as if the floor beneath had been lined. Plain enough that a hasty and fairly complete search had been carried out here.

For what purpose? Bobby's mind leaped back to that other room where he had found Mona Leigh only just in time to save her from further injury. There, too, just such a search as this had taken place, and what strange link of fact or doubt was there between the very modernistic and expensive flat occupied by Lady Geraldine and this small working-class house in a Kilburn side street?

A sense of urgency sent him hurrying into the entrance passage. He noticed a 'phone, but did not stop to use it. The house was very still—still with the strong silence of the house where no living creature stirs. He hurried down the short passage into the kitchen. That, too, bore all the signs of having endured a rapid, eager search, a search indifferent to concealment or to damage done. Yet it could still be seen that this had been the general living-room, and that it had been a pleasant, friendly room where family life had flowed in contented peace. A door banged. It was the back door, leading to the small garden behind the house from the rear kitchen or scullery, where cooking and other household tasks were carried out.

Bobby ran through it into the garden. There was no exit; but the garden walls were low and the houses beyond were larger and semi-detached, with passages round them leading to the street. Perfectly easy to clamber over the garden wall into the next garden, from it reach that street, and by now be walking quietly away, even if no car had been in waiting. Pursuit would probably be quite useless, and Bobby felt his first care must be to find out what actually had happened. There might be those here in just such desperate need of help as had been Monica Leigh.

He ran back into the house and upstairs. There were three bedrooms, all originally clean, tidy, well kept, and all now in extreme confusion and disarray. In the front room was a double bed, pyjamas and night-dress neatly laid out in their cases on a rather gaudy satin bed-cover. The middle room held two small cots, and there was a toy cupboard, the contents of which had been flung on the floor in the course of the same rough and hurried search that had been carried out upstairs as thoroughly as in the ground-floor rooms. The third room, at the back, evidently intended for visitors, was in the same condition.

There was something oddly sinister in this disturbing contrast between the so evident signs of what had been the prim orderliness of a well-conducted, self-respecting household, and these plain signs of a desperate and anxious search. What cause could there be for the irruption into the placid stream of such a calm, quiet existence of this angry violence?

And where were they who have lived here? The man might still be at work; but the mother, the children? What had become of the woman of whose daily toil and loving care every room showed proof? Where were the children whose toys Bobby had noticed thrown on the floor in a pathetic heap?

No hint, save only Bobby's memory of the pale and evil face he had seen staring at him from the downstairs window and that other memory of how he had found Mona Leigh in Lady Geraldine's flat.

CHAPTER XIV

UNAVAILING SEARCH

BOBBY HURRIED downstairs again, meaning to summon help before doing anything more. He rang up the nearest police station, and had just received their promise to send assistance immediately when there came a loud knocking at the front door. Bobby went to answer it. On the doorstep was a policeman in uniform. Bobby said cheerfully:

"Well, that's what I call service."

"Eh?" said the policeman suspiciously. "You live here?"

"No," answered Bobby. "Something very wrong, though. I've just rung up to say so, and some of our people should be here almost any minute. You don't know me, do you?"

He gave his name and status, and the constable looked very impressed but still a little suspicious.

"A lady told me she had seen a man climbing in at the front window," he explained.

"Me," said Bobby. "There's no one here, but take a look inside the front room, and you'll see what I mean. Is that the lady who spoke to you?" he asked, indicating a woman hovering excitedly in the distance.

The constable said it was. Then he looked in the front room, and when he saw the chaos there he said simply: 'Lummy.' A car with two plain-clothes men in it, but with a uniformed man as driver, now appeared. The hovering woman, who had been eyeing Bobby doubtfully, not quite certain whether to scream and run in case he had murdered the now unseen constable and she might be the next, acquired confidence and drew nearer. In her hearing Bobby said to the alighting plain-clothes men:

"This is the lady who gave the alarm. She spoke to the man on the beat, and he came at once. A very great help. I only wish every one was as quick and alert." Speaking directly to her, he said: "There seems no one at home. Can you tell us who lives here?"

"It's Mr and Mrs Porter," she informed him. "Mr Porter is away on business. They've two children, and they've all been to the pictures, she and the children. They got back half an hour ago, and Mrs Porter said what a nice picture it was. She would never take them out again now it's so late."

The constable who had arrived first came to the door.

"There's no one in," he said. "I've looked everywhere. The whole place is upset."

"We had better look again," Bobby said, his underlying uneasiness not diminished in any way by what he had been told.

"There isn't any one, and nowhere where any one could be," the constable repeated.

Bobby went back into the house. The others followed him. He had noticed a door under the stairs, though in his rapid survey of the house he had done no more than pull it open to make sure no one was hiding behind it. It had been too dark to see more. He went back to it now. He had to stoop to pass through, and came at once to the head of some steps, evidently leading down to a small cellar. He called, but got no answer. He went down the steps, and by the light of his torch he switched on, he saw crouching in a corner a woman with two children clasped in her arms. She was staring up at him with frightened eyes, and the moment she saw him she began to scream. Bobby, addressing her by name, tried to say something reassuring. She continued to scream. Bobby retreated.

"Ask that woman outside to come, will you?" he said to the uniformed constable. "The one who gave you the alarm, I mean. Mrs. Porter will know her. I suppose it's Mrs Porter down there. She's all right, and the kids, too, I think, but she's scared into hysterics."

The woman came as asked. She was a Mrs Bigge. She lived next door, she said, and she succeeded in inducing Mrs Porter to believe that she was now quite safe. The poor woman was in a highly nervous condition. Her disjointed and tearful story was to the effect that as soon as she and the children entered the house on their return from the cinema a masked man had come out of the sitting-room. He poked a knife in her face and threatened that if she made a sound he would cut her throat and those of the children as well. In additional menace he had put his knife to the throat of one child. When she tried to pull it away she had cut her hand badly. She and the two children had then been hustled into the cellar under lurid threats of instant death if they made the least sound. When Bobby appeared she had been convinced that these threats were to be put into instant execution. Even yet she seemed by no means sure that they were all quite safe again. She clung pitifully to Mrs Bigge, comforted to think that among all these large, strange men there was at least one familiar face.

She was clearly in no condition to be questioned further until she had recovered more fully from the ordeal she had endured. Mrs Bigge undertook to put her to bed. Doctor and nurse were summoned. A more thorough search of the house was made with no result. No finger-prints. Gloves had probably been worn. Mrs Porter's store of household money was untouched in the usual place—an old teapot on a dresser shelf where no doubt Mrs Porter had always been convinced no one would ever dream of looking. It had been looked at, however, for it was overturned, and the lid was lying broken on the floor, but the contents—a few pounds only—had not been touched. Mrs Bigge, coming downstairs for something she wanted, said all Mrs Porter's jewellery—not very much of it or very valuable—was lying on the bedroom floor. Apparently it had not been thought worth taking.

"Disturbed," said one of the plain-clothes men. "Means the bloke heard Mr Owen knocking and was off as fast as he knew how."

"Means," said Bobby, "he was looking for something much more important than a few bits of jewellery or one-pound notes—and I wish I knew for certain what it was. I can guess, of course, but guessing isn't much good. We have to know in our job, and then we have to prove we know."

"Mrs Porter should be able to tell us," suggested the plain-clothes man.

Bobby thought that doubtful and said so. Mrs Bigge appeared, having left Mrs Porter in charge of a newly arrived nurse. The doctor, who had arrived at the same time, had already left again, promising to send at once a mild sleeping-draught. He thought Mrs Porter, though at the moment suffering from shock, only needed rest and sleep. Bobby asked Mrs Bigge what she could tell them of the Porters.

"Is Mr Porter away, or is he on night work?" he asked. "We ought to get in touch with him if we can."

It appeared that Mr Porter was often away. He was employed by a leading firm of turf agents, and his job was to estimate the form and prospects of thoroughbreds, more especially colts. He also advised prospective buyers of promising young stock. His employers, said Mrs Bigge, attached great importance to his opinion when it came to fixing odds. But Mr Porter himself never bet, though once or twice he had given Mrs Bigge valuable tips. A very nice gentleman, Mrs Bigge said, and such a home-lover. He often complained of the frequent and occasionally prolonged absences from home his work entailed, and he even spoke of getting other employment. But that would be difficult. The demand for such specialized knowledge as his was limited. So he and his family had to make the best of it, since providing for his family must be a married man's first concern.

Bobby agreed on both counts. But he had never heard of any one employed as was apparently Mr Porter. But also he could see that such an explanation provided very satisfactory reasons for absences from home and for the provision of a telephone. There are, of course, plenty of racing touts and tipsters; but the Porter background did not seem that to be expected of such persons, nor are they ever in the employ of large firms of turf agents—a much nicer name than bookmaker, for, pace Shakespeare, the smell of a rose depends much upon its name.

Possibly something he said suggested he had his doubts, for
Mrs Bigge launched, somewhat indignantly, into a eulogy of Mr
Porter's personal character. A gentleman such as you seldom met
in these days, one in a thousand. Ten thousand, she corrected
herself, apparently feeling that she had been guilty of a bad un-
der-statement. She could not, she said, speak of him too highly.
The best of husbands, the best of fathers, the best of neighbours.
He neither drank nor smoked, and he never—this was said a little
enviously—visited the local public-houses. That particular about
the children, too. He insisted that they should go regularly to
Sunday School; and, though not much of a church-goer himself,
he paid for sittings for them all at a neighbouring church. He even
encouraged Mrs Porter to attend service on the Sundays when
he was at home, and he would look after the Sunday dinner himself in order to allow her to do so. How many men, demanded
Mrs Bigge, would do that? Not many, Bobby had to admit. In Mrs
Bigge's opinion, Mrs Porter was a lucky woman, and she said so
herself. The only fly in her ointment was that Mr Porter had to
be away so often. Still, a man had to do his job, and it was all the
nicer when he was at home.

Bobby produced his photograph of dead Joey Parsons. Mrs
Bigge identified it at once. It was certainly Mr Porter, and her curiosity as to how and why it had come into the hands of the police
had to be gently suppressed.

The renewed search of the house had now been completed—without result. Mrs Porter was sleeping soundly. The children, young enough to recover quickly from a terrifying but
only half-understood experience, were also by now comfortably
asleep. Mrs Bigge returned to her own home and family. A local newspaper man who had turned up was provided with a very
watered-down account of what had happened—Bobby had no
desire for publicity at this stage of the investigation. There also
appeared a brother of Mrs Porter's. He had been working near—
he was a foreman road-sweeper under the local borough council—and a rumour of what had happened had reached him. He
seemed a sensible, responsible person, a sergeant in an infantry
regiment during the war, and he promised to bring his wife round

to stay the night. The plain-clothes men went off to make their report. Bobby drove home to find awaiting him a message from head-quarters. It was to inform him that a brown-paper parcel delivered at Wharton House, Mayfair, through the post had contained all the Duchess of Wharton's lost jewellery, as well as a good deal more recently reported stolen.

"What do you make of that?" asked Olive; and Bobby said he didn't know, and as it was late and he was feeling tired, he would go to bed and see if inspiration came in his dreams.

CHAPTER XV

AN UNEXPECTED VISIT

COLONEL HAROLD GODWINSSON, D.S.O., O.B.E., J.P., came into Bobby's room, and Bobby rose to greet him.

An impressive personality. Bobby thought he had seldom seen one more striking. In his youth the colonel must have been as handsome as his son, that dream youth, Gurth, whom Bobby had seen at Lady Geraldine's flat. Now age had taken its inevitable toll, but if something of youthful bloom had been lost, it had been replaced by an air of power and authority. A big man bigly made, he overtopped Bobby by two or three inches, and Bobby measured a good six feet; he had strongly marked, well-shaped features—those, indeed, of the ancient Viking chief of tradition or Wagnerian hero. His once-golden hair had lost much of its first lustre, but could still shine and glimmer when the sunlight caught it, and the loss of one eye only served to make more noticeable the clear, strong, piercing gaze of the other that made one think involuntarily of the solitary eagle watching from some lofty peak. The mouth, close-set and firm, seemed one that could smile on friends, but also one that would set into grim lines at any hint or sign of opposition.

As he stood there silently, the piercing gaze of his one eye fixed, whether in challenge or in question, upon Bobby, it was almost as though the room were too small to hold his tremendous personality. About him, indeed, it seemed as though pride hung like a garment, a pride so great, so much a part of himself as by natural right, that he himself was altogether unaware of its existence.

For a moment or two thus the two men stood, looking silently at each other. Bobby, accustomed to form swift judgments of others, was aware that this time he himself was being considered, judged, placed inevitably in some category or another. He wondered what—and why. He became aware of a feeling of tension in the air, as though were now beginning some strange and dark drama of which he did not understand the beginning, could not foresee the development, but knew none the less that to it there would be an ill ending.

A little absurd, though, that they should stand there facing each other like two old Norse warriors joining in ancient holmgang. Yet so they still remained, and their mutual gaze was direct and strong. Then Bobby pushed forward a chair and offered a cigarette. The chair was accepted, the cigarette refused—with perfect courtesy, indeed, but still with the faint aroma of a suggestion that in making the offer a slight liberty had been taken.

It had been a great surprise to Bobby to find on his desk, on his arrival this morning at Scotland Yard, a note not asking for ™ appointment, but simply stating that Colonel Godwinsson would be glad of a few minutes conversation with Mr Owen and for that purpose would call at ten o'clock. The wording of the note had been entirely normal, and yet it did somehow manage to convey the impression of being a command rather than a request. But, then, there was something almost regal about Colonel Godwinsson's every word and action. Oddly impressive in its way. All the more so because it was so entirely natural, so completely unselfconscious.

"I understand," he said now in slow, deep tones through which there sounded reverberations of controlled power, "that you had some conversation recently with my son, Mr Gurth Godwinsson."

"At the flat of Lady Geraldine Rafe," Bobby agreed. "Where an attack was soon after made on Miss Monica Leigh. Miss Leigh is a friend of Mr Gurth Godwinsson's, I think."

"They are acquainted," the colonel said, but not as though he altogether approved. "Lady Geraldine was my ward till she came of age. She left her flat some days ago and she has not returned.

Nor has she written. It is somewhat disturbing, more especially in view of this attack on Miss Leigh."

"A puzzling affair," Bobby agreed. "Miss Leigh's assailant seemed exceedingly anxious to know where Lady Geraldine was. You know he used great brutality in trying to make Miss Leigh tell him? We are quite in the dark as to what the fellow was after or why he was so anxious to know about Lady Geraldine. The flat was ransacked, but nothing much seems to be missing. Then something very similar took place yesterday in Kilburn."

"Indeed," said the colonel gravely. "The same sort of thing? In what way?"

"There is a resemblance," Bobby said. "A puzzling resemblance. The Kilburn house, like the flat, was entered by a masked man armed with a knife he used to emphasize his threats. And the house was ransacked. Why is not plain, since again nothing seems to have been taken." He produced another copy of the Joey Parson's photograph "This man has been identified as the occupier of the Kilburn house, and he seems also to have visited Lady Geraldine's flat. Do you recognize it as that of any one you have seen at any time? I would ask you," Bobby said formally, "to try your best to remember."

Colonel Godwinsson took the photograph, just a little with an air of rather expecting it to have been offered on bended knee. He said:

"I think I have seen the photograph before. I seem to remember noticing either it or one very like it on the porter's desk at my club. Who is it?"

"It is not that of any one you have ever seen?"

"No," the colonel answered. "No," he said again, and added sternly: "I said I thought I had seen the photograph before, not the original. Is there any reason why you should think it likely it was some one I had seen at any time?"

"We are doing our best," Bobby explained, "to find out who it is. So far we haven't had much luck. Like Lady Geraldine, he left his Kilburn home recently and has not returned. Can you give us any information about Lady Geraldine? I think you said she had been your ward till she came of age. But I think I remember hearing that her father—Lord Sands, wasn't he?—died heavily in debt."

"That is so," agreed Colonel Godwinsson, "though I don't think he realized it. Unfortunately he interested himself in business." This last word was pronounced with a faint and aloof distaste, as it might have been said: 'he interested himself in sweeping the streets.' "Naturally he lost all his money. Lady Geraldine was left in my care. Her education was provided for by her friends. After she came of age she wished to be independent."

"She seems to have lived in very good style," Bobby remarked. "Can you tell me where her income comes from?"

"I did not inquire," the colonel answered. "She was of age and fully responsible." But he spoke with a touch of hesitation this time, and Bobby had the impression that the question was one that had troubled him considerably. "From what she said at times, I understood that she earned considerable sums by advising the big shops and dressmakers on the trend of coming fashions. I think also at times she wrote for the papers. Apparently many people are willing to do that in these modern days. And I remember her telling me once she had been very lucky in bringing off a double—the Leicestershire Handicap and the Grand National, I think," and this time Colonel Godwinsson's voice was less frosty, as if he felt it much more suitable that a person of birth and breeding should obtain money by betting on horse-racing rather than by work for dressmakers or newspapers.

"It all sounds a trifle precarious and uncertain," Bobby remarked thoughtfully. "One would have thought that with her influential connections something more satisfactory could have been managed."

"Had she been willing, that could certainly have been done," Godwinsson agreed. "There were suggestions. The Duchess of Wharton made a most friendly and valuable offer."

"It wasn't accepted?"

"Unfortunately, no. I regretted it. Her Grace was willing to provide everything in return for such small services as any girl would naturally offer in her own home. I am afraid Lady Geraldine took offence—a wilful personality. She even told me that

when she wanted a job as lady's-maid she would put an advertise-
ment in the papers."

This time Bobby's sympathy was with Lady Geraldine, wilful
as she might have shown herself. It did sound to him very much
as if Her Grace of Wharton had been trying to get a 'lady help'
on the cheap. Indeed, the duchess had the reputation of being a
hard bargainer who considered that every ducal guinea should be
worth at least twenty-five shillings of more plebeian money. He
asked a few more questions and learnt that though Lady Geraldine was connected in one way or another with half the aristoc-
racy in the country there were no nearer relatives that some first
cousins living in Peru.

"You understand," Bobby explained, "that we must have some
authority for making inquiries, though in the circumstances I
think what you have told us, as her former guardian, is sufficient
ground. Though we may get into very hot water indeed if the
young lady turns up safe and sound from—well, for example from
a holiday with friends or a trip abroad. People don't always like it
if police start making inquiries about them. If that happens this
time we shall most likely try to push off the responsibility on you.
Of course, in this case, there is the rather disturbing coincidence
of these two affairs, the one at Lady Geraldine's flat and at the
Kilburn house. There's a lot that needs clearing up. Oh, by the
way, did you wonder how that photograph came on the porter's
desk in your club?"

"No," the colonel answered. "Why should I? I noticed it.
No more."

"You remembered it," Bobby observed. "It was there because
we had information that the original of the photograph had been
seen in the company of a gentleman of military appearance near
a car park from which recently cars had been vanishing rather
too often."

"Perhaps you will explain yourself more fully," Colonel Godwinsson remarked, very much as though he were asking a specially bad defaulter in the orderly room what he had to say for himself.

"We were hoping," Bobby said, "that some member of one or other of the Service clubs might recognize it and be able to give us some help. A very long shot, of course."

"No doubt fully justifiable in the circumstances," agreed the colonel, less coldly this time. "It had no success?"

"None," Bobby admitted. "Can you tell us anything about Miss Leigh? She is hardly in a condition at present to be questioned very closely, but she doesn't seem to have any idea of who attacked her or why."

"I am afraid I can't tell you very much there, either," answered the colonel. "I know nothing of the young lady except for meeting her once or twice at Lady Geraldine's flat. I believe they were old school-fellows and that Miss Leigh served till recently in one of the women's corps. Lady Geraldine asked her to stay with her for a time till she got settled. I gathered that it hadn't worked out very satisfactorily, and that Miss Leigh was leaving almost at once."

"Oh, indeed," Bobby said. "She didn't tell me that. No wonder, perhaps, after what she has been through. It's a rather troubling fact that Miss Leigh seems to answer to the description of a young lady seen recently in an East End district of London."

"Again I fail to follow you," Colonel Godwinsson said in his most aloof, most regal manner. "Will you be so good as to explain yourself? At present I am inclined to find some of your remarks obscure—unsatisfactorily obscure." He said this very quietly, but also very much as if any expression of dissatisfaction he made must necessarily carry great weight—the weight of a ton of bricks was how Bobby expressed it to himself. "Do you usually try to follow up descriptions of young ladies you may chance to see in an East End district of London?"

"When they seem as if they were strangers there," Bobby answered in a voice as quiet as the colonel's own, "and when the body of a murdered man is found near by."

CHAPTER XVI
SEARCH BEGUN

BOBBY, THE MOMENT he had said this, was aware of a sudden increase of tension. Hard to say exactly why, for Colonel Godwinsson's expression did not change, only his one eye seemed to fix itself on Bobby with an added force and intensity, his voice to take on a deeper note as he said:

"Murder? A murdered man?" He put out his hand and took up again the Joey Parsons photograph, and now his gaze upon it was of such concentrated power it was as though he commanded that inanimate bit of cardboard to speak and answer. "This man?" he asked, and then, and there was almost a challenge in his voice, he said: "Are you sure that he was murdered?"

"He was found shot," Bobby answered, slightly puzzled by the question.

"Was it murder?" the colonel asked once more, as though he had not heard Bobby's reply. He laid the photo down, and for a moment there was silence. When he spoke next his voice had regained all its former aloof, almost unearthly pride. "As for murder," he said, "I do not think that either I myself or Miss Leigh is likely to commit murder."

"Murder," Bobby commented, "except in those cases when it is merely an outburst of brute or beast, of anger or of passion, is so abnormal that what is 'likely' has to be largely forgotten. I think I mentioned we had information that a tall gentleman of military appearance had been seen near where the murder occurred. I don't think I said our report also stated that he appeared to have lost one eye. I must put this question to you. Was that man you?"

"I remember now," Colonel Godwinsson answered, "noticing a paragraph in the papers about an unknown man having been found dead in the East End in a street—a curious name. I forget it for the moment. Let me see."

"Angel Alley," Bobby said.

"Ah, yes, yes. Of course. I have seldom visited the district you mention. I am not quite sure where Angel Alley is or Canon Square, where you say some one more or less resembling myself was seen." He paused with his aloof and haughty smile, a smile that seemed as if it made all further comment unnecessary. But then he went on: "I have certainly never to my knowledge been near either place."

"Thank you, that is quite explicit," Bobby said. "If it was Miss Leigh who was seen near there, can you suggest any reason for her presence?"

"Have you any substantial cause for supposing it was her?"

"She practically admitted it," Bobby explained, "though in a somewhat emotional moment when I think she felt we had saved her from a very unpleasant situation. But she tacked on a flat denial. I take that to mean that she was there, but she doesn't mean to say why. I have a high idea of Miss Leigh's courage and will-power. I can think of only two explanations. Either she knows or suspects who is guilty or else she is guilty herself."

The colonel smiled again, a grim and wintry smile.

"I can't take that last suggestion seriously," he said. "Miss Leigh is no more likely to commit a murder than I am. The idea is unthinkable. I might say—foolish."

"I said just now," Bobby reminded him, "that in this sort of case we have to forget the 'likely'. Murder is never likely."

"You have spoken of murder several times," Colonel God-winsson went on. "It startled me. For more reasons than one. It is—well, disturbing that nothing has been heard of Lady Geraldine. It is disturbing, too, that you showed, though you have not thought fit to say so, this photograph to Miss Leigh, and that both she and the housekeeper at the flat seemed to think it was like a Mr Brown, a clergyman who used to get Lady Geraldine to subscribe to charities he was interested in. You seem to suggest that the same man is mixed up in this Kilburn affair you mentioned. It all seems most disturbing. I thought at first Gurth—my son, I think you met him at Lady Geraldine's flat—was worrying himself more than there was any need to. I only agreed to call to see you because he asked me to. It seems now as if he might have more reason for being disturbed than I realized."

He was silent then, and Bobby also was silent, so that this silence lay heavily between them and it was as though the shadow of death crept into the room. At last Bobby said:

"Is it in your mind that Lady Geraldine may have been murdered, too?"

"No," the colonel answered, and immediately corrected himself. "Well, yes. It is fantastic, incredible, utterly impossible. All the same, one can't help—you keep talking of murder," he said rebukingly. "It is disturbing to have such a word pushed atone. You say Miss Leigh was seen. I will speak to her myself as soon as possible. Can she have had some idea of following Geraldine, of getting to know where she was or what had happened? That's the only suggestion I can make."

"Is it possible that it was Lady Geraldine who shot this man and that that is why she has disappeared?"

"Good God, no!" exclaimed the colonel with vehemence. "What an idea!!"

"Can you suggest any reason why a young woman in Lady Geraldine's position should vanish so completely?" Bobby asked.

"Loss of memory?" Colonel Godwinsson suggested, though somewhat hesitatingly.

"I suppose it does happen," Bobby remarked. "I think only very rarely, though, and then only in a limited way and for a short time. When people come to us and tell us they have lost their memories, we have our doubts. Sometimes it is just a little too convenient. I am not inclined to take that idea very seriously at present. And if there had been an accident or sudden illness we should almost certainly have heard by now. There is always the possibility of some love affair. Was there anything of that kind between Lady Geraldine and your son?"

"I believe he would have liked there to be," the colonel admitted. "She has a most magnetic personality—strangely so. But she gave Gurth no encouragement, I am glad to say. In any case, that would be no reason for disappearing."

"I suppose not," agreed Bobby, even while there fluttered into his mind a vague thought or suspicion, though one that he felt could hardly be taken very seriously—not yet, at least. He went on: "Or was there anything of the sort between Mr Gurth and Miss Leigh? He struck me as a young man liable to turn the head of any girl."

"Well," admitted the colonel with a smile slightly more human than usual, "I suppose that has happened. Our family is supposed to have a reputation for good looks—especially among the boys. I am old enough now to claim that I had my share as a youngster. Gurth has more than his. He has even been pestered to go to Hollywood. But there I did put my foot down, and fortunately I still have some authority in my family."

That Bobby felt he could well believe. Colonel Godwinsson seemed, indeed, to be surrounded by a kind of aura of authority and command. It was as though he assumed so completely that there could be no opposition to his will that others had to feel the same. Indeed, Bobby himself was aware of the sort of compelling power that appeared to emanate from the man's personality.

"Do you think Lady Geraldine was attracted to any one else?" he asked.

"Gurth told me he was certain there was some one," replied the colonel. "He had no idea who. Lady Geraldine has many friends, but none intimate, as far as I know."

"You see, Colonel Godwinsson," Bobby said, "there are apt to be complications when two young ladies like Lady Geraldine and Miss Leigh and such a very handsome young man as your son are concerned. You have another son, haven't you? Has he the same good looks?"

"Well, hardly," the colonel answered, with again that more human smile which showed the father behind the mask of almost intolerable pride. "Leofric himself always says that the family ration of good looks was exhausted before he arrived on the scene. Harold, my eldest boy, he is dead—" Colonel Godwinsson paused, and for the moment—for the moment only—he was no longer the proud, self-possessed, self-contained patrician, but a father remembering the loss of his first born. Very plain was it that that was a loss as vivid still as if it had happened only that week. He conquered his passing show of emotion and went on: "Both he and Gurth were unusual, in Gurth's case even embarrassingly so. But you have seen Gurth. Harold you shall judge for yourself."

He fumbled in his pocket and produced a small photograph of some half-dozen or so young men, grouped together before what seemed a very fine old Elizabethan manor-house. So quickly in these days do styles and fashions change that already the photograph had a quaint, old-fashioned air, reminding Bobby of some he had seen in an old family album he still possessed. There were straw hats—'boaters'—for instance, and several of the young men were displaying in their lapels small union jacks or buttons showing photographs of popular generals—a fashion hardly seen since the last days of the Victorian era. Several moustaches too—thick, luxuriant moustaches. It was not difficult to pick out the young Godwinsson. His tall and more than handsome personality dominated the whole group, and his attitude told plainly enough that he was quite aware of the fact. A chieftain surrounded by his followers. Bobby examined the photograph with care and interest and then handed it back to the colonel.

"Remarkable," he said. "Most remarkable—and interesting."

"Leofric," the colonel said, carefully putting the photograph away again, "is more ordinary, though a fine, upstanding lad. More of an athlete, indeed, than either of his brothers."

"I suppose he was friendly with Lady Geraldine, too?"

"Leofric. Well, hardly that—acquaintances. I believe he visited the flat occasionally."

"A tall young man, better dressed than most of the people about there, and so much a stranger he had to ask his way, was looking for Angel Alley about the time of the murder," Bobby remarked. "He could hardly have been Mr Gurth. Good looks like his would be remembered and spoken of. Could it have been your other son—Leofric I think you said?"

"That appears to me a most extravagant idea—incredible."

"Unfortunately, the incredible is also sometimes factual," retorted Bobby. "It did just strike me there might be a connection with Miss Leigh's visit. I remember thinking that the young man was a stranger there and tall, and Miss Leigh a stranger there and small. And of course it is often said that tall men are attracted by small women. The other way round as well."

"Most far-fetched," the colonel said severely. "If you conduct your inquiries on such lines I don't wonder at a certain lack of success much commented on in the Press lately."

"The Press is always severe," admitted Bobby sadly. "A kind of general attitude of 'Hold out your hand'. No doubt it does us good, and hurts them more than it does us. In the meantime, I think there is sufficient reason to make inquiries about Lady Geraldine, and that will be put in hand at once." He went on to express conventional thanks for Colonel Godwinsson's visit, thanks which were accepted with aloof and distant dignity. After the colonel's departure, Bobby made full notes of their conversation and then went to show them to a colleague.

"A remarkable old boy," Bobby observed of the colonel, "though a little apt to get himself confused with God Almighty. I am wondering a lot what it was he was really after."

"You think there was something besides anxiety over this missing young woman?"

"I am sure there was," Bobby said, and he looked very worried indeed. "All the time I felt there was something a bit artificial, not quite in keeping, in his attitude. If he had merely been worried about this ex-ward of his, I should have expected him simply to say so and would we get on with the job at once. Instead he talked all round the shop. My feeling is that there was something he was anxious for us to know but that he didn't want to say outright. If we go over what he said very carefully, it may be possible to spot what it is."

"Suppose it is something intended to mislead?" the colleague asked.

"That would be splendid," Bobby declared with enthusiasm. "Then we should know at once where we weren't." The other did not share this point of view, and said so emphatically. While they were still talking there came a message from the nurse looking after Mrs. Porter. It was to the effect that, in the doctor's opinion, Mrs Porter was now in a fit condition, after a good night's rest, to face the ordeal of establishing the identity of dead Joey Parsons as her husband, Joseph Porter.

"Good," said Bobby. "I'll go at once."

"Need you go yourself?" disapprovingly asked the colleague, who thought Bobby had plenty of work on his desk without going off on an errand any competent sergeant could discharge just as well.

"I think so," Bobby answered. "This is one of those cases when there are no material clues and it all hangs on a good knowledge of the background. Make up your mind what people are and their probable behaviour according to character and circumstance, and then you know what questions to ask. Which means you know the answers, too."

"Psychological stuff," grumbled the other. "Give me the good old-fashioned magnifying-glass and the grain of dust found on the scene of the crime that tells you all about everything at once."

Bobby laughed, pointed out that such grains of dust weren't always there, but people inevitably had to be, and so departed.

CHAPTER XVII

THE SHOP OFF EMMETT STREET

BOBBY HAD FELT it his duty—a difficult and grievous duty—to prepare Mrs Porter for the inevitable recognition that he was sure awaited her. The identity of the dead Joey Parsons, 'spiv', 'layabout' or worse, with the respectable, home-loving Mr Porter of Kilburn seemed to him to be certain, and it needed but Mrs Porter's first low cry of dismay and horror to confirm that impression.

It was perhaps a measure of the shock given her by so sudden an intrusion of lawless violence into her calm and seemly life that what appeared to be most on her mind was a kind of puzzled and even slightly resentful bewilderment at her husband's presence in the East End of London. Realization of her personal loss had as yet hardly begun, though once or twice she remarked in a detached way: "He was always good to me and the children." Then she would begin again to wonder what business had taken him to this crowded, poverty-stricken district of the town.

"He always told me everything," she said more than once as they were driving back to Kilburn. She looked out of the car window at the teeming, squalid streets through which they were passing, as different from the quiet respectability of Kilburn as was Kilburn from Mayfair. She said: "He always said where he had been and how he had got on, and it was always the horses and stables and things in country parts. There's none here."

"You never knew Mr Porter to have any business or any friends in this part?" Bobby asked as he slowed down to permit a traffic block in front of them to dissolve.

"Oh, no, never," she answered. "There was the time we nearly got summonsed because of a policeman saying we had been stopped too long, only Joey came back, and he always had away with him, and he made the policeman laugh so he never did."

"When was this?" Bobby asked.

"When we were coming back from Southend last year. It wasn't our car, of course, though Mr Porter always made good money and free with it to all, but his boss let us have it sometimes for special times like going to Southend for our wedding day because it was there we met, and I never knew him look the way he did when he saw the lady, and him so good-tempered always. It gave me a turn, fair frightening it was."

"Who was the lady?" Bobby asked, making his voice as casual as he could.

"It was along of her husband owing him five pounds and never paying, though well able, with their shop doing so well, and smart she did look, like you see them in Bond Street. Putting it all on her back, as some do, and sorry I am for their husbands. Joey said most like it was that way and why he hadn't never been paid and he wasn't going to stand for it any longer. I wouldn't have liked him to look that way when he was talking to me."

Bobby wondered if there had been a touch of doubt and suspicion in her mind when her husband left her, apparently so abruptly, to speak to such a smart-looking stranger? Was it that had made the incident stay in her memory? And had his black looks, though impressing her so much, relieved her misgivings only slightly. Had she perhaps dimly perceived a certain inconsistency between his anger over the delayed repayment of a comparatively small debt and his customary liberality with his money-? Not that it seemed very helpful to know that the dead man had once spoken to a smartly dressed woman in this district. Bobby wondered if she could have been Mona Leigh, the only smartly dressed woman who so far in the case had been heard of as visiting this part of the town? But more likely to be some one entirely unconnected with recent happenings.

"Did Mr Porter say what kind of shop it was?" he asked.

"Well, he said if it had been nearer I could have taken it out in tea and sugar and such like, so it must have been groceries. Joking like, he was," she explained. She paused and seemed to remember. "Joking like, he was," she repeated; "but he won't no more now he's gone and been killed, will he?" Bobby did not answer, for there was none to make. She went on in a puzzled, hesitating voice as if something quite fresh had just occurred to her. "I'll have to tell the children, and them that fond of him— ever so excited when he came home, and always with something for them."

When they reached the little Kilburn house, Bobby told the nurse, still on duty, that Mrs Porter had better be put to bed again. He thought her on the verge of a fresh breakdown. She had been talking far too much, and was more than likely to collapse again as she began to realize more clearly her husband's death and how strangely he had died. Didn't the nurse agree that for the present she ought to be kept as quiet as possible; and wouldn't a sedative of some kind, or even a mild sleeping draught, be advisable? However, that was the business of nurse and doctor. He went on to say that probably a fresh search of the house would be thought necessary. The officers in charge of the case would almost certainly want to do that in order to find out if anything had been taken, and also, though Bobby did not stress the point, to obtain any scrap of fresh information they could about a man who was so plainly leading a double life. Interrogation of Mrs Porter would have to wait for the time, though Bobby did not think it likely there was much she could tell. She seemed a simple-minded woman; the other side of her husband's life had been kept carefully hidden, and she had plainly been willing to accept with complete trust everything he thought fit to tell her.

From Kilburn Bobby returned to the Angel Alley district. He had great faith—a faith tested and proved—in the local knowledge of the man on the beat. True, what Mrs Porter had said was vague enough. A doubtful hint at the best. But her story of the smartly dressed woman whose husband was a grocer owing money to the Joey Parsons-cum-Porter personality seemed on the whole worth some kind of an attempt at a follow up. 'Real vexed', Mrs Porter had said, almost as though the memory still frightened her, and had that 'real' vexation been for a reason more serious than a mere question of an unpaid debt? Bobby had drawn up a list of questions he wanted answered. They caused some discreet amusement, so much did they seem shafts shot at random into the blue. One, underlined, was a request to be informed of any (a) grocer's (b) other—shop where an outstandingly smart young woman was employed. Another was for a list of shops suspected of being either engaged in unlawful activities or used as a cover therefor. A third was for any grocer's shop about which anything in any way unusual had been noticed.

A net with meshes too wide, Bobby felt, to catch any worthwhile fish. Only his authority and prestige persuaded the district G.I.D. to take it at all seriously. Nevertheless a fish was caught; and in a long report, which at least did credit to the plodding industry of the officers concerned, there was a reference to a grocer's shop in a small side street off Emmett Street. It was a bad position, facing the blank wall of a warehouse. It was exposed to neighbouring energetic and well-established rivalry, and it had never done well. There had been rapid changes until some years previously when a Mr and Mrs Yates had taken it. They were still there. What puzzled the man on the beat, though, was the fact that the Yates seemed to neglect their business, were very unpopular in the neighbourhood, had acquired a reputation for being even more autocratic, overbearing, and generally rude to their customers than even the worst of war-time shopkeepers, and yet appeared to be making a very good living.

Bobby mused over this report for some time. The man who had made it happened to be in the station at the time, and Bobby asked him what Mrs Yates was like: did she in any way answer to the description of 'a real tip topper'? The constable grinned broadly and replied that the woman was a notorious slattern, couldn't even keep the shop clean, and, like her husband, spent far too much time at public-houses near.

"Open late, shut early, and close in the middle of the day for a lot more than an hour," said the constable. "It beats me how they manage to carry on, even the way things are with every shopkeeper thinking it's a favour to take your money."

Bobby thought all this sounded interesting. What it all meant he could not imagine, but there certainly seemed matter for investigation. No telling what might lurk behind anything in any way unusual in a case that seemed to present so much that was much more than unusual. He borrowed a uniform man both as a guide and for effect and drove off to the address given. The shop presented a sufficiently forlorn appearance, grubby and neglected. The windows had plainly not been dressed for some time, and what goods were displayed seemed to have been thrown in almost at random. When Bobby opened the door, a jangling bell announcing his entrance, a frowsy, sullen-faced, elderly woman shuffled forward, looking distrustfully from Bobby to the uniform man and then back at Bobby.

"If it's about them points," she began, "we done our best and what I say is—"

Bobby cut her short, little interested in what she had to say about 'points', though he could well believe shops like these drove many food officials to a premature grave.

"Nothing to do with points," he told her. "I take it you are Mrs Yates."

"Well, what about it?" the woman demanded. "Suppose I am?"

Bobby turned to his companion.

"I'm not in uniform," he said. "You are. Ask this lady to show you her identity card."

She duly produced it, though sulkily enough. The constable examined it and passed it to Bobby.

"Apparently in order, sir," he said.

"I see you don't live here," Bobby remarked. "Who occupies the premises over the shop?"

"It's Mr Potter," she answered. "He's the landlord. We don't have nothing to do with him except pay the rent, as we do regular as clockwork."

"Is he married? Is there any one there now?" Bobby asked.

"We don't know nothing about him," Mrs Yates insisted. "We pays our rent, and that's all. Sometimes he's there and sometimes he ain't. Travels in a big way for a big firm, so he told Mr Yates once."

"See if you can get any answer," Bobby said to the constable. "I noticed a side door." To Mrs Yates he said: "Is your husband here?"

She shuffled off. He heard her voice in the back regions calling angrily for 'Abel' to come and talk to the gentleman instead of leaving it all to her, same as he always did. Mr Yates appeared, and proved to be a kind of masculine replica of his wife, though perhaps even a trifle more frowsy, more slipshod, more beery, more sullenly suspicious.

"What's up now?" he demanded. "Funny thing if a bloke can't earn an honest living without busies on his doorstep all day long."

Bobby said he was sorry to trouble them, even though he didn't notice any great press of customers at the moment. In any case, his own business was important. He produced the Joey Parsons photograph.

"Is this any one you know?" he asked. "Please look well before you say."

They looked at it and at each other and then at Bobby. His impression was that they had recognized it at once, but were hesitating whether to say so or to lie. Finally the man seemed to make up his mind that the truth would be safer. He said:

"Mr Potter, ain't it, missis?"

"Couldn't say," she answered. "I ain't hardly never seen him. It was always you paid the rent. It might be," she added.

"Have you seen him lately?" Bobby asked.

They both denied it. Very often from one quarter day to another they never set eyes on him. He went and came by the side door, and they were in the shop. He might be in out a dozen times a day without their knowing or any reason why they should. Sometimes they could hear him moving about overhead, but that was all. They couldn't say when they had seen him last, but not for weeks. Nor did they know if he had visitors. There might be plenty after they had closed the shop and gone home. Nor did further questioning produce much more than professions of ignorance. Bobby gave it up. They might really know no more than they professed, had perhaps been careful not to know. In any case, there would very likely be occasion for further questioning, when there might be more to go on. For one thing was fairly plain: they would say no more than they were forced to. However, he did impress upon them that if Mr Potter returned he was to be asked to communicate with the police at once.

"Not that he ever will return, either here or anywhere else upon this earth," Bobby said to his companion as they drove away. "But as soon as it is dark we'll come back and see what we can find. Quite clear, I think, there are sufficient grounds for a breaking in."

"Well, sir," observed the uniform man, for this is rather a sore point with some of the police, "we could always ask a food inspector to come along. We may have to be careful what we do, but seems as if they can walk in anywhere they want any time."

CHAPTER XVIII

THE ROOM OF THE SEVEN LUSTS

As soon as it was dark—for he had no desire to attract undue attention—Bobby set out again. This time he was accompanied by Inspector Hall, the D.D.I.'s chief assistant, Ulyett himself being still on the sick list, by a sergeant chosen because locks and keys had been his life-long hobby, and by the constable-driver of the car.

The Yates shop was situated in a side street, just round the corner from Emmett Street. Even in pre-war days the street lighting here had been bad. Then had come the black-out; and even now it was not much better, with the need for fuel economy restricting lighting to one lamp halfway down the street and with the high blank wall of the warehouse opposite throwing down its dense and obscuring shadow.

"Carefully chosen," Bobby remarked. "Easy to slip into that side doorway of the Yates shop without being seen, and easy to hang about opposite in the shadows to make sure of not being followed. And yet there seems enough traffic up and down for there to be no likelihood of any one passer-by being specially noticed."

"It's a bit of a short cut," the sergeant explained, "for people going shopping in the High Street."

He was already busy on the lock. Yale locks are secure enough as a general rule. But there are ways of dealing with them, ways which are well enough known, but which perhaps it is better not to describe in detail. In a very few minutes the door was open and the three of them entered. Not till the door had been closed behind them did Bobby flash his torch to show steep and shabby stairs, covered by worn linoleum. Followed by his two companions, Bobby ascended them, and found them closed at the top by another door, strongly made, and, Bobby guessed, of more recent construction. It was not locked, however, and admitted to a small landing, dingy and dark, the wall-paper dirty, old, and worn. There was an aged hatstand—on it neither hat nor coat—and a still more aged umbrella-stand in which stood a smart silk umbrella, beautifully rolled, with a gold-mounted handle. They all regarded it with interest. An umbrella like that ought to be identifiable. From the landing there opened three doors. Bobby pushed back the nearest, and in doing so evidently operated a switch, for at once the room within was lighted by soft fluorescent strips that ran in wavy patterns here and there about the walls and showed a room furnished in a very extremity of a decadent and evil luxury.

"Gosh!" said the sergeant, and repeated: "Gosh!"

"Some style," said the inspector, more restrained, as befitted one who felt himself marked for promotion.

Bobby, being more senior still, said nothing at all, but looked the more.

The room was large, covering as it did the whole of the shop below. The walls were decorated with a continuous painting of considerable artistic merit, or so Bobby thought at this first glance, and of that kind, nature, and species which second-hand booksellers describe as 'curious'—in this case very curious indeed, and even meriting a stronger epithet.

"Gosh!" said the sergeant once again as he began to take in the full import of this mural painting.

The inspector followed Bobby's example and said nothing, but he shook a gravely disapproving head over each fresh detail as he studied it with close attention in case a full report was required.

Not, by the way, until some moments later did they notice that the wavy fluorescent lighting gave in rather fantastic lettering the title and description of this remarkable work of art as 'The capture and destruction of youth by the seven lusts'.

The furnishing of the room was unusual. It consisted almost entirely of low, luxurious divans and of cushions—innumerable cushions, piled high everywhere, on the divans, in the corners, everywhere, and all of a bewildering variety of rich and diverse colouring and material. There were also two or three cabinets in ivory and ebony, of extremely fine Chinese workmanship, and evidently of very considerable value. Museum pieces indeed. On the floor was a carpet into which the feet seemed to sink as though to the ankles. Bobby thought its value must run into the hundreds. The windows were covered by heavy curtains of a golden silk. An elaborate and expensive radio set and an equally elaborate and expensive cocktail bar provided an up-to-date touch, and the air in the room was heavy, lifeless, and scented.

"Some one with money to splash about," said the inspector, dragging his disapproving eyes with difficulty from those abominable wall-paintings.

The sergeant, by the way, had lost even the capacity to say 'gosh' and could only stand and stare, though whether the sort of standing and staring that Mr W. H. Davies meant, may be doubted.

"Not only with money, but with the taste and knowledge to get what was wanted," Bobby commented. He added: "Where did the money come from?" but expected no answer, nor received one.

He had noticed that a part of the wall-painting represented a door on which was a scroll reading: 'Paradise enow: admission by ticket of leave only.' It was perhaps the only bit of the whole work that, on grounds of decency, not of art, did not merit immediate obliteration; and even to this door the artist, by the surrounding pattern of peeping fauns and other inventions, had managed to convey a suggestion of still stranger things, upon which it opened.

Bobby gave it a more careful look. He beckoned to the sergeant, still lost in a kind of hazy doubt and wonder. The sergeant came and looked where Bobby pointed.

"Gosh!" he said, reverting to his favourite exclamation he had picked up listening, as he always did when he had the chance, to the children's hour on the B.B.C. home programme.

For the door showed a keyhole, a very realistic keyhole—so realistic, in fact, as to be real. The sergeant produced a fine steel instrument. In a moment or two he had the door open. Within was a small, luxurious bedroom, fitted up in the Louis Quinze style, all slender gilt and gay silk hangings. The carpet, Aubusson this time, was again a lovely thing. About the room small golden cherubs held golden candelabra before shining oval mirrors, and the air was even more scented, dull, and lifeless than in the larger room. In one corner there had been fitted up a small silver fountain, and Bobby guessed that the water was heavily perfumed when in action. In a large wardrobe was a variety of both men's and women's clothing. Of the two other doors the room possessed, one opened on the drab and shabby landing they had already seen, and one admitted to a bathroom fitted up in equally luxurious style, with silver fittings to the porcelain bath and tiled walls showing mermaids disporting themselves in a fashion that made the shocked inspector look even more disapprovingly and closely than before.

Bobby left this room, crossed the landing, and opened the third door. Beyond was a long, narrow room of which the farther end seemed a kitchen, the middle portion an office, with filing cabinet, a typewriter and so on, and the nearer end arranged as for a conference with a narrow table, on it half a dozen writing-pads and stationery, and swivel chairs drawn up to it. Possibly to the more exotic rooms all visitors were not admitted. The room was lighted, though not well, by a window at the farther or kitchen end, and here Bobby noticed an arrangement of a pulley and rope. He went across to look more closely, and guessed that supplies—more than supplies, perhaps—came this way. Probably casual visitors were not much encouraged, even if they were only carmen or messenger-boys and so forth. Probably, too, it was not desired that the delivery of goods here should attract even the slightest notice. All packages could be deposited in the yard behind the shop, as though ordinary trade goods, and those meant for Mr Potter—otherwise probably Joey Parsons or Joseph Porter or the Rev Mr Brown, or plain Mr Brown of the city—could be placed under this kitchen window and hauled up. Exit and entry could also be effected in the same way, if necessary. Climbing either in or out by the aid of the lowered rope would be easy for any normally active person.

"Yates must have known what was going on," Inspector Hall said as he joined Bobby in examining this contraption.

"Oh, yes," agreed Bobby, "but probably well paid not to know too much, all the same. He would say he thought it was all merely Mr Potter having a good time, and no business of his. And he thought the occasional deliveries were merely cases of champagne and other good-time necessities. Never, never dreamed there was anything else in them."

"A good deal more here than merely a love nest," Hall remarked.

"A lot more," Bobby agreed again. "An ingenious cover for much more serious activities. For the love-nest business any West-End flat would have done, but this is what we've been looking for, for so long. The place where these recent robberies have been planned and the centre where the loot was collected and disposed of. I wonder what's in that filing cabinet."

He went across to it and gave a swift glance at some of the contents. There was an odd variety. Some of the entries were in cypher. Others were rough notes, probably meaningless to all except the man who made them. There were plans of West-End flats and country mansions and notes about their inhabitants. Bobby supposed the plan made of his own flat had been destined to find a place here. Then there were notes about various personalities, including a good many of members of the police forces, a large proportion with photographs attached. There was an exceptionally good one of Bobby. He read the comment on himself with much annoyance. It ran: "Stolid, dull, routine ridden; somehow gets there all the same." He thought this verdict unjust, and would have liked to argue the point. He turned up the 'S's' to see if there was any reference to Stokes. There was. It gave his address and the simple comment 'O.K.' Then he looked to see if there was any reference to the missing Lady Geraldine Rafe, but there was nothing. He said to Hall:

"Lots of useful information here. I think you had better arrange for it to be sent to Centre at once. It ought to be gone through as soon as possible."

Hall said he would have it seen to immediately. He was a little excited. He said it was like capturing an enemy headquarters during the war. The sergeant who had been looking round the room came up and said:

"There's a good-size packing-case in the corner, all corded up ready to be sent off."

"Where to?" Bobby asked.

"There's no address," the sergeant answered. "Shall I see what's in it?"

"Yes, do," Bobby answered, still absorbed in his examination of the contents of the filing cabinet, and inclined to believe it the most valuable discovery yet made in the fight against the post-war crime wave.

The sergeant busied himself with the opening of the packing-case. It was not easy. It had been nailed up very effectively, and was itself strongly made. Presently, however, he got the lid off, and found the contents wrapped in a heavy tarpaulin covering, carefully sewn. He cut the stitches, and disclosed beneath a fresh covering, this time a linen sheet. Nervously, for he was beginning to be uneasy, he drew it aside. He gave a loud and sudden cry.

"It's a woman, a dead woman!" he shouted.

Bobby was at his side in a moment.

"I think we have found Lady Geraldine Rafe," he said gravely.

CHAPTER XIX
TIM STOKES AGAIN

As CAREFULLY AND reverently as might be, they removed the body from its unseemly resting-place. It was fully clothed, the eyes had been closed; except for the bluish, unnatural colour of the skin, it might have been thought that she slept. It almost seemed as if, after all, care had been taken to treat the dead woman's body with a certain amount of respect and care.

"Lady Geraldine Rafe?" Hall repeated. "Her there's been talk about in the papers and then that affair at her flat?"

"I think there can be no doubt," Bobby said.

"No sign of violence," Hall said. "Could it be poison? Or a natural death?" he added doubtfully.

"Suffocation, I think," Bobby said. "The doctors will be able to say. Probably done while she was asleep, and very likely after she had had too much to drink."

The sergeant produced a handbag from the bottom of the packing-case. Bobby opened it. It contained money, cigarettes, the usual small accessories a woman generally carries with her, other odds and ends, and a very much crumpled letter. It was addressed only to 'darling'; its terms were those of a passionate but not confident lover, it was signed with the initials 'G. G.', and Bobby had no doubt but that it came from Gurth Godwinsson, though of course that would need formal identification. He put it away carefully.

Hall began to give his sergeant instructions to return at once to the local police station, to inform Scotland Yard of this new development, and to see that the customary procedure in such cases was put into action. Bobby listened, making one or two suggestions. While they were still talking the door-bell rang. The sergeant said:

"I'll go, shall I?"

"I'll go, too," Bobby said. "Better be two of us. It may be some of Mr Potter's pals, and they may run for it when they see us—or try to make trouble."

"Excuse me, sir," interposed Hall. "They may turn awkward—dangerous lot. Hadn't I better go instead?"

Bobby squashed him with such a look as only really senior officers can produce, and began to descend the stairs, waving back as he did so the sergeant who had presumptuously tried to go first.

He flung open the front door. It was dark, but Bobby thought he recognized the squat, burly figure standing on the doorstep.

The recognition was not mutual, for here, at the foot of the stairs, inside the door, the darkness was complete and absolute. Bobby did not speak. The newcomer said:

"Any business doing?"

"Oh, quite a lot," Bobby answered. "Tim Stokes, isn't it? Come inside, won't you?"

"I might have known it would be you," Stokes sighed, and looked over his shoulder as if calculating his chances of escape.

He gave up the idea, knowing well that for such a move Bobby was fully prepared. He said: "I saw a light show. Through the curtains. I thought it might be some of Joey's pals. I might have guessed it would be you," he said again and with resignation.

"Well, we had better have a talk now you're here," Bobby said. "Come along in."

Stokes complied, his gloom, like the darkness at the foot of the stairs, such that it could be almost felt. When they reached the small and shabby landing above, Bobby hesitated a moment, and then opened the door of that exotic front room. Stokes stood still and gaped. Fairly evident he had never seen that interior before. Bobby closed the door again. He did not wish to take Stokes into the back room, where there still remained the body of the unfortunate Lady Geraldine. Standing on the landing, he said:

"Well, how do you come to be here, and what do you want?"

"Nice little hide-out," Stokes said. "I've seen some things, but never the like of that," and he jerked his head towards the now closed door of the front room.

"How did you know about it?" Bobby asked.

"I never did," Stokes asserted. "Of course, all the boys knew there was some place not so far from Angel Alley as was general H.Q., so to say, same as for D. day. I've heard more than one say so, but even them as had been there didn't know exact, because they was driven round and round in a car, and it was always dark as blazes."

Bobby did not stop to inquire how dark 'blazes' might be. He asked instead:

"Who drove?"

"Joey—it was always Joey. What they all said was he stopped the car after you hadn't an earthly where you were and put a bag over your head, and when you took it off you was in a sort of kitchen, with a table and chairs at one end—a long, narrow room. That's what they all said, but none of 'em said a word about any place like that." He nodded again, and now in a half-frightened manner, towards the closed door behind. He said: "I never saw the like, never."

"I suppose you mean that's what happened when you were brought here," Bobby remarked. "Not merely what others told you. No, never mind denying it. If you didn't know about this place, how is it you rang to-night?"

"All the boys said it couldn't be so far from Angel Alley, as was where they waited like when Joey told 'em they was wanted," Stokes explained. "So I mooched around a bit, and I noticed how the curtains were always drawn here, so when to-night I saw a spot of light showing through a chink I thought as I would just see if there was any one."

"Hadn't you better tell the truth?" Bobby suggested. "A bit serious to be mixed up in a murder case, you know. More serious than a discipline board, for instance. If there's anything you can tell us—"

"So help me," Stokes interrupted with an appearance of earnestness and sincerity that did to some degree impress Bobby, "if I did, I would split quick like. So would plenty others of the boys. But none of 'em has any idea who did poor Joey in or what for. He was a good sort. You could always touch him for half a dollar, if you were up against it—or more. If he put up your name for a job—well, you knew it was a good job, well planned, everything as it should be, and good money at the end. Sort of honour to be in on his jobs—showed you were a live wire. Even Cy King and his pals as Joey always said the boss wouldn't ever have anything to do with, because of being too given to violence, as Joey never held with, it showing lack of brains—even them would pass on who did him in if they knew."

"Perhaps it was one of them," Bobby suggested. "Cy King himself?"

"I've thought of that," Stokes said. "I've thought of that," he repeated. Then he said: "I don't reckon it was that way. Why should Cy? He wouldn't want any gang war, reprisals and all that. His lot and Joey's didn't ever mix. They had their own lays, and kept to 'em, not interfering."

"What was Cy doing at Angel Alley, then?" demanded Bobby.

"He never looked for to find you there," Stokes said. "All the blokes knew there was good stuff somewhere waiting to be shipped abroad, and when it got about as Joey had been done in, and where, they guessed maybe that was where it was. So they went to have a look see, meaning no harm; only you being there and cutting up rough, they didn't get no chance."

"By good stuff, I suppose you mean the Wharton jewels?" Bobby remarked.

"It might be," Stokes admitted.

"And I suppose that's why you were prowling around to night?" Bobby suggested.

"There's a reward been offered," Stokes protested. "Come in handy all right, and me unemployed, as you might say, after twenty years faithful service, only for one slip—"

"Yes, we know all about that," Bobby interrupted unsympathetically. "Who was Joey Parsons?"

"Mr Owen, sir," Stokes declared, "I don't know, and that's a fact. I don't know any more than the blessed babe unborn. I don't know as any one knows. The boys all knew it wasn't healthy to ask, and they didn't try. There was some said Cy King knew, but it wasn't too healthy either to ask him things he didn't tell you."

"Nonsense," Bobby retorted. "The men Joey worked with must have known a good deal."

"Not them," Stokes insisted. "Joey always said it was orders from the boss he handed on, but he never let on who he meant. Some of the boys said the boss was Joey himself, but it didn't seem like it, him always quiet and timid like and never saying much on his own."

"Why didn't they think it healthy to ask him questions, then?" Bobby asked.

"Because," Stokes explained, "if you did he would smile, timid like, and say he would tell the boss you were asking. That meant trouble—a beating up, perhaps, or a give away. When the boys reported, it was always Joey passed on the orders." Stokes glanced at the door of the room of which he had been given a glimpse in order to see if he showed signs of having known it before. He went on: "There was times when I felt sure all that about a boss was only Joey trying to cover himself. But that room—I never seen the like." He turned to look once more at the closed door, not without the hint of a suggestion in his manner that he would very much appreciate another peep. "I never seen the like," he repeated, "and it can't have been Joey. Joey wasn't that sort—simple sort of bloke, liked his glass of beer and half a crown on the gee-gees and a game of darts. Just like you and me. Never bothered about women, neither. None of that sort of fancy stuff."

Bobby listened to all this with some suspicion. No time now, though, for further questioning. Photographers, finger-print-men, other specialists, too, would soon be arriving, snatched from their homes or even from their beds, for by now it was beginning to grow late. Above all, he needed the famous "murder-bag" kept always in instant readiness and containing everything, down to a packet of pins, likely to be required in such inquiries. The whole busy routine of a murder investigation would soon be in operation, to continue all through the night. He decided Stokes would have to be held for questioning at a more convenient time. It was a decision that moved Stokes to bitter protest.

"You haven't any cause," he said sulkily. "I'm trying to help."

"There's more than enough to hold you on for questioning," Bobby told him. "Suspicion of being concerned in murder, as principal or as accessory."

"Murder? What murder?" Stokes asked sharply and uneasily. Then, speaking slowly and hesitatingly and watching Bobby closely, so that Bobby felt sure he had either knowledge or suspicion of the crime just discovered, he said: "I wasn't nowhere near; I can prove it—not when Joey was done in, nor this place neither."

"The useful alibi?" Bobby smiled. "I'm not going to take any risk of letting you go and then being told you've been called out of town on important business, and you didn't say where. You are going to be questioned, and pretty closely questioned. You'll be asked to make a statement. Think it over."

"You ain't treating me fair," Stokes grumbled again. "Just one slip in twenty years, and treated worse than dirt ever after." He hesitated. Then he said: "Is it about Lady Geraldine Rafe? Have you found her?"

"Why do you ask?"

"I'm not a fool," Stokes said angrily. "Doesn't every one know she's missing? Isn't it plain there's something up with you here and all?" When Bobby waited, feeling there was more to come, Stokes went on: "Murder? Not me. No, thanks. I don't mean to swing. O.K., Mr Owen, I'll tell you something. While you are wasting time bullying me as only wants to help, as like as not there's murder being done right now upon the doorstep here, so to speak."

CHAPTER XX

FIGHT IN THE DARK

Bobby had listened to all this with both disquiet and distrust. He was not sure whether Stokes spoke with knowledge or from vague foreboding, or whether in an attempt to escape from that inconvenient questioning the prospect of which he so clearly disliked. Bobby said sharply:

"Out with it. There's no time to waste if that's true. You'll be held responsible now, you know, if anything happens."

"That's the thanks I get," Stokes complained. "There's been another bloke around, that's all. Same as me. I mean, doing a look-see. A tall bloke, a toff."

"What age?" Bobby asked. "Old? Young?"

"Youngish. Asking questions. On the job every night. Stands drinks all round in pubs, letting on to have had a drop too much, which he hasn't ever. Not him; sober as you like the moment he got outside."

"What sort of questions?"

"Clever they were. The dogs at first, and then getting round to Joey, and who did him in, and some one doing mighty well out of all the jewel robberies, and the police must be asleep, and then after a bit how he was looking for a girl friend who lived in these parts but he didn't know where exactly. Some of the other blokes got to thinking he was a busy himself, and used to sheer off. But he wasn't, not him. The complete amateur. West End he was all right, and never been outside, except like visiting the Zoo."

"Did he describe the girl he was looking for?"

"He showed a photo. It was Lady Geraldine Rafe."

"All the same," Bobby remarked thoughtfully, "I don't quite follow why you should think there's a risk of murder."

"You would, Mr Owen, sir," Stokes answered, "if you had seen Cy King waiting for the young toff to come out and looking the way he did as he followed close behind."

"Do you mean to-night?"

"That's right. I started to follow, too, but I saw Cy King look round, and so I thought I wouldn't any more."

"I'll send out a warning," Bobby said. "I think I know the young man you mean. He had better be picked up. There's no 'phone here. Where's the nearest box, do you know?"

It was three or four hundred yards away. Stokes gave Bobby directions how best to reach it and added:

"I've seen Pitcher Barnes, too. And there's a car that stands at street corners—waiting."

"Waiting? What for?"

"My idea is they think it's this young toff himself as outed Joey, because they all reckon there was some one in the know used to tip the boys off where the real stuff was and how best to do the job. And they think maybe it's him that's got the Wharton stuff. So Cy King is aiming to get hold of him and make him turn it up. And afterwards drop him in the river most like, with a lump of iron round his neck."

"If it's like that, why should he be still hanging about here, and why should he be trying to find Lady Geraldine?"

"May be he never got the stuff, and only her knows where it is. Or it might be her bumped off Joey, or again it might be her tipped off the boys. Wheels within wheels, that's what I think, Mr Owen."

"So do I," agreed Bobby. "Very much so. You've quite ingenious ideas, Stokes. Pity you couldn't make up your mind to run straight. You would have done well. As it is, I won't forget you've been useful—unless I find you've let me down, and then I won't forget that either. Wait here till I get back. I must put a call through at once. We had better have some of the Flying Squad here."

He told Inspector Hall of his intention, asked him to keep an eye on Stokes, and ran down the stairs into the blackness of the street outside where lay the enormous darkness thrown by the shadow of the tall, blank warehouse wall opposite. He hurried in the direction Stokes had indicated. The second turning on the right, about a hundred yards down the street, would lead him straight to a call-box some distance farther on, Stokes had said. Here too, at the indicated corner the darkness lay heavily in the shadows cast by tall buildings on either hand and relieved only by one street lamp showing a faint gleam some distance away. But he could distinguish the outline of a car that was waiting near. He stood still. It was all very quiet, and he could hear distinctly a shuffling of heavy feet approaching and a muttering of low, hoarse voices. He flashed his torch. In its light he saw a group of three men, of whom two were partly supporting, partly carrying, partly dragging, the inert body of a third towards that waiting car of which he saw now that the door hung open.

Only a momentary glimpse was he allowed, for at the instant that he stood and flashed his torch a violent blow from behind sent him reeling. With difficulty did he keep his footing, and only because by good luck he was brought up by a lamp-post—unlighted for economy's sake, but affording a support that saved him from falling. He clutched it, swung round it for protection, as instinct rather than sight warned him another blow was coming. He still held his torch. He flung it hard and straight, and by good luck it struck his assailant full in the face, checking effectually any attempt to follow up that first attack. But Bobby, too, though he had recovered his footing, made no effort to follow up his own attack. Instead he shouted at the top of his voice, in the hope of attracting attention and help, and ran towards the little group now nearing the waiting car. His shout, however, was lost at once in the reverberating report of a pistol shot. He found out later that that fortunate throw of the torch had made his assailant drop a big Luger pistol that then a subsequent kick had exploded.

The thought flashed into his mind that this shot would give the alarm very effectually, and that he need waste no more breath in shouting. Just as well. Probably he was about to need it all and more. There was shouting enough, in any case, going on now, for the man behind him was yelling a warning to those in front, and they, in their turn, were shouting to know what was happening, what the shot had been fired for, and at the same time to each other to get their victim or prisoner or injured companion, whichever he was, into the waiting car.

He lay limp and helpless in their grasp—whether dead or unconscious or drugged, Bobby could not tell. Now they were trying to bundle him into the car. One of them snarled a hoarse order to Bobby to keep out or it would be worse for him, and another thinner, shriller voice cried: 'Cosh him—quick.' Bobby said: 'Stop it', and made a grab at a protruding leg sticking out through the open car door. In the confusion and the darkness no one was quite sure what was happening, who was friend or enemy. Somebody tried to push Bobby away, and in return Bobby thrust him violently against his companion, who hit out viciously, apparently taking him for Bobby, and was hit himself in return before each of them discovered who the other was. Meanwhile Bobby was pulling away at that protruding leg, but without great effect, for some one inside the car was pulling with equal vigour the opposite way. The same thin voice Bobby had heard before screamed through the darkness and the noise and the confusion:

"Steady, you fools. It's Pitcher Barnes. Look out, look out; he'll have him out of the car in a minute."

Bobby did now, in fact, with a final yank, get both legs and a part of the body outside. It came incongruously into his mind that so Trojan and Greek contended for the bodies of slain comrades. Then he had to turn to meet a rush from the two who had given up fighting each other for a joint attack on him. He dodged aside and hit out with what aim he could in that baffling darkness. The impact told him that one blow at least had got well home. But now the inert body he had succeeded in getting half out of the car was back within it, huddled on the floor, and over it came trampling a burly figure that Bobby thought was that of Pitcher Barnes. He greeted it with a violent punch below the belt, for this was no time for Queensberry rules, and whoever it was—Pitcher Barnes or another—sat down suddenly. There was neither wind nor fight left in him. But at the same time some one from behind caught Bobby in an expert wrestling grip, tripped him; he found himself flat on his back, and some one else took the opportunity to deal him a hearty kick in the ribs. He was on his feet again almost at once, but the interval had been enough for the gangsters to pile into their car, and it went roaring away just as a Flying Squad car came roaring up from the opposite direction. Bobby had only time to escape being run over by flattening himself against the wall. He was still a little dazed and breathless. The Flying Squad crew jumped out. Bobby shouted to them to get in again and follow the car that had just escaped.

"It's Cy King and Pitcher Barnes," he said. "They've a kidnapped man with them—or else a dead man. Send out a general alarm."

The car departed, though on a hopeless errand, for the fugitives had a start that made escape almost certain. In the silence that followed the disappearance of the two cars, a voice from the darkness said calmly:

"You've got it all wrong. I've not been kidnapped, and I'm jolly well not dead. But I've a lump on my head the size of the dome of St Paul's—bigger probably," the voice added thoughtfully.

Bobby, a good deal surprised by this unexpected development, went across to where he could make out a figure sitting on a doorstep.

"What happened?" he asked. "How did you manage to get out?"

"I don't know quite what did happen. I suppose I got knocked out. I remember hearing some one behind, and next thing I knew I was on the floor of a car with two blighters swearing at each other and trying to pull me in half. One of them won and got me inside, and he started to scramble over me, only he sat down instead. I think something must have hit him."

"It did," said Bobby, not without complacence.

"He seemed quite busy trying to hold himself together," the other continued. "So I wriggled from under, got the other door open, and tumbled out just as the car went off. That's all I know. Are you chaps police?"

"Yes. You are Mr Leofric Godwinsson, aren't you?"

"That's right. How did you know? I say, I feel awfully groggy."

"There's a doctor coming. I'll ask him to have a look at you, and then we'll send you home. There's a car coming now," Bobby added.

It was the Flying Squad men back. One of them jumped out and reported that the pursued car had been abandoned and the occupants had escaped in the maze of dark, ill-lighted side streets near which they had stopped. There had been no chance of overtaking them. The Flying Squad man was interrupted by Leofric saying suddenly:

"I'm awfully sorry. I think I'm going to faint or something."

Promptly he fitted fact to word. The Flying Squad man flashed his torch. He said:

"Hullo. I know him. It's the young gent, we picked up outside Wharton House the night of the jewel robbery there. We had to let him go though. Nothing definite we could hold him on, though it smelt a mile off."

CHAPTER XXI

SEVEN GOLDEN WHYS

THE NEXT DAY was a Sunday, and though a police investigation must go on, Sunday or weekday, Sundays generally bring a considerable slackening of routine work. Incidentally, reporters are occasionally just a little less active on Sundays than on other days, and for this brief and partial respite Bobby was grateful. He had been anxious to keep the news of the strange return of the Wharton jewels from general knowledge as long as possible. No good this time adopting the usual plan of telling the reporters in confidence; the only way, as Bobby was ruefully aware, of keeping a newspaper man quiet. Because it was perfectly certain that by this time the news had already leaked out, whispered, in a confidence not at all likely to be respected, from one member of the Wharton household to another, and then again to those outside, till by now it was sure to be widely known and sure to be in every paper soon.

However, though it was Sunday, a conference had been called of all those actively engaged in this case of so many strange ramifications. It was to be held in the afternoon, and Bobby, wandering in and out of the kitchen, was seriously interfering with the preparations for dinner—Olive knew too well what conferences meant for her to consider for even one moment having that meal at night as usual. Lucky she would be, she told herself resignedly, if she saw Bobby back by midnight.

"The whole thing will be splashed in all the papers tomorrow," he was saying moodily. "They haven't taken much notice of the Joey Parsons murder yet—crowded out by this latest political crisis. But it won't take them long to link it up with the death of Lady Geraldine and the return of the Wharton stuff."

"Well, of course, that's obvious," agreed Olive. "I wish I knew what time you are likely to be back. There'll be some corned beef, but when I asked Mrs Vere de Vere in the flat opposite if she would go shares in a cabbage she said they couldn't afford."

Bobby said abstractedly: "Who could?" Olive said she had put the arnica on the table in his room and he had better apply it again to his ribs where he had been kicked. Bobby accordingly wandered back, but forgot about the arnica. Presently he emerged, and found Olive on the brink of tears.

"Look," she said, "there are three points left in your ration book I had forgotten all about, and now they aren't any good any more, now it's the end of the period."

Bobby took the ration books from her and placed them on the top of a cupboard, where she couldn't reach them except by standing on a chair.

"Never mind all that," he said. "I've got to clear my mind. You listen."

"Yes, sir," said Olive meekly, but all the same eyeing wistfully her out-of-reach ration books.

"To begin with," said Bobby, "it's clear there's some connection between the deaths of Joey Parsons and Lady Geraldine and the jewel robberies that have been going on. But which comes first—which is, so to say, the prime mover? There isn't much we know so far to suggest what is cause and what is consequence."

"All three both cause and consequence, perhaps," suggested Olive, wondering if she could slip a chair near the cupboard of the ration books without Bobby noticing, and deciding it would be worth trying.

"Joey Parsons," Bobby said. "Who was he? Is there some one else in the background, or was he the mainspring of the whole affair?"

"If he was," Olive asked, "why is it still going on? He isn't, and a watch doesn't go on if the mainspring is broken."

"False analogy," Bobby told her. "Cut off a hen's head and it will still go on running round in circles. The difference between life and a machine. The noticeable thing about Joey Parsons is the entirely different character he seems to have presented to every one he met. In Kilburn the admirable, hard-working, conventional, eminently respectable householder, devoted to wife and family. At Lady Geraldine's flat and among her friends, the strict, severe, somewhat puritanical clergyman. At the boys' club the jolly, hail-fellow-well-met social worker. For Stokes, he was at first the go-between, the errand-boy of the gang, a timid, frightened sort of bloke, liking to keep in the background as much as possible. The rest of the gang don't seem to have been so sure. But all contrasting and opposed characters. And how are you to compose a whole out of so many opposites? Notice, too, this sort of secret rendezvous over the Yates shop—the same violent contrasts. A sort of super luxury flat that must have cost a lot to fit up in what is one of the worst slum districts in London. How to pick the truth out of that medley of contradiction?"

"Perhaps", Olive remarked, "it isn't contradiction, but a question of the point of view—just as a soldier may be decorative or dreadful. He may have been a quiet, respectable householder in

Kilburn, and a narrow-minded puritan, and a jolly pal among boys, and a secret roué, and the scared errand-boy of a criminal gang, all in turn, all real for the time."

"Well, then, in which of those characters was he killed?" Bobby asked, "and why? And by whom?"

"Better bring in those seven golden whys you are always talking about in those lectures of yours," suggested Olive, not without the faintest possible touch of malice in her voice, for she was still feeling very sore about her ration books so unfairly placed where she couldn't reach them.

"Lectures?" Bobby repeated, slightly surprised that any one should think of taking them seriously. "Talk," he said, and dismissed them with a gesture. "All that counts is experience—and luck. Of course," he conceded, "they do buck the chaps up a bit. Gives them more self-confidence, because they think they've learnt something."

"The Seven Golden Whys," repeated Olive, who always read over Bobby's lectures for him, so as to be sure he had made his meaning plain. "What? Who? When? Where? In What Way? What with? Why? There you are."

"Theory, that's all," Bobby commented. "But take them in turn. What happened? Answer. Two deaths and a whole lot of stolen jewellery returned to its owners. Who? An enigmatic personality and a young society woman and what else were they? When? Well, we know that more or less accurately, thanks to the medical evidence, and apparently both within twenty-four hours of each other, but the doctors aren't sure which was first. Where? In a deserted room in a bombed house, marked dangerous, and in a luxury hide-out in an East-End slum. In what way? The man shot at close range, the woman suffocated, probably while in a stupor from drink. What with? An old style automatic and a cushion filled with down. Why? Yes. Why? Nothing to show. Joey may have been double-crossing his pals—an errand-boy has his opportunities. Rival gangsters may have been trying to get hold of the Wharton stuff—hi-jacking, I think they used to call it in the States in prohibition days. Or for some reason we know nothing about—and perhaps never shall."

"Don't you think," Olive asked, "that just possibly Lady Geraldine wasn't there on her own account? Couldn't they have got her there by some sort of trick—or kidnapping, like last night with Mr Godwinsson?"

"She was living in good style, spending a lot of money," Bobby pointed out. "No known source of income, so where did it come from? We've always been inclined to think that in most of these recent robberies the thieves had good inside information. They know where the key of the safe is kept or when the family jewels are taken out of the bank for special occasions. Who told them? Was it Lady Geraldine? And her money, her share of the loot, perhaps?"

"You don't like to think it could be that," Olive protested. "Not her own friends."

"There's plenty going on just now you don't like to think," Bobby answered. "There is the possibility of an illicit love affair. If there really is a 'boss' in the background, Lady Geraldine may have been his mistress, and he may have given her money. If it was that, then there's the possibility of her death resulting from jealousy, or even some drunken quarrel. That sort of connection does sometimes end in tragedy if one or the other grows tired of it or if the woman gets troublesome—wants marriage, for instance. But that's bringing in an entirely new element. And nothing much to show there really was a 'boss'. Quite likely it was Joey himself, using an imaginary figure as cover."

"Could the boss be Cy King?" Olive asked.

"I suppose there's that," Bobby admitted. "That would mean it was probably Cy King who committed the murders. He's capable of it all right. But I can't see Cy in connection with that extraordinary hide-out over the Yates shop. Cy is only an ordinary vicious little street rat—rattlesnake, rather. Clever enough in his cunning little way, but that's all."

"Isn't there enough for you to act on?" Olive asked.

"No; I wish there was. I am sure it was Cy who was trying to put a knife into me in that scrap at Angel Alley. But I couldn't swear to it. Masked all the time. It was certainly Cy again at Lady Geraldine's flat, but only Miss Leigh saw him, and again he was masked and Miss Leigh couldn't swear to him. At Kilburn, Mrs Porter only saw him masked, and I only had a glimpse of him looking at me through a window. Same thing last night, too dark to be sure who anybody was. In any case I can't relate him to the strange dark hidden personality you seem to glimpse behind the scenes in all this affair. In my idea all Cy has been trying to do is to get his fingers on the Wharton loot."

"Does that mean," Olive asked, "that was why he was trying to get hold of Mr Godwinsson last night? Because Mr Godwinsson might have it or know where it was?"

"Most likely. The Godwinssons come into it somewhere. It may be only as friends of Lady Geraldine's concerned about what's happened to her. Leofric was trying to find her. Perhaps he knew, though, and was merely laying down a smokescreen against discovery. But again it might have been the stolen jewellery he was trying to track. The colonel and both his sons know something. I told you one of our men spotted Leofric as having been picked up the night the Wharton stuff was stolen. Nothing in that, perhaps. Interesting, though, and worth remembering. None of the Godwinssons will talk, but that may be only because they are trying in their old-world, gentlemanly way to protect Lady Geraldine's reputation. Or is there some other reason?"

"I thought there were three sons," said Olive, who by now had managed to edge a chair up to the cupboard on whose top reposed her ration books.

"Gurth and Leofric," Bobby said. "Old family tradition to give the sons ancient Saxon names—Harold, Gurth, Leofric, Athelstane, always in strict order of birth. I don't know what number five would be. Hengist or Horsa, perhaps." He paused and stared with intense concentration at nothing at all. "Is there a hint there?" he asked.

"Where?" Olive asked.

"In that list of ancient names," Bobby answered slowly.

"For the moment I thought I saw—" He was silent. He said again: "I thought for a moment I had a glimpse—" and then once more he was silent. "Oh, well," he said, picking up the chair Olive had so cunningly sidled up against the cupboard and removing it to the farther end of the room.

"Beast," said Olive dispassionately.

"Old family tradition," Bobby repeated. "Keeping up their claim to be the rightful representatives of the last Saxon king by direct descent. Big claim. Not many families go back beyond Elizabeth—if any. Interesting all of them—father and sons, too. What strikes you most about them?"

"Good looks," said Olive promptly. "I should love to see Gurth," she added. "I mean, if he is anything like as handsome as you say." She clasped her hands and a far-away look came into her eyes. "A dream man," she sighed, and told herself with satisfaction that anyhow she had got a bit of her own back over that chair business.

"Eyes in the boat," commanded Bobby, very sternly, "and never mind good looks. They aren't evidence."

"Quite sure?" Olive asked. "A handsome boy and two girls—Miss Leigh and poor Lady Geraldine. Aren't there possibilities there?"

"Means," grumbled Bobby, "another entirely different line to follow up. But I didn't mean good looks, or Leofric being picked up, or anything like that. I meant the old man's family pride. It doesn't show so much in the sons. Perhaps it only develops when one of them becomes head of the family and custodian of its traditions. With the old man—old Colonel Godwinsson—it's almost crazy. He might really be a royalty of a hundred years ago before royalty got as democratic as the rest of us. He gives you the idea of not being quite sure you're the same flesh and blood."

"You mean," Olive suggested, "like a shopkeeper talking to a customer?"

"No, that's merely being rude. I can't imagine Colonel Godwinsson being rude—he wouldn't know how. It's more an intense reverence for his own blood—'the divinity that doth hedge a king about'. That sort of thing."

"I think that's most awfully nice," declared Olive with enthusiasm. "I think anything that goes back hundreds and hundreds of years is always awfully nice."

"Including fossils?" asked Bobby.

"That's only silly," declared Olive, dignified now.

"Well, so long as you don't take it too seriously," Bobby conceded.

"You've never said anything about Stokes," Olive remarked. "He seems to keep popping in and out just like the masked man you think is Cy King."

"I'm sure is Cy King," Bobby corrected her, "though I can't prove it. I'm not forgetting Stokes. He can't be left out of any list of suspects. There are three questions we have to answer if we can. Who killed Joey Parsons—and why? Who killed Lady Geraldine—and why? Who returned the Wharton jewels—and why? And one fundamental question more important than all—why did Colonel Godwinsson come to see me at the Yard?"

"Yes, I know," agreed Olive thoughtfully. "But what he did shows that, doesn't it?"

"I shall have to check up in Punch," Bobby remarked, and Olive said that would be the best way of making sure.

CHAPTER XXII
ROYAL BLOOD

THE CONFERENCE that Sunday afternoon went on and on, as conferences do, and arrived at various generally vague and often contradictory conclusions, as conferences and committees often do. But it was decided that Bobby should visit Colonel Godwinsson, and that he should go alone, since it was desirable at the present stage of the inquiry that as friendly and unofficial an attitude as possible should be adopted.

"Got to handle the old boy tactfully," said one of those present. "All this descent from ancient Saxon kings. Romantic. Sentimental. The great British public would lap it up. Be on his side to a man, bless their innocent hearts. Stir up a hornet's nest there if we aren't careful."

"Surely we can depend on full co-operation from a man in his position," said in a slightly shocked voice the most junior of them all.

"Unless," said the oldest and most cynical member, "he is doing the chivalrous stunt and risking all for a woman's name."

"Impossible," pronounced the very most senior of them all, "to suspect a man like Colonel Godwinsson of being concerned with criminal activities—murder, robbery, so forth. I was at school with him myself, though he was in the sixth and I was only in the lower fourth. Utterly impossible. You agree, Owen?"

"Oh, yes. Utterly impossible," Bobby answered promptly. "Even though the impossible does sometimes happen," he added.

The remark was not well received. It was pointed out that by definition the impossible is what does not happen. Bobby agreed, and withdrew the observation—with mental reservations. The meeting broke up, as the very most senior of them all had a train to catch. Otherwise the conference would probably have continued till the next morning. Bobby returned home, where, beyond his deserts, considering the way he had behaved over those ration books, he was given a large-size omelette for supper.

Next morning, accordingly, after a pleasant drive through a quiet countryside where it looked as though nothing ever changed, he presented himself at the residence of the county Chief Constable. That gentleman, warned by 'phone to expect his visit, was waiting for him in a mood of mingled amusement, surprise and resentment.

"What's it all about?" he demanded as soon almost as Bobby arrived. "I've known Godwinsson all my life. A man of the highest standing, of the utmost integrity. You might as well suspect a bishop of leading a double life, bishoping by day, burgling by night, as suspect Godwinsson of doing anything he thought dishonourable or dishonest."

"I am as convinced of it as you are," Bobby said, and he spoke with complete sincerity.

"Well, then," said the Chief Constable.

"A former ward of his," Bobby said, "Lady Geraldine Rafe—you may have heard of her—was found dead in London on Saturday night."

"Good God!" said the Chief Constable.

"We held the news back," Bobby continued, "until identity was established, though there was never any real doubt. All the morning papers have got is a paragraph about the body of an unknown woman having been found in the East End and foul play being suspected. Never any real doubt either about its having been murder, but we had to wait for the medical report, to be on the safe side. There might possibly have been a condition of heart disease or something, or even suicide. But the medical report is quite clear. Almost at the same time when her dead body was found an attempt was being made to kidnap Leofric Godwinsson. Colonel Godwinsson's second son, isn't he?"

The county Chief Constable had listened to all this, his eyes, his mouth opening wider and wider, till at last they could no wider go. Then he said feebly: "Dear me." This, however, appearing to him to be an inadequate comment, he tried to think of something more appropriate, but failed to do so. So he said "Dear me," again and lapsed into silence. Bobby continued: "Naturally we feel Colonel Godwinsson may be able to help. And then, too, we felt it would be more considerate if he were informed personally of what had happened, rather than let him see it in the papers. It's sure to be in the evening papers, and they are sure to splash it big. You may expect every crime reporter in London down here before long. With a man like Colonel Godwinsson it's important to get the background right. Could you give me—well, a sort of character sketch?"

But before the county Chief Constable would do this he had to express at some length his amazement and distress. He had, he said, known Lady Geraldine since she was that high—'that' being about twelve inches from the floor. Evidently this fact increased greatly both his horror and his surprise. Incredible that such a thing should happen to one he had known, etc., etc. Bobby listened patiently, agreeing gravely with every comment, except with a half-hearted suggestion that there must be some mistake about Leofric and the alleged kidnapping attempt.

"A pleasant, easy-going lad," declared the Chief Constable. "Even though he has been in a little trouble once or twice. Oh, nothing much. His father took an unnecessarily severe view. Just a little youthful kicking over the traces. Wild oats and all that, you understand. Why on earth should any one want to kidnap him? Are you sure there isn't some confusion of identity."

Bobby didn't think that was possible. He said one of the things he very much wanted to know was what was behind this kidnapping attempt. The young man had been rather badly hurt, was in hospital, and the doctors would not allow questioning for the present. In the meantime, what information could the Chief Constable give?

Very little, the Chief Constable thought. He was quite unable to suggest any possible explanation of what had happened. Indeed, it was clear that, as the philosophers and psychologists would say, he believed intellectually, not emotionally. Or, in more common language, that he hadn't really got it into his head as yet. He repeated that Colonel Godwinsson was a man of the highest possible character, more respected perhaps than loved, though that was not to say that he was in any way unpopular. But he did keep people rather in awe, so to speak. And as much above suspicion as any Caesar's wife that ever was. The Chief Constable, a little pleased with this comparison, repeated it more than once.

"Caesar's wife," he said firmly. "A little too conscious of his family and his descent, perhaps. He does rather give you the idea that he feels his ancestry puts him apart from other men. I expect you know he claims direct descent from Earl Godwin, the father of the King Harold killed at the Battle of Hastings, and that therefore, by right of blood, he is the rightful heir to the English throne."

"He takes that seriously?"

"Oh, very seriously. William the Conqueror seized the crown by force, but that makes no difference to the greater right of blood. Nor does lapse of time make any difference or give force any more right than it had at first. That's Colonel Godwinsson's position. Really," added the Chief Constable, with a slightly rueful laugh, "I don't believe the old boy would be in the least surprised if some day a deputation arrived to offer him the Crown."

"He seems a little mad about it," Bobby remarked. "Is he quite sane in other ways?"

"He is perfectly sane in every way," retorted the Chief Constable. "No doubt of that whatever. If a man considers he has a right to a piece of property stolen from him at some time, but can't establish his claim because of some technical point or another, you can't call him mad because he does his best to keep his claim in being."

"I suppose not," agreed Bobby thoughtfully.

"That's all it amounts to," the Chief Constable insisted. "What he does is simply to try to keep the old tradition alive. The sons are all given Saxon names in the proper order—Harold, Gurth, Leofric, so forth. He has a sort of mystic reverence for his own blood. *Noblesse oblige*. That sort of thing. And I take it he feels royalty obliges still more."

"I suppose so," agreed Bobby again. "Interesting," he repeated. "Takes one back into the centuries. Have the sons the same sort of ideas?"

"I'm afraid," said the Chief Constable with some regret, "they are both inclined to be a little cynical about it. A pity. Leofric—the boy you mentioned just now—turned Socialist at one time. It upset his father terribly. Luckily, as he had been at a public school and the university, he was classed with the intelligentsia. So he got out. Rather more than he could stand, he said."

"There was an elder son, wasn't there?" Bobby asked. "I think Colonel Godwinsson said so once. Harold. Isn't he dead?"

"Yes—by Godwinsson's first marriage. Poor lad! He was in France at the time of the German break-through in 1940, and they shot him as a spy. Apparently they took him for his father. There were letters addressed to Colonel Godwinsson in his possession. As he was in mufti he was clearly a spy, so they shot him out of hand. Later on they apologized and offered to pay compensation. It was while they were still in the stage of being 'correct'. Of course, the compensation offer wasn't accepted. But there was what I must say I thought a very feeling, sympathetic letter from a Count von Pierrus. Apparently he had known Harold in America, where they had been at Yale together, and then he met Gurth at Oxford, and he had stayed at Ing Wain. And Harold had stayed with him at the Pierrus Schloss on the Rhine. Apparently there had been some kind of half-recognized love affair between Harold and Von Pierrus's sister. The letter spoke most feelingly of the loss he and his sister felt they had sustained. He had secured an order postponing the execution, but it had arrived too late, or hadn't been opened, or something of the sort. The letter hinted at a carelessness or neglect which would be suitably dealt with, and said he had hurried at once, as soon as he knew, to make sure such a ghastly mistake didn't happen. Unfortunately he arrived two or three minutes too late. The young fellow, even if he was a German, wrote with a good deal of very proper feeling. Evidently he was very upset; both on personal grounds and because of the stain on the German army. He said he had arranged for a decent funeral and for the poor lad's personal effects to be sent through the Red Cross—his wrist watch, papers, and so on. There was a photograph of the grave, too. When they arrived it was my job to take them to Colonel Godwinsson and give him all that was left of his eldest son. A tragedy."

"I'm afraid there were many tragedies about that time," Bobby said conventionally. "Interesting story, though—very." And the Chief Constable thought with some impatience that the Scotland Yard man's trick of calling everything 'interesting' was a rather dull mannerism. Of course it was 'interesting', but what a word to use of such a tragedy, relieved only by the humanity and good feeling shown by the young German, von Pierrus. 'Interesting', the Chief Constable told himself was no very sympathetic or intelligent comment on so moving a story. Unfortunately at this point Bobby said 'Interesting' once more, and seemed to find it so much so as to have no more to say. The Chief Constable ventured a cough as a reminder. Bobby woke from his abstraction and said: "Then Gurth is now heir, and I suppose his firstborn will be a Harold. Interesting. I told you I met Gurth in town. The handsomest lad I've ever seen, I think—give any girl a start and a beating in the good-looks handicap. Film star type, only more so. Had the poor boy the Germans shot the same good looks?"

"I believe so. I never saw him myself, but his father seemed to think him better-looking even than Gurth. They met in France once or twice."

"Well, if he could outshine his brother he was certainly a world beater," Bobby agreed. "Gurth's looks are enough to make any husband uneasy, and Harold at that rate must have spread panic around. But why met in France? Didn't Harold live here?"

"The first Mrs Godwinsson took him off to America and never came back. When Harold was a baby. She was an American, and apparently married Godwinsson largely on account of the glamour of his Saxon royal blood. She seems to have had an idea she would be recognized as England's uncrowned queen. Of course, it wasn't like that at all. She wasn't even supposed to mention it in public, and yet in private her husband expected her to live up to it. She got fed up and went off home. She must have been ill at the time, for she died soon after, and left all her private fortune to trustees to pay the income to Harold on condition that he never set foot in Great Britain till he was thirty. To preserve his democratic American heritage, the will said. Odd the way things turn out. It was that clause most likely cost him his life. If he escaped from the Germans to England he might forfeit his money. He hesitated too long, and was captured and shot. Ironical, and even more so that coming to England and forfeiting his money wouldn't have mattered. When it was gone into after the news of his death came through, the trustees melted away into the blue and the money with them. They had been doing a bit of speculating on their own, and what they hadn't already lost they took with them."

"Interesting," said Bobby once more; and the Chief Constable was confirmed in his opinion that Bobby's intellectual powers permitted him to make no comment more profound.

CHAPTER XXIII
COLONEL GODWINSSON'S DREAM

ING WAIN, Colonel Godwinsson's home, mentioned under that name in Domesday Book, was about half an hour's drive distant. The name was Saxon, was supposed to mean 'men of the wagon', and to refer to a time when a Saxon family had arrived in a wagon and established itself on the site. The house, though, was Elizabethan, said to be only the third that in fifteen hundred years had stood there, and was a lovely building. Bobby, remembering the impression made on him by the photograph shown him by Colonel Godwinsson, thought it as fine a piece of domestic architecture as he had ever seen, none the less so because the architect, if there had been one, the master builder more likely, had aimed so little at what he had achieved—beauty. Not alone in politics and statecraft does he travel the farthest who knows least to what goal he journeys.

The large—very large—garden, or small—very small—park in which the house stood had been carefully laid out and, in spite of all labour shortages, was still well kept. The lawn was one of those only to be seen in England—mown, rolled, watered, tended through the centuries till to-day it lay like a still carpet of green velvet. Colonel Godwinsson had nearly, though with pain and grief, brought himself to the point of allowing it to be dug up during the war for growing cabbages, but had been spared the necessity when it became plain that neither for the digging nor the proposed cabbage cultivation was there available labour. A famous, much admired feature of the garden was a superb and extensive stretch of rhododendron bushes, extending to the orchard wall at the west of the house.

Bobby's knock was answered by an ancient and very deaf butler, who, though regarding him with evident suspicion, finally consented to show him into the library, there to wait till the colonel could be found and informed.

The library was a fine, spacious apartment with large windows affording a pleasant outlook over the rhododendron bushes to the orchard and the road beyond. On the lawn, between the house and the rhododendrons, an elderly woman was sitting sewing in an invalid chair. On a table close by were some books and papers, and there was an unoccupied basket chair. Bobby guessed the lady was Mrs Godwinsson. The Chief Constable had mentioned that she was an invalid. Probably the basket chair had been or would be occupied by the colonel. Bobby turned his attention to the bookshelves that lined the walls from the floor nearly to the ceiling. They were filled with ancient tomes, including many of those volumes of sermons which seem to have provided the light reading of our ancestors. There were, too, what Bobby thought were first editions of such works as *Clarissa* and *Tom Jones*. He noticed also a first edition in five or six volumes of Pope's *Homer*, in which, in the list of subscribers appeared the name of Harold Godwinsson, Esq., of Ing Wain. There were a great number of legal books, both old and new, these last being the only modern works visible. Apparently the Godwinssons had always studied law, possibly with the idea of being sufficiently instructed to be able to sustain their claim by an ability to cite analogy and precedent. There was, for example, a formidable eighteenth-century 'presentation' in nine volumes of Roman law, and next to it in two volumes a study, published about the same time, of the *'patria potestas'* which the author evidently approved. Another volume, published about half a century ago, discussed the same subject very learnedly, and with special reference to Sir Henry Maine's theories. Maine's own work, *Ancient Law*, was itself represented in three different editions.

"Legal minded," Bobby told himself. "Think too much of formal rights and precedents and all the rest of it."

The door opened and Colonel Godwinsson came slowly in. At least, he always somehow gave the impression of moving with slow dignity, though in fact he moved as quickly as most people. He waved Bobby, who turned away from the bookshelves on his entrance, to a seat; a little with the air of finding it proper and commendable that Bobby had remained standing while waiting for him. He seated himself at the big writing-table that stood near one of the long, straight, rather narrow windows. He said:

"I understand you have a communication to make."

"I am afraid," Bobby said, "it is one that will distress you." He paused. The colonel waited impassively. Bobby said: "Your former ward, Lady Geraldine Rafe, has been found dead."

The colonel remained silent. He might not have heard. Only a tightening of his hands clasped before him till the fingers showed white under the strain betrayed emotion. Bobby waited, watching intently. At last the colonel spoke, in slow, level tones.

"In what circumstances?" he asked.

"In circumstances that suggest murder," Bobby answered.

Again there was no apparent reaction, no sign of emotion or surprise. Only the clasped hands clasped each other more closely still, and Bobby saw a spurt of blood appear where the nail of one finger dug more deeply into the flesh. Again Bobby waited. At last the colonel said in the same quiet, level tones, dropping each word slowly, one by one:

"Can you give me any further details?"

"You do not seem surprised," Bobby remarked, wondering at such iron self-control.

"The possibility has been present in my mind for some time," the colonel answered. "Lady Geraldine was passionate, reckless, avid of experience and yet knowing little of life. I considered it probable that she had made undesirable acquaintances of whose real character she had no knowledge. Her disappearance seemed inexplicable. I had begun to contemplate the possibility of such an eventuality as you tell me has occurred."

"Can you give any information likely to help in the discovery of her murderer?" Bobby asked.

"I am afraid not," came the slow answer. "I have known for a long time that she was not giving me her full confidence. She said her life was her own."

"Her death, too," Bobby said. "I understand, then, you think there is nothing you can tell us?"

"Nothing," said the colonel. He was not looking at Bobby. He said again, and he made the word sound like a pronouncement of doom: "Nothing." Then he added: "Except, indeed, that killing does not go unpunished."

Bobby was not so sure. In a higher sense, true. No crime, no sin can go unpunished, since their punishment is in themselves. In a lower sense, who can say, since who knows what murders are committed and never come to light? Bobby went on:

"I should tell you further that near the place where Lady Geraldine's body was discovered, and at about the same time, on Saturday night, an attack was made on your son, Mr Leofric Godwinsson. Apparently a kidnapping attempt. We were in time to prevent it from succeeding. The attackers escaped. Mr Leofric was injured, and is in hospital. I understand there is no danger, but the doctors forbid questioning at present."

For the first time the colonel allowed himself to show surprise, alarm, even bewilderment or incredulity.

"Leofric? Kidnap Leofric? Why should any one want to do that? Are you sure? Isn't there some mistake?"

"Very sure," answered Bobby, and nearly said very sore instead as he felt his bruised ribs. "I had a hand in the affair. Quite lively while it lasted. They actually had your son in their car. I tried to pull him out. In the end he managed to jump out just as the men were driving off."

"You let them escape?" the colonel asked with severity.

"I don't know that there was much 'let' about it," Bobby answered ruefully. "Anyhow, they didn't get your son, which seems to have been their object. Can you suggest any reason?"

"None whatever. The whole thing seems incredible, fantastic."

"It happened," Bobby remarked. "Incredible, fantastic perhaps, but it happened, and for the incredible and fantastic, as for everything else—indeed, more especially for the incredible and fantastic—there must be a sufficient reason."

"If this happened on Saturday night," the colonel said, with increased severity, "I should have been informed before this."

"It was felt necessary first to make certain preliminary inquiries," Bobby explained. "To be certain of Lady Geraldine's identity, for instance. Of Mr Leofric's identity we had immediate evidence, as he was recognized by one of our men as having been detained for questioning at the time of the theft of the Wharton jewels."

"That was a misunderstanding," the colonel said quickly. "He was released at once with apologies."

"Quite so," agreed Bobby. "Merely coincidence. Another coincidence that he was there, close to the place where presumably the murder was committed, at the very time when it was discovered. He will have to be asked for an explanation. In the meantime he is in no danger, and no visitors or questioning are allowed. One of our men is waiting on the spot ready for any information he can give us to help to identify the men who attacked him. We think we have a good idea who they are, but we have no certain proof, unless he can supply it, and we are quite in the dark as to the motive."

"You can't suspect—" began the colonel, and stopped.

He was plainly much disturbed. "You can't—" he began again, but got no further. He seemed oddly shrunken; he had lost his customary air of dignity—aloof, unassailable. Only too-clearly he had been shaken to the depths. Bobby was not watching him now. Rising to his feet, Bobby went to stand in the corner by the nearest window, looking out over the rhododendrons. It was on these now that his eyes were fixed intently. Stammering a little, the colonel said: "My boy ... Leofric ... a good lad ... you can't imagine, you can't suspect him of smothering a woman and pushing her body into a packing-case."

"Colonel Godwinsson," Bobby said, but still it was the rhododendron bushes that he watched, "I told you nothing about smothering, nothing about a packing-case. How did you know?"

"How did I know?" the colonel repeated. "How did I know? I wonder. It was a dream I had. I dreamed I saw a man put a cushion over a woman's face, and then I thought I saw him lifting her body into a packing-case."

"Who was the man?" Bobby asked.

"In my dream that man was I," the colonel answered.

CHAPTER XXIV

CY KING AGAIN

BOBBY REMAINED standing motionless by the window. His eyes were intent upon the rhododendron bushes, his mind intent upon what he had just heard.

His eager, searching glance allowed no least movement in the bushes to escape his notice. His eager, searching thoughts ranged over every possible interpretation of the colonel's strange statement. Had it been, he asked himself, a veiled confession, giving relief to the mind without being a complete commitment? Or could it be a subtle attempt to explain away the knowledge shown of the circumstances of Lady Geraldine's death? Or was it a father's desperate attempt to divert suspicion from a beloved son, known, or at least feared, to be guilty? Or, again, could it be that in some paranormal way Colonel Godwinsson had indeed seen in dream what had occurred in fact?

Bobby had known too much that was strange to feel able to rule out this last explanation, however doubtful and suspicious it might be. Even science, though not every scientist, has grown humble in admitting that the processes of nature include uncertainty. Colonel Godwinsson had not spoken again. He sat impassive and immobile, it was as though he was no longer there. Presently Bobby, his eyes still as intent and watchful as before upon those rhododendron bushes, said as if to himself: "Dreams may be true."

"It seems this was," the colonel answered.

"Was it a dream?" Bobby asked.

"What else?" the colonel asked in return.

With sudden flashing movements Bobby tore open the window and hurled himself through it. With all the speed his long legs could provide him with, he raced towards the bushes. He saw a small figure he thought he recognized emerge from among them, and, agile as a monkey, swing itself over the orchard wall. Bobby ran harder still. But now he had reached the rhododendrons, and they barred his progress. One cannot hope to rival the hundred yards record while dodging through and round a tangle of bushes. By the time he had reached the orchard wall and climbed it, the sound of a motor cycle starting up had become audible. Bobby ran across the orchard, climbed the farther wall, dropped into the road beyond, and was just in time to see a cloud of dust diminishing in the far distance. He watched ruefully.

"Of all the elusive eels in or out of Christendom," he told himself, "that fellow takes the cake."

He sighed, a frustrated man. Then he examined anxiously the knees of his trousers, for he knew only too well what Olive would say if he had to ask her to mend torn knees, and no more coupons available. To his relief, no damage was visible. After so happy an escape, he was not going to risk his trouser knees again by climbing any more walls, so he walked on to the Ing Wain entrance gate.

It was a fair distance, and took some time. However, when he was admitted by a butler whose worst suspicions had now evidently been confirmed, he found Colonel Godwinsson still seated in the same position, as if he had not stirred or moved. He seemed as remote, as withdrawn as before. Indeed, there was that about him which made Bobby feel that dreams and visions and the second sight were from him just now to be expected. He did not even look up when the ancient butler, opening the door to admit Bobby, announced:

"The person has returned."

Bobby crossed the room and seated himself in the chair he had occupied before. The colonel took no notice. Bobby said formally:

"I must apologize. I had for some minutes noticed movements in the rhododendrons that made me think some one was hiding there, and then I saw a man evidently trying to slip away, so I went after him. But he was too quick and he had a motor cycle waiting. I had my run for nothing."

The colonel seemed less remote now. It was as if his spirit had returned from the remote and awful regions into which it had wandered and was beginning again to concern itself with mundane matters. He said:

"I think I remember hearing about a man asking questions in the village. It is not unusual, but apparently he was rather persistent. This house interests many people, and it is known that my family is one of the most ancient in the world. I gathered, though, that this man hardly seemed a person likely to be interested normally in such things."

"Were any steps taken?" Bobby asked. "Were the police informed?"

"What of?" the colonel retorted. "There was nothing unusual. Many people visit the village and seem to think my house is a show place open to the public. It isn't, though I am always prepared to allow visits from persons with proper credentials."

"Yes, I see," Bobby said. "Most likely it was the same man I saw. If so, he was up to something. If I had been able to catch him I could have charged him with being found on enclosed premises for a presumed unlawful purpose. It would at least have given a chance to search him and take his fingerprints. We have never been able to do that so far. A slippery customer."

"If you know him, why can't you arrest him now?" the colonel asked, evidently suspecting lack of energy and zeal.

"No charge," Bobby answered. "I think I know who it was all right, but I couldn't swear to it. I never saw his face, and no court would accept recognition of a backside and a pair of vanishing legs."

"But who is he? And why does he want to hide in my rhododendrons?"

"Cy King's his name," Bobby answered. "Dangerous as well as slippery. He's the boss of one of the post-war gangs that infest London. He tried to murder me once, and will again, given the favourable opportunity I intend to see he doesn't get. He is rather more than suspected of one or two murders already."

"But surely in that case—"

"No proof," Bobby answered. "The Public Prosecutor wouldn't even be amused if we took it to him. No proof even that the missing men are dead. But that is what is being said in the underworld, and they generally know. If the attempt on your son had succeeded, I think it more than probable he would never have been heard of again. Cy King is one of those rare killers who like to kill. His luck was out that he never got the chance of a job in a German concentration camp. Suited him down to the ground. I can assure you that he would cut your throat—he specializes in knife-play, considers guns clumsy, noisy, inartistic—as soon as look at you if he got half a chance, either with or without any sort of reason."

"I shall have to be careful," the colonel remarked with a faint smile, "but I can't understand either why he was paying us a visit or, for that matter, what any criminal gang should want with Leofric."

"Colonel Godwinsson," Bobby said, "I will ask you a question—who returned the Wharton jewellery?"

"I did not even know it had been returned," the colonel answered. "I haven't seen anything in the papers. Naturally, I heard about the robbery, and I remember admiring the jewellery the duchess was wearing at a ball shortly before the second German war. Of course, too, Leofric, told me of his own absurd misadventure and of the ample apology he had received. I was annoyed, I admit, but I know mistakes do happen. I am glad to know the jewellery has been returned. Have you any idea why?"

"Possibly because the thieves found things getting too warm for them," Bobby said. "There's nothing to show. It happens sometimes. There was one case when an extremely valuable pearl necklace was stolen, and finally discovered in a matchbox in the gutter. The thieves found it too difficult to dispose of, the pursuit growing too hot, and at last got rid of it like that. Or there may be some other reason. In this case one seems to catch a glimpse of many different and complicated, and even contrasting motives."

"Is it generally known that the Wharton jewels have been returned?"

"We want to keep it quiet as long as possible. We had reason to believe rival gangsters were fighting for possession. There has been one killing, though we don't know whether it is a result or a cause of what was going on in the underworld. Of course, we knew we couldn't keep the return of the Wharton stuff quiet for long, and it's getting known now. We stopped the mouths of the newspaper men by telling them in confidence, poor dears. They do hate that, and now they want a release. We shall have to agree. But we are trying to put it about that the Whartons haven't got the famous Wharton blackamoor pendant—the three black pearls, you know. Everyone's heard of them. And that they haven't the Charlemagne jewel either. I take it the Charlemagne jewel is one of the best-known things in the world; worth any amount almost."

"You mean the thieves have still got them?" the colonel asked. "That's bad."

"Well, no," Bobby answered. "Neither the thieves nor the Whartons have them, for the very good reason that we asked permission to take charge of them ourselves for a time. We hope the gangster hunt—if there is one, as we believe—will still go on and some move will be made to give us a chance to act. I am telling you this in confidence, of course. I thought it necessary as Cy King is showing himself in the neighbourhood, and I think you would be wise to take precautions. I think, too, it would be as well to warn your other son—Mr Gurth is his name, isn't it? It may be that whoever made the attack on his brother will turn their attention to him next."

"It hardly seems possible," said the colonel. "I don't pretend to understand all this—not in the least. If this Cy King you speak of does try to pay me a visit, I shall certainly take care to be ready for him."

"There's just one other thing," Bobby went on. "One never knows how an investigation of this sort is going to develop. My visit to-day has been more or less unofficial. It was thought you might be able to help us over the attempt on Mr Leofric. Possibly it may be thought well to ask you for a formal statement. That would probably be for the county police—" and Bobby named the Chief Constable whom he had talked to earlier in the day.

"An old friend," Colonel Godwinsson commented. "Always glad to see him."

"Which means," Bobby thought, "you know any inquiry he has anything to do with will be carried out in the most friendly, 'dear-old-boy' style possible. Well, as to that, there may be someone else on the job as well."

CHAPTER XXV
STOKES IS AFRAID

BOBBY DROVE AWAY from Ing Wain in a very troubled and disturbed state of mind. That Colonel Godwinsson was to some extent implicated in recent events seemed clear, but it was by no means clear how far he was directly concerned and how far he was merely trying to protect others. Or, indeed, whether it was the actual criminals he wished to shield, or only someone more or less innocently concerned. But, then, who was that someone? One or both of his sons? Was it Gurth, the strangely handsome lad whose good looks might well have had their own disturbing effect and who was said to have been in love with Lady Geraldine? Or Leofric, seen more than once in the Angel Alley district and once already 'held for questioning'? Or did the colonel think it his duty—'up to him' in the current slang of the day—to guard the reputation and good name of the dead girl who once had been his ward? Considering the colonel's old-world ideas of chivalry and the duty of a gentleman to go to all lengths to protect a woman's reputation, here might be a powerful, indeed a compelling, motive. There was Monica Leigh, too. There had apparently been a quarrel between her and Lady Geraldine, sufficiently serious for Miss Leigh to decide to leave the flat. Was jealousy the cause? Bobby had to remember that the murder of Lady Geraldine could easily have been carried out by a woman. Easy to hold a cushion over the face of an unconscious person till unconsciousness lapsed into death. But though Mona had been seen in the district and had admitted, though not in words, that she knew about Angel Alley, there was nothing so far to show she had any knowledge of that remarkable flat over the Yates grocery.

That the colonel was responsible for the return of the Wharton jewellery, Bobby was fairly certain. But he was by no means certain whether that return had been made directly or as a result of pressure the colonel had exercised. Not a very important point. What was important was to know how the jewellery had come into his possession, or, in the alternative, how he had known on whom to exercise pressure and what form that pressure had taken.

However, the Wharton jewels had now become relatively uninteresting. They had been recovered; and presumably there would now be fewer nasty remarks darkly muttered in ducal circles about the incompetence, negligence, and other faults of Scotland Yard. The pressing problem was to bring to justice whoever might be guilty of the cold-blooded murder of Lady Geraldine Rafe. And to discover in what way, if any, that shocking crime was connected with the almost simultaneous killing of the enigmatic Joey Parsons, as mysterious in death as in life, still guarding his secret so that it was still uncertain whether he had been prime mover in what had happened, or a mere errand-boy and go-between.

Upon these points Bobby felt attention should be concentrated. Yet there were clearly others concerned, others whose activities seemed to centre strangely on Colonel Godwinsson; on Colonel Godwinsson with his unblemished reputation, his high sense of responsibility, his excessive pride of birth, superb or fantastic according to the view taken. Ex-Sergeant Stokes, for example, hovering assiduously on the outskirts of the affair, evidently knowing something, though impossible as yet to say whether that something was much or little. Or indeed anything, since it might well be his sole motive was a vague hope that he might pick up something or another of which he might make use. A share in the offered reward, perhaps—the innocent motive he had himself put forward. And behind him the sinister and doubtful figure of Cy King, whose sudden appearance in the Ing Wain grounds seemed to Bobby disturbing and menacing in the extreme.

Was he there, for instance, by appointment, so to say? Colonel Godwinsson had shown no great surprise, or even interest in his appearance. Almost certainly Cy King and his associates would have heard by now of the return of the Wharton jewellery, so the hope of laying hands upon it could not be the reason for the visit.

Bobby was not even sure that there was much truth in the stories of bitter enmity between the Cy King gangsters and those with whom Joey Parsons had been connected, whether as leader or subordinate. As good business men, gangsters do not often waste much energy upon feuds, though of course it happens at times when one gang tries to intrude upon another gang's private preserves. Or they may be at feud one day, carrying on fierce warfare, and in firm alliance the next—just like the Great Powers of the world. In this bewildering jungle of doubt, intrigue, and treachery, it was even possible that Joey Parsons had been one of Cy King's men, used as a 'stooge' to deceive the police and even, for that matter, others of the gang.

In that case Joey might have met his death as a result of such activities, and that again might mean there was no connection between his murder and that of Lady Geraldine Rafe.

Gloomily did Bobby contemplate this welter of conflicting and contradictory facts and theories. True, now and again, as he went over and over them in his mind, he did think he caught a glimpse of what seemed for the moment as if it might turn out to be a thread leading to the heart of the labyrinth. But only for a moment or two. Then again all seemed hopeless confusion. He tried to comfort himself with the reflection that at least there were a few things certain, a few facts. Some confirmation at least he had obtained this morning. But was the interpretation he was inclined to put upon them the true one? Doubtful, startling, improbable even; but what else was there to work on for a starting point?

Of one thing only was he sure—that the appearance of Cy King at Ing Wain was ominous in the extreme. Where Cy went, death was apt to follow. If there really was any connection between him and Colonel Godwinsson, then the colonel was in danger—danger much greater than he knew.

Bobby began to drive faster, as though responding un-consciously to the sense of urgency he felt. Colonel Godwinsson, wrapped in the innocence of his pride of family; his belief that by right of the royal and ancient descent he claimed, he was in some sort set apart from other men; his deep instinct that he had a right to expect deference and respect from all, would be like a child in any dealings he might have with such a man as Cy King. All kinds of inhibitions, scruples, traditional restraints, on one hand. None on the other. The colonel would be like a country clergyman dealing with a city shark; like a young girl thinking to amuse herself in the company of an experienced roué; like a sheep before the shearers. Or would he? Which was his part? The first in each pair or the second?

Was it possible he merely felt himself at war with a society refusing to admit the claims he believed so well founded?

Faster and faster Bobby drove, as these doubts and speculations drove in upon his mind—at least till he came to a built-up area and slowed down just in time as he noticed the disapproving eye of a policeman on, fortunately, the hither side of a warning notice. But there was no built-up area to set a barrier against the rushing tide of fear and doubt that was flooding in upon his thoughts.

He had reached Town now, but he did not go direct to Scotland Yard. He wanted his lunch—wanted it badly—and he knew if he showed himself at headquarters he would be immediately caught up in a flurry of reports and interviews and probably get no lunch at all. So instead he drove home. Olive would not be expecting him, but she was trained to endure with resignation his sudden arrivals and departures, and he could take her out to a neighbouring restaurant. Of course, by this time she would have had her own lunch, but as he knew she had been intending that morning to do something she called turning out a room, it was fairly certain that that lunch had consisted of a cup of tea and a bun—woman's favourite meal for that matter. So she ought to be able to deal with a more reasonable repast; and anyhow he wanted badly some one to talk to, some one before whom he could lay all the different possibilities he saw, the varying theories and beliefs in his mind, including one so strange, so doubtful, he felt he would not dare mention it to anybody else.

But there was to be no lunch for him just yet, for as he drew near he saw Stokes lounging close by the entrance to the flats. Bobby, not pleased, greeted him with little cordiality.

"Well, what is it now?" he demanded.

"I'm only trying to help, Mr Owen, sir," Stokes protested in his most injured voice. "I don't hold with murder. Nasty. Bad publicity. Means every one on the *qui vive*, and a bloke getting no chance to go about quiet and peaceful like. I don't hold with it. Not with killing I don't," and this time into his rather whining voice came a note of what seemed like sincerity and real feeling.

"Well?" Bobby asked when Stokes paused.

"Cy King," said Stokes, and was silent.

"What about him?"

"There's something made him murderous mad," Stokes said slowly. "He was at Mike's last night. You know Mike's?" Bobby nodded. All the police knew Mike's. It was a Soho cafe, utterly respectable under another name in front, very much other than respectable at the back, where it was known to the initiated as 'Mike's'. Stokes went on: "He came in looking like all the devils in hell. He didn't say nothing, but some of the boys as was there just looked at him and got up and went out and none of them that stayed said a word. I wanted to go out too, only I would have had to go right in front where he was, and I didn't want, and then I was sitting in a corner and hoped maybe he wouldn't notice. He had that knife of his, and he was stropping it, loving like. Mike brought him a drink—a special. Well, you know what Mike calls his special. Cy King don't drink much as a rule, but he had two specials right off and asked for a third. Mike hesitated in a way because rightly speaking two specials is enough for most; but Cy sort of looked, and Mike fair tumbled over himself to get that third one. Cy downed it like it was nothing at all, but it did sort of loosen him up. Made him talkative, and you wished it hadn't. He said he had been double-crossed. He asked if we knew what he did to blokes who double-crossed him. He saw me and he said: 'You tell 'em, Tim Stokes, what I do to them that double-cross me.' I said I didn't rightly know, and he said: 'You don't know, don't you? I'll show you,' and he got up from where he was sitting, but I beat it—in quick time I beat it. I heard him laughing, and I've not been near Mike's since, and don't mean to. He means it, Mr Owen. He means it all right, same as a snake means it when it puts its head up and back."

"Who has double-crossed him?" Bobby asked. "What does he mean?"

"It's to do with the Wharton stuff," Stokes answered. "Is it true you've got it back? It's what some of the boys are saying."

"Well, they can go on saying," Bobby answered. "No business of theirs. Have you any idea who Cy King means?"

Stokes shook his head.

"Whoever it is," he said, "had better mind or he won't be alive much longer."

"Is it you?" Bobby asked, and Stokes denied it with vehemence; but his face was very pale, and when he went away he stumbled a little, walking like a drunken man.

CHAPTER XVI
HELD FOR QUESTIONING

AN UNLUCKY DAY for lunches. Olive, having finished turning out her room, had apparently then turned herself out, and was probably now standing in a queue somewhere. A used teacup and a plate with a few crumbs on it in the sculleryette (why not? if there's a kitchenette) gave evidence that Bobby's suspicions about her probable lunch had been well founded.

Nursing a distinct sense of grievance—for why a wife if she isn't there when you want her?—he went off to lunch alone. Nothing much left, though, since now it was late, except some cold corned beef and a salad that once no doubt had been young and fresh and gay, but was so no longer. Moodily he ate, thinking how much easier it would have been if he could have put all his different, conflicting theories and beliefs to Olive. Brought into the open, expressed in plain language, some would have appeared more, some less, plausible. Still more moodily he reflected that the case seemed to be developing from the problem of who had committed two murders in the past to that of whom was to be murdered in the future.

Stokes certainly feared it might be he, but Stokes was an egotist who always thought of himself as the centre of all things. No doubt Cy King had heard of the return of the Wharton jewellery, was furious to think he had no longer any prospect of being able to lay his hands upon loot he had searched for so long and at such risk, and perhaps intended revenge upon whomsoever he chose to think responsible for his disappointment. Especially if he had heard and believed that two such valuable pieces as the Blackamoor pendant and the Charlemagne jewel had been held back. Double-crossing he might call that, though in criminal circles 'double-cross' means generally not double treachery, but any trickery one rogue carries out upon another. If, in fact, Cy King had been tricked in any way, not only his prestige among his friends would suffer, but his vanity as well, and vanity is the chief ingredient in every criminal's make-up.

Possibly that was behind the attempt to kidnap Leofric Godwinsson. Could it also explain Cy's visit to Ing Wain? He might have thought to find Leofric there, or get news of where he was, or he might have been hoping to get on the scent of the two supposedly missing pieces of the Wharton loot.

Impossible to take any action. There was no charge that could be brought against Cy King—none, at least, supported by any evidence at which a magistrate would look for a moment. Bobby gave it up, paid for his corned beef at the pre-war rate for grouse on toast or smoked salmon, and departed for his office, wondering unhappily what the next development was likely to be.

He had not long to wait. Almost the first thing he learned when, still hungry, he arrived at the Yard was that Mona Leigh was being 'held for questioning'—that convenient euphemism for an arrest, though one that might possibly not be followed by a formal charge.

The news had just come in from the Angel Alley district police station. Bobby got on the 'phone at once. What had happened was that police officers, continuing their examination of the flat over the Yates grocery, heard a ring at the door, answered it and found Miss Leigh there. She received a pressing invitation to enter and was questioned. She had refused to answer except in the presence of her lawyer, who was also her uncle. His office, when rung up, replied that he was out of town and would not return till the next day. Mona had then decided to wait for him rather than accept the services of either of his partners, even though told that that meant her remaining in custody for the time.

Bobby rubbed the end of his nose defiantly. If Olive couldn't be there for lunch when he wanted her so badly, then he didn't care how much she disapproved that gesture. He rubbed it, indeed, so hard he seemed to want to rub it off altogether. Then he decided, leaving all the work piled up on his table and clamouring for attention, to interview Mona himself. She might, remembering the small service he had once done her, be more willing to talk to him. Not if she were guilty, of course, but if she were innocent. Probably her uncle-lawyer, concerned only for her immediate interests, would advise her to say nothing—always a lawyer's first instinct and last resource. But Bobby was thinking also of that dark warning he had just received, and it seemed to him possible that Mona might be able to give some intimation of where the threatened blow was likely to fall.

At the police station he found a very scared-looking girl in charge of an amiable, fussing matron who kept calling her 'dearie', advising her not to worry, and providing her with cups of tea for which Mona had not the least desire. She brightened up a little when Bobby appeared. He told her frankly that not only was she entirely within her rights in refusing to speak till her lawyer arrived, but that also it was probably much the wisest thing to do, whether she were innocent or guilty—

But at this last word Mona broke in with a cry of indignation that was either genuine or at least a wonderfully good imitation thereof.

"Oh, I'm not ... it's awful ... you can't think ... no one could really ..." she protested, and clearly she was having some difficulty in keeping back her tears.

"My dear young lady," Bobby said gravely, "when a person turns up at what seems to have been a most carefully concealed hide-out where a murder has just been committed, that person is bound to be asked for an explanation. I was going to say that as regards yourself and your own interests, you are very right and wise to say nothing till your lawyer gets here. But I've been warned—information received is what we say—that there is a very real risk of another murder happening. I don't know of whom, and I don't know why. But there's some connection with what's been going on. I've no right to say more than that I think you might be able to help."

She was staring at him with great, wide-open eyes. She was clearly both puzzled and apprehensive, and it was a moment or two before she answered.

"I don't think ..." she began hesitatingly. "I don't ... understand. How can I help?"

"By being willing to answer a few questions," Bobby told her.

"Oh, but ..." said Mona and paused again.

"If you would like time to think it over," Bobby said, "I will come back whenever you wish. Or not at all if you say so. I would like to repeat that, to the best of my belief, a man's life may hang on it. A man's life—or it may be a woman's."

"Oh, but ..." said Mona again, and again paused.

"Shall I make you a nice cup of tea, dearie?" asked the matron.

"Oh, please," said Mona; and the matron looked hurt, so negative had been that 'please' and the accompanying gesture, so plainly had they meant: 'Oh, for goodness' sake, leave me alone.'

"You have known yourself," Bobby said, "what it is to be in danger."

"Oh, yes," said Mona; and looked still more frightened, and became so pale that it was all the matron could do not to repeat her suggestion of a nice cup of hot tea.

"It is the same man," Bobby said. "I've seen him hanging about near Colonel Godwinsson's place. A man named Cy King."

Mona seemed to make up her mind.

"What do you want to know?" she asked, the words tumbling out as if they had to come in a hurry or not at all.

"You see," Bobby explained, "it's all badly mixed up with these jewel robberies that have been going on. I haven't had much to do with them myself, but I know our people began to suspect that the thieves were getting inside information. At first we thought it was servants. At present people are so glad to get domestic help they are inclined to take any one. Possibly sometimes it was like that. But overall study made it clear it couldn't always be servants. The staffs were different each time, and it wasn't likely any gang could always manage to plant an accomplice, and always a different one. Our people began to feel there must be some one else who was giving the information. Some one in society itself, some one who got invitations to big houses. Nothing to show who. Delicate, too, to accuse influential, well-connected people. A short list was drawn up. Not so short, either. Astonishing how many society people are living beyond their means—or on no means at all. One of the names was that of Lady Geraldine Rafe. Only on general principles. There was nothing definite against her. Only that she was living in good style and it wasn't very clear where her money came from. But that is sometimes true of other good-looking young women, and nobody's business but their own. Also she seemed rather rackety and it was noticed that she was on the spot when the loss of the Wharton jewellery was discovered. Now she's dead."

"Yes," Mona said in a whisper. "Yes," she repeated.

"We are fairly certain this man, Cy King, is the man who tried to make you tell him where Lady Geraldine was."

"I didn't know," Mona said.

"The same Cy King broke into a house in Kilburn where a man called Joey Parsons lived—the man who was killed just about the same time as Lady Geraldine. Now I've seen him hanging about Ing Wain—Colonel Godwinsson's place, you know. He seems to have been asking a good many questions in the village—some of them apparently about you."

"About me?" stammered Mona; and if she didn't look even more frightened than before, it was because that was not possible.

"It's pretty clear," Bobby continued, "that Cy King was on the track of the Wharton jewellery—other loot, too, perhaps. The difficulty is to know whether he was in on the theft itself or whether he was trying, so to say, to gate-crash. Hi-jacking, the Americans used to call it. That is, he may have been trying to grab for himself stuff that another gang stole in the first place. It happens. Rogues rob rogues soon enough if they see their chance. Or if he was one of the original thieves, it may have been the other way round. One of his pals may have thought it a good idea to try to make a get-away with all the stuff. Possibly that some one was Joey Parsons and that is why he was killed. All that is certain, or fairly certain, is that Cy King is in a very dangerous mood, threatening murder. We have to take that seriously. He is a killer by instinct. You don't often get them, but you do sometimes. Nasty when you do."

"But why? Why should he want to kill any one?"

"He thinks he has been what he calls 'double-crossed', and he wants his revenge. Vanity comes into it, too. He wants to let his pals see what happens to any one who gets in his way. I suppose it's a form of the power urge that some psychologists tell us is the strongest motive of all, the most fundamental." Mona was moistening dry lips, and, when she tried to speak, the words did not come very easily at first. The matron made sure that the kettle was boiling on the gas ring, the tea-pot warm, the tea-caddy close at hand. Mona said:

"Who … ?" She said again: "Who … ?" Then she said "Who does he mean … want to … ?"

"If we knew that," Bobby answered gravely, "it would be much easier. We could take precautions. But it may be any one of half a dozen or more. It might even be me."

"Oh," said Mona; and Bobby hoped he was wrong in thinking he detected a note of relief in Mona's voice, or, alternatively, as the lawyers say, that it only meant she was sure he could look after himself.

So was he, for that matter; but he saw no reason why others should be so cheerfully confident of the fact. Even though on occasion he wished Olive was, instead of sometimes appearing to regard him as a kind of half wit, unfit to be trusted out of her sight for more than an hour at a time.

"I don't think," Bobby went on slowly, "that we can even exclude you. There has been one attack on you, and Cy was asking questions about you in the Ing Wain village. More probably it is one of the Godwinssons. There's the attempt on Leofric. Then there's a man called Stokes who is badly frightened in case he may be meant. Or there may be some one we've never even heard of. Or an old prize-fighter called Pitcher Barnes. Or even a wretched little guttersnipe, Eddie Heron, who has been trying to get himself locked up, evidently because he wants to be in a nice safe place. A wide choice, you see. For the moment it's a more pressing problem than finding out who killed Lady Geraldine and who killed Joey Parsons, if it wasn't the same murderer in each case. We are very much in the dark at present, except for two or three hints Colonel Godwinsson has given, and they may not mean much. If we can find out who Cy King wants to kill, it ought to help us to find out who did the other two killings—and why."

"What do you want to know?" Mona asked; and this time the matron made up her mind and went resolutely to make the nice, hot cup of tea she was sure would soon be wanted.

CHAPTER XXVII
MONA'S STORY

"WELL," Bobby answered slowly, "I would like to say first of all that I'm not asking you to make a statement. This is unofficial in a way. If necessary, you will be asked to make a formal statement. It will be taken down in writing, and you will be asked to sign it. But that's something for the future. What I want now is if you'll tell me a few things that may help to give me an idea of the background, the general atmosphere of the thing. I shan't try to take any note of anything you tell me."

He paused, wondering what the effect would be of this attempt to put their interview on the footing of a friendly chat. He was glad to notice that Mona looked immensely relieved. Putting things in writing often, indeed generally, has an intimidating effect. So much care is given to the effort to be precise that the undertones may get forgotten, and often there is more truth in undertone than in precision. Few things more deceptive than a fact. Mona did not speak, but she was plainly waiting for him to continue. He said:

"Well, first of all, could you tell me how you knew about the rooms over the Yates shop?"

"She took me there once," Mona answered in a low voice. "It was horrid," and she became very red, as if at the memory of what she had seen.

"When was that?"

"About two or three weeks ago. I'm not sure exactly."

"You realize," Bobby said, "that you are making a very grave admission. If you knew where this place was, surely when Lady Geraldine disappeared—"

"Oh, but I didn't," Mona interrupted. "That was what was so funny. I mean, know where it was. She took me in her car one night after we had had a most awful row, and it was pitch dark. I couldn't see anything. Except when she used her torch to find the key-hole. She had been drinking rather a lot. She did sometimes. The torch showed up a shop window for a moment, and I remembered afterwards it looked like a grocer's. And I thought it must be somewhere in the East End, because of some of the streets we had been through. That was all."

"But you went there to-day?"

"That was Leofric. I told him how frightfully worried I was about Gerry. It was after that awful man tried to make me tell him about her. I began to wonder if she could be at that dreadful place where she took me. Only if she was, why didn't she let us know? Leofric was worried, too. He said there had been a murder and it might be the same district. He went several evenings to look, and he rang up to say he thought he had found it. He said he couldn't get any answer when he knocked, but when he had made sure it was the right place he would come to tell me and we would have to think what to do. But he never came. I thought I had better try to find out what had happened. So I went where he said he thought it was, only when I rang some men came and they said they were policemen and they said Gerry was dead. They brought me here."

Bobby made a mental note to emphasize in his next lecture that a detective's business is to receive information, not to give it. Now he had no chance of seeing for himself how Mona would react to the news of Lady Geraldine's murder. He said presently:

"I think you were at school with Lady Geraldine, weren't you?"

"We were special friends. Gerry was lovely to me. I was older than most girls are when they go to boarding school, and awfully backward, and I was simply miserable. I think I might have tried to run away, or something, only for Gerry. When we left we both joined the Wrens; only I got pushed out to Ceylon, and Gerry was such a good driver they kept her at home to drive V.I.P.'s. When I was demobbed at last, long after she was, I suppose I did rather wish myself on her. I mean I didn't give her much chance to say she didn't want me. I wanted to be in London to look for a job, and I hadn't anywhere else to go, and I suppose it seemed natural."

"Yes?" Bobby said when she paused.

"I think she was glad to see me at first," Mona went on, rather hesitatingly, "but after a time I began to feel there was something wrong."

"Was that when you had the quarrel you spoke about?" Bobby asked, and wondered again if she realized how damaging an admission that might seem.

He felt she was either very simple or very cunning. He was not quite sure which. He knew extreme simplicity and candour can often seem extreme cunning, just as the innocence of the simple-minded and the uninstructed can often reach a truer conclusion than the wisdom of the scholar and the philosopher. His impression so far was that Mona was telling the truth, but how well he knew that sometimes the most innocent-looking, sweet-faced young girl can outlie the very father of lies himself. He suspended judgment. Mona was speaking. She said:

"It was awful. You can't imagine how ashamed I felt afterwards. It was almost worse than it was sometimes when our girls quarrelled in the Wrens. You couldn't help picking up words, and we both began using them. Once you hear them you can't forget them. I wish you could."

"What was it about?"

"She said I was jealous. It wasn't true a bit. Of course, she knew ..."

"Yes," Bobby encouraged her.

"You see," Mona explained hesitatingly, "Leofric and I were in Ceylon at the same time. We didn't see much of each other, because of course he was generally away in his ship, but we did sometimes, and once he had a long shore spell when he had a poisoned arm. Gerry said all I wanted was to use her so I could get my claws on him again. I told you we were saying the most awful things to each other. It was true I did want to see Leofric again so as to know if he still liked me, because he had said things in Ceylon. Only that's different. Ceylon, I mean. I knew people often felt quite differently about each other when they got back home. I thought perhaps we might, too. That wasn't being jealous."

"Was this before or after she took you to the Yates flat?"

"It was why. Because of the things we said. I expect we both got a bit ashamed. I know I did. And I said so, and then she said there was only one man for her, and there would never be another. I told you she had had too much to drink. She said they weren't married; it was better than that, grander than that. It was perfect freedom for both, and so it was perfect belonging, each to each. I told her that was what men said to our Wrens when they wanted to get their own way with them, and that made her cry. She was getting a bit maudlin, and she said I must come with her and she would show me. I didn't want to, but she made me. It didn't matter how much she had drunk, she could always drive, and she got her car out. She said I was a silly little school-girl straight from the kindergarten class, and now I was going to learn something. I told her there wasn't much you didn't know after you had served with the Wrens. It was an awfully dark night. I hadn't any idea where she took me. She could drive better in her sleep than most people when they were awake. I told you all I noticed was the shop window when the light from her torch showed it for a moment. She took me upstairs in a room. It was ... I can't tell you."

"I've seen it," Bobby said.

"I never knew ..." Mona began, and paused. In spite of her boasted Wrens and Ceylon experience, it was evident she had been thoroughly surprised and bewildered. She said: "I can't think why ... I mean what for ... why should any one ... ?" She paused again, searching for a word. She found it at last, and brought it out with emphasis. "Silly," she said loudly.

"So it is," agreed Bobby.

"She was laughing a lot, she kept laughing. She wanted to explain it all—all those things on the wall. I told her to be quiet. I said I was going. Then we heard the door open and some one coming up the stairs. Gerry seemed to go all sober all at once. She said to wait where I was, and she went out on the landing. I could hear them talking. Gerry came back. She said it was a man with a message from her friend to say he couldn't come and she was to meet him at a night club, so I had better go home. The man who had come with the message could drive me home and then come back for her."

"Didn't you ask her who her friend was?"

"No. I knew."

"You knew? How? Who was it?"

"Gurth."

"Gurth? Gurth Godwinsson?" Bobby exclaimed, and when she nodded he asked: "Are you sure? Did she say so?"

"It was his umbrella," Mona explained.

"Umbrella?" Bobby repeated, puzzled.

"It was almost the first thing I saw when we got there. In a stand on the landing. I knew it at once. It had a rather special gold-mounted handle. When I saw it, I said it was Gurth's. Gerry didn't take any notice. She began to show me that awful room, and I forgot about the umbrella. But of course then I knew."

"I see," Bobby said thoughtfully. "Can you describe the man who came with the message to Lady Geraldine? He drove you home?"

"I didn't see him clearly. He was in the driver's seat when I got into the car to go home, and I only saw his back. It was Gerry's big car, you know. He had on a big coat. I didn't notice him much. I was worried about Geiry and about Gurth. It all seemed—horrid. I heard the driver say to her: 'Bad enough that other time. Worse coming in a car. Anyone may have seen it. A swell car like this. It would be noticed. You promised you never would again.' It was funny the way he spoke. As if he were most awfully angry, but didn't want to show it. Why should he mind if any one saw the car?"

"Well, it does rather sound," Bobby suggested, "as if he had been trying to keep their meeting-place a secret; and he thought a big car in a side street in a poor district like that might be remembered and set neighbours talking. There may have been—I think there was—something of the sort before and she had promised not to again. Did it seem a long drive home?"

"Oh, yes. I've thought afterwards that he must have been driving round and round. I don't know. There was another thing."

"Yes?" Bobby said. "Yes. What was it?"

"He stopped on a bridge. He said it was the back tyre, and he got down to look at it. I think it must have been Putney Bridge. I don't know. I was thinking about Gerry and that awful place. I wanted to help her, and I knew I couldn't. And then it was just like a voice, only of course it wasn't one, only imagination, but it was just like a voice saying close by: 'Well, you could say a prayer, couldn't you?' It was almost like telling me to. The voice said— of course not really, it was only my fancy. It said: 'The car has stopped and the driver is attending to the back tyre, so no one would see you if you did it now,' and I did. I got down on my knees and I began to say something out loud. I know it sounds awfully odd and silly."

"Go on," Bobby said. "What happened next?"

"It was the driver. He had finished with the tyre, and he came back and opened the door. It was very awkward. You see, I was on my knees. He said: 'What are you doing?' I said: 'I am trying to say a prayer for Gerry and for the man she loves.' He said: 'Why?' and I said: 'I think they need it.' Now, wasn't that a funny way to talk to a strange man on Putney Bridge?"

"Did he say anything?"

"No. Not then. He had a big sack he was carrying. He threw it inside on the floor. There was something awfully heavy in it. When he threw it down it shook the whole car. I asked what it was, but he didn't answer. He just stood there. I heard a clock a long way off strike twelve."

"Did anything else happen?"

"No. He shut the door and got back into his seat and we drove home. When we got there he said he was sorry he had been so long but he had missed his way. He said he began to think he would never get me home at all. It was funny the way he said that. I tried to find my purse to give him half a crown, and he began to laugh. He said: 'Don't trouble, miss. You've got here safe, and that's the main thing.' He drove away then, and after I got in the flat I began to feel most awfully frightened."

"Well, you were quite all right and safe there," Bobby said brightly. "Have a cigarette?"

She took it, but she did not light it, though he held a match for her till it began to burn his fingers. She said:

"I dream about it sometimes. About the sack and there being something heavy in it." Her voice sank to a whisper. It shook slightly and she was trembling. She said: "Do you think perhaps he meant to put me in it and drop me in the river?"

"Well, he didn't," Bobby said still more brightly as he struck another match for her. "I shouldn't think about it any more if I were you."

"No," she said, "no." After a moment she added: "It's the dream keeps coming back."

CHAPTER XXVIII

IDENTIFIED UMBRELLA

THAT ENDED the interview, Bobby reflecting gloomily that he was no nearer than before to knowing whose life was threatened. Nor had he learnt anything to help to show on whom rested the guilt of the murders of Joey Parsons and of Lady Geraldine.

For that matter, he could not even be certain that Mona's dramatic tale was true. Only her word for it, and Bobby's first principle was to accept no story without corroboration. Undoubtedly it was coherent, and it was consistent with what else he knew. All the same, he told himself cautiously, he must suspend judgment. The other two actors in the scenes Mona had described were both dead; that is, if, as Bobby thought might fairly be assumed, the driver of the car had been the man known as Joey Parsons and by other names. And Mona's story, even if accepted, left it still most maddeningly uncertain whether he were chief and 'leader', or merely an unimportant hanger-on. If this last were the case, then it might even be that his failure to dispose of Mona on Putney Bridge had been the cause of his own death. Gang parasites who omit to carry out their orders do occasionally come to a swift and messy end.

Plainly the next thing to do was to have a talk with Gurth. He must be questioned about that umbrella Mona said she had noticed at the 'love nest' flat. Presumably this was the same umbrella that Bobby, too, had seen there, and that was now in the hands of the police, who had been trying, without success, to trace its owner. And if that owner were Gurth, then considerable explanation would be required. This, however, had to be postponed for the time. Gurth, it seemed, was away on a motor trip, and it was not known when he would return. Leofric, too, must be questioned, but that again would have to wait. He had developed pneumonia and was now on the danger list. Bobby decided, as the best that could be done in the circumstances, to recommend that a plain-clothes man should remain on duty at the hospital. It might well be that Cy King's threats were aimed at Leofric.

Nor did that mean, Bobby reflected, that Leofric was innocent. Whoever Cy King considered had 'double-crossed' him over the Wharton jewellery might well be the murderer of one or other of the two victims, or even, indeed, of both. So, neither Gurth nor Leofric being available, Bobby was able to get a quiet evening at home—and there annoyed Olive very much by pointing out that Mona's story could only be accepted provisionally. At the moment there was nothing to support it except her own word.

"I think that's being rather absurd," Olive declared with dignity. "I'm sure no young girl could invent such a story."

"Ever hear of Elizabeth Canning?" Bobby asked.

"We aren't talking about Elizabeth Canning, whoever she is," retorted Olive, still more dignified. "We are talking about Mona Leigh."

"Well," Bobby said, "if she is guilty, as is possible, of two murders, one out of jealousy, and the other to cover up the first and she is clearly under suspicion—she would probably be more than equal to a spot of invention. One thing certain is that she is in love with Leofric. Love can lead into strange places."

"It can," agreed Olive, slightly vicious now. "To darning socks, for instance, and washing up, and sweeping floors. And even," said Olive, looking very bewildered, "it can make you rather like it—at least sometimes."

But Bobby was not listening. He said:

"There is one thing to remember. Mona did seem to be suffering from a sort of delayed-action panic. It did rather seem as if she had not realized at first what that weighted sack might mean. As if only much later, and rather slowly, had she taken in the idea that it might have meant being knocked on the head, pushed in the sack, and dropped over the Putney Bridge parapet into the river."

"Bobby, don't," Olive exclaimed; and Bobby said he wouldn't, and anyhow it was time for bed, though he didn't suppose, he added sadly, that he would sleep a wink.

Olive had heard this prognostication before, but remained unaffected, since she had never known it fulfilled. Her own belief was that if Bobby remained awake two minutes after getting into bed before going to sleep and remaining asleep for the rest of the night, that was the full extent of his insomnia. Incidentally, her own idea of the perfect husband was of one who would never sleep so soundly while his wife lay and counted endless sheep—without result.

Next morning, Gurth, in response both to a letter and to a 'phone call, was early at Scotland Yard. He looked pale and ill; and his eyes were red-rimmed and bloodshot, yet that fine physical beauty he possessed seemed by this rather enhanced than diminished. He expressed regret for not having answered the earlier summons sent him the night before, but he had been out motoring. Asked if he had been to visit his father at Ing Wain, he said he had merely driven straight into the country without much caring where, and then back again.

"I wanted to be alone," he said. He added after a momentary pause, as if feeling the need of further explanation: "I had only just heard about Geraldine Rafe. She was a friend of mine," and in spite of all the self-control and suppression of emotion that was in the tradition of his class and country, he had difficulty in getting out those last few words.

Bobby did not try to express sympathy. For all he knew, he was talking to her murderer. Not the first time, if so, that a murderer has wept at his victim's fate. For a moment or two he talked more or less at random, to give Gurth a chance to recover. Then he explained that he wished to ask a very few questions. Nothing formal. No question of making a statement at present. He always found that when a will to co-operate existed, a friendly chat was the best way of getting at the truth. Of course, purely voluntary. Later on perhaps the procedure would be formal, question and answer taken down in shorthand and typed out for signature. At the moment, though, the chief need was for speed. Two murders had been committed, and now a third was threatened.

"A third? Who of?" Gurth asked; and he looked startled, and, if not more pale than before, since that was impossible, at least more uneasy.

"That is what we want to know—very badly," Bobby answered. "Police duty is not so much to bring criminals to justice as to prevent their becoming criminals by preventing crime—if we can. A difficult job. Can you make any suggestion? Apparently a man named Cy King—have you ever heard of him?" Gurth shook his head. Bobby resumed: "He seems to think he was double-crossed, as he calls it, by one of his accomplices when the Wharton jewels were returned, and he threatens reprisals. A question of his prestige with his pals. And then a big disappointment, no doubt. Those jewels might have brought enough for him to retire on, or to visit one of the South American countries, where there is said to be considerable scope for gentlemen like himself."

"I don't see the connection," Gurth grumbled. "I don't know anything about it."

"Some cases," Bobby went on, "are difficult because there are too many clues. Some because there are few or none. This case is exceptionally difficult for both reasons. There are no physical clues. Any there may have been at Angel Alley were destroyed when the flooring collapsed—unfortunately before any thorough examination had been made. But the case simply bristles with motives of all kinds. We can pin a motive on almost every one concerned. But of course a motive isn't proof, or anywhere near it. Any one may have a motive for murder without ever even dreaming of committing it."

"Lady Geraldine's body was found in some sort of hide-out in the East End, I believe," Gurth said, and now his voice was perfectly steady and equable.

"A hide-out very carefully hidden," Bobby agreed. "Most elaborate precautions were taken, and the place itself was care-fully chosen. A high blank wall opposite, which meant no inquisitive neighbours on the watch. The shop people say they saw nothing and know nothing. In working hours they were always busy in the shop, and outside working hours they never went near the place. They don't think there was often any one upstairs during the day. Gas, electricity, water, were all laid on from the shop services, so that even the gas and water people and so on didn't call at the flat upstairs. They generally paid their rent, after deducting payment for gas and the rest of it, by dropping what was due through the letter-box of the side door. The whole business thought out to the last detail."

"I don't know anything about it," Gurth repeated. "I had no idea anything of the sort was going on."

"I must ask you a personal question," Bobby said. "I ask it because a letter was found in Lady Geraldine's bag. It was from you. I think it may fairly be described as a love-letter—even a passionate love-letter."

"I suppose you had to read it," Gurth said angrily.

"Letters found in a murdered woman's handbag can hardly be regarded as private," Bobby answered. "What were your relations with Lady Geraldine?"

"I wanted to marry her," Gurth said. "She wouldn't say anything. That's all."

"I must apologize for mentioning it," Bobby said. "But I'm probably not the first to have noticed your unusual good looks. I'm told it's hereditary in your family. Certainly Colonel Godwinsson had them when he was a young man, and he's a most striking, impressive figure still. Your brother Leofric, too. I imagine that you've often found women aware of it."

"It didn't seem to make any difference to Gerry," answered Gurth. "All she did was to rag me about it. Plenty of girls wanted to flirt, if that's what you are getting at. Some of them made beastly nuisances of themselves—especially the older ones. Made me sick, some of them. Gerry wasn't like that," and again his voice shook with an emotion he could not wholly control.

Bobby found himself wondering if Lady Geraldine's in-difference to Gurth's good looks had not been a main factor in attracting him to her. And that that attraction had been strong, possibly even passionate, Bobby felt convinced. Probably Gurth had grown tired of the easy conquests he so often experienced, and had found a challenge and an incentive in her indifference. Into what strange and dreadful paths might not that passion—if indeed so strong a word could be justly used—have led him?

Grim possibilities there, Bobby felt, and yet at present suppositions only. On a sudden impulse he got up and from behind a filing cabinet, where it had been inconspicuously hidden, he took out the umbrella found in the rooms over the Yates shop. He laid it on his table. Gurth said:

"That's mine. How did you get hold of it?"

FRIENDLY CHAT

"So I UNDERSTAND," Bobby said. "We'll come to that later on."

"Why?" Gurth asked. He had a challenging and uneasy air. "What about it?" he demanded. "It's my umbrella all right. What's the idea?"

"The truth, the facts," Bobby told him. "Two murders committed, and perhaps a third in contemplation. It entitles me, I think, to ask for full co-operation. Police are pretty helpless without the help of the public. It is they who do the work. We only take the pay and the credit—or blame. Generally the latter."

"Well," Gurth muttered. "Well."

"I am taking it for granted," Bobby went on, "that you wish to see the murderer of Lady Geraldine brought to justice. It seems to have been a very specially brutal affair, very deliberate. I am sorry to press you, but this may be important, and I do beg of you to give me a perfectly candid answer. Had you any reason, even the slightest, to think that any one else was more fortunate? With Lady Geraldine, I mean."

"Well, of course, I wondered," Gurth admitted. "She always said there wasn't. Plenty of chaps hung around her, but she never seemed to take much notice of any of them."

"There seems to have been a clergyman, a Mr Brown, who came to see her fairly often," Bobby remarked, and this produced from Gurth a faint and passing smile.

"That blighter?" Gurth said. "Sort of religious maniac. He came to cadge for subscriptions—pretended he wanted to convert her, but it was her money he was after. He tried to convert me once. I'm afraid he hadn't much success. I shut him up. I told Gerry to cut him out. He used to upset her with his talk of hell fire and all the rest of it. My own idea is she paid up as a kind of insurance. Regular fanatic—tried to look shocked if any one even said 'damn.' I expect he said it himself and worse when he was alone."

It was Bobby's turn to smile now, for, if his own suspicions were right, he thought Gurth's remark was much nearer the truth than Gurth himself probably imagined. He opened a drawer of his table and took out the photograph of dead Joey Parsons, taken in the hospital mortuary and touched up later to make it look as much as possible like that of a living man. He passed it across the table to Gurth.

"Do you recognize that now?" he asked. "I showed it you once before."

"There's a likeness," Gurth said after he had studied it for some moments in silence. "I told you so. I'm not sure. I only saw him once or twice. Different somehow. There's a queer sort of look about it. It isn't that Cy King man you were talking about, is it?"

"We haven't established identity yet," Bobby answered, "but it's not Cy King. So far as you know, then, though Lady Geraldine had plenty of admirers, there was no one she seemed to favour?"

"No, there wasn't," Gurth said positively, and Bobby was inclined to think that his eager and jealous eye would soon have noted and resented any sign of preference Lady Geraldine had shown.

"What about your brother, Leofric?"

"Leofric?" Gurth repeated. "Good Lord, no! What on earth made you think of him? You do get some cracked ideas."

"Oh, yes, rather," Bobby agreed whole-heartedly. "And sometimes the most cracked of the whole lot turns out the right one. You feel sure, then, that Leofric ..."

"He hardly knew her. He was away on foreign service nearly all the war years. Besides, he was Mona Leigh's meat, poor devil."

"You mean she was in love with him?"

"Oh, definitely."

"More so than he was with her?"

"Definitely. But he hadn't a chance. That girl knows just what she wants and means to get it. I told him once his only chance was to run for it."

"What did he say?"

"He said she could run faster."

"I think you know he is in hospital after a somewhat mysterious attack on him near the place where Lady Geraldine's body was found?"

"Yes I've been there. They won't let anyone see him—not to talk, that is."

"You know, too, that he was held for questioning after the theft of the Wharton jewellery?"

"So was every one else, weren't they?"

"No. Questioned, yes. But not held."

"Well, they let him go again—with apologies."

"You know also that he is believed to have been seen near Angel Alley shortly before a man named Joey Parsons was. murdered there."

"No, I don't, and I don't believe it," Gurth answered. But he had paused before speaking, and his manner was not very convincing. "Look," he said more firmly, "I'm not going to say anything about Leofric. Ask him yourself anything you want to know. I don't think you have any right to cross-examine me about him."

"None at all," agreed Bobby. "But I haven't. For one thing, our talk hasn't been a cross-examination at all—an examination-in-chief, if anything. Cross-examination doesn't mean close questioning. I should have preferred to say we had been having a friendly chat. And I haven't asked you any questions about your brother. I asked about your personal knowledge of certain facts concerning him, facts that seem both relevant and important."

"What you mean, I take it," Gurth said, speaking slowly and deliberately, as if he felt a need to choose his words, "is that you've heard Leofric has been a bit rackety. He's not the only one. It takes a bit of time to settle down after you're demobbed. Especially when it's been foreign service nearly all the time. Has Mona been saying anything? I expect you would try to get it out of her. That Wharton jewel business did it. After that she felt it was her mission in life to save him."

"Save him from what?"

"Oh, bad companions."

"She never hinted anything of the sort to me," Bobby said.

"Didn't she? She tried with the dad once, and got put where she belonged. The dad wouldn't stand for any one trying to come between him and one of us. Pretty big ideas he has of the rights and duties of the head of the family."

"The 'patria potestas'?" Bobby asked, smiling; and Gurth looked surprised, as if wondering how a mere policeman could ever have heard of it, but said nothing. Bobby went on: "You had an elder brother, hadn't you?"

"You mean Harold? A half-brother. The dad's been married twice. The Germans got hold of the poor devil at the beginning of the war and shot him out of hand. Called him a spy, and afterwards said it was all a mistake and how sorry they were. I never saw him."

"How was that?"

"Oh, under his mother's will he forfeited his money if he came to England before he was thirty, I think it was. I forget. To preserve him from the 'corrupting influence of outworn British feudalism and keep his American democratic instincts uncontaminated'. I think that's how the will put it. France was as near as he dared come. The dad went to Paris once or twice to see him there. I don't gather they hit it off very well."

"To go back a little," Bobby said. "Did Colonel Godwinsson share Miss Leigh's feeling that your brother was getting mixed up with bad companions?"

"Ask him," Gurth said with a shrug of the shoulders. "There's not much he does miss, and not much he says till he has it all, and then he drops on you like a ton of bricks. Well, if that's all, what about my umbrella? Can I have it now?"

"Sorry," Bobby answered, "but I think for the present we must ask you to let us keep it—exhibit so and so. When did you lose it?"

"I don't know exactly. I missed it a few days ago. How did you get hold of it?"

"It was on the landing outside the room where Lady Geraldine's dead body was found."

Gurth hesitated, stared, was silent. It was evident that he was slowly beginning to appreciate the significance of this. Bobby waited. There was a long pause before Gurth said:

"I don't even know where that is—Angel Alley, I take it, or thereabouts." He stared at Bobby defiantly. "All I can say is that I lost the thing and I can't say when or where."

"Did you report the loss to the police? It seems quite valuable, and good umbrellas are as scarce as most things."

"No. I never thought of the police. I was expecting it to turn up somewhere. Look. Has all this anything to do with the Cy King, was it, you were talking about?"

"Not that I know of," Bobby answered. "Why?"

"I've noticed a rather shady-looking customer hanging about the garage where I keep my car. I didn't take much notice beyond wondering what he wanted. But then later I thought I saw him again near where I live, and after that I noticed him in the Tube. I rather thought I would speak to him if I saw him again. Anyhow, I haven't. Of course, it may have been only my fancy."

Bobby asked him to describe the man. Gurth's description was as vague as is that given as a rule by the untrained observer. But it could have applied to Cy King, though no doubt also to many thousands of others. Nothing at first sight to distinguish Cy King from any other of those shabby, furtive inhabitants of the borderland between crime and just not-crime who are only too plentiful in London at present. All the same, disquieting in view of the threats that Tim Stokes had reported and so clearly believed in so implicitly.

"If you see him again," Bobby said, "let us know at once. Mention my name, so that I can be told immediately. Cy has gone underground. There's no charge we can bring against him at present, but we could pick him up for questioning. Not that that will do much good. Still, it would let him know we were watching. It might prevent his carrying out his threats—that is, if he has really made them. I don't think I need trouble you any longer, Mr Godwinsson, though I may have to bother you again. In the meantime I am deeply grateful for the information you've given."

"I didn't know I had," Gurth said with a slightly disconcerted air, as though that was the last thing he wished to do. He got up to go. "I don't see what right you have to stick to my umbrella," he complained.

"Oh, I do hope you won't object," Bobby said amiably. "You see, it really is important. Of course, it will be returned in time. Meanwhile, if you could remember when and where you lost it, it would be a great help."

"I've no idea," Gurth repeated. "I may have left it anywhere. I may have forgotten it at the office, and one of the cleaners may have taken it. Or one of the clients, for that matter. You get some queer customers sometimes in a stockbroker's office. I don't know. Or, for that matter, I might have left it in Gerry's car. She gave me a lift sometimes."

Bobby let this pass without comment. It was a possible explanation, of course. But also a suspiciously convenient one. As with Mona's story, no confirmation. Gurth was on his way to the door now, Bobby having filled in the slip that would take him past the constable on duty at the entrance. With his hand on the door-knob, Gurth said:

"I suppose what all this means is that you think I may have done it?"

"Every one connected with the case is under suspicion," Bobby answered gravely. "We can't be sure of any one's innocence till we are sure of some one's guilt."

"Well, now, then," Gurth muttered; and, with sudden passion breaking through the self-restraint he had hitherto preserved, he burst out: "God in Heaven, man, I loved her!"

"Even love is sometimes a reason," Bobby said, and Gurth made no answer but went slowly away.

CHAPTER XXX

CONSULTATION

LEFT ALONE, Bobby sat for some time, doing his best to sort out in his mind the impressions received from his talk with Gurth. He had he felt learnt this time things that were probably both important and significant. Presently he took a half-sheet of paper and on it wrote down slowly the names of all those who, so far as he knew, had been in any way concerned with recent events.

First the Godwinsson family, the colonel and his sons. Next the others, Monica Leigh, Ex-Sergeant Stokes, Cy King, even Pitcher Barnes; and, finally, the two victims, Lady Geraldine Rafe and Joey Parsons, since the part these two had played seemed essential to understanding the problem. Underneath, in block letters, the very care with which he formed them indicating, by an odd contradiction, the doubts and hesitations in his mind, he wrote:

"Motive: (A) Jealousy. (B) Theft. (C) Mixed A and B. (D) Unknown."

With this in his hand he went to consult a senior colleague. Not that he wanted to, or hoped for any special result, but he knew his own highly individual methods were often criticized severely, and that he was sometimes accused of playing for himself and not for the team. He suspected that this was one reason why his position in the police hierarchy was not yet very clearly defined and why he was still chiefly employed as what he himself called a 'back-room boy'—that is, in lecturing to new entrants and in refresher courses to men back from the services.

Now his senior colleague, glancing at Bobby's half-sheet of paper, shook a doubtful head. He expected a report to be submitted in triplicate, with plenty of red-ink headings, a wide margin for notes, and to be at least a dozen pages long. Half-sheets of paper he could not help regarding as highly irregular.

He said finally:

"When you stress motive and insert '(B) Theft', presumably you are referring to the Wharton case?"

"That and others," Bobby answered.

"Although the Wharton jewels have been returned?"

"I think," Bobby explained, "that it is precisely their return which is causing the new trouble. Whether Cy King was one of the original gang I don't know. But I'm sure that he is in it up to the neck now. Hi-jacking, very likely. I don't know. But it's clear he thinks he has been what he calls double-crossed. Hurt his vanity, lowered his prestige with his pals, disappointed his hopes. He may feel he has got to reassert himself at all costs, so as to stop the rot. Afraid of being given away by one of our contacts unless he keeps them all in terror. His sort rule by terror, and if he doesn't keep it up he won't be able to trust his pals to do what he wants."

"Shouldn't wonder," the senior colleague commented, "if Cy King hadn't been the prime mover from the start."

"It's possible," agreed Bobby cautiously.

"Got one or two murders to his credit already," said the other. "Not much doubt of that."

"Very little," agreed Bobby again, less cautiously this time. "Don't want another, do we?" declared the senior colleague, and glared at Bobby as if challenging him to deny it.

Bobby didn't. It was indeed his chief preoccupation at the moment. He said:

"That's the danger. Anyhow, he is the prime mover at the moment, whether he was from the start or not."

"Only there's this," remarked the other doubtfully. "Is he the type to fit up the sort of place you found? Room of the Seven Lusts, that sort of set up?"

"That may have been Lady Geraldine's doing," Bobby suggested. "No telling. Lot of careful planning there, and Cy King's speciality is action—tactics, not long-term strategy." The senior colleague grunted and turned again to that half-sheet of paper he privately so strongly disapproved of. He said:

"How much do we really know about these Godwinssons—the colonel and his sons?"

"Not very much," Bobby answered. "I feel sure it was Colonel Godwinsson who was seen talking to Joey Parsons in Canon Square, at the car park there, shortly before Joey was killed. He denies it. I don't accept his denial. He was clearly very worried about, and felt responsible for, Lady Geraldine. He knew she hadn't returned home. He may simply—and innocently—have been trying to find out where she was. If so, while he wouldn't tell a lie to save himself, he very likely would lie himself black in the face, in his old-fashioned way, to save her. A point of honour to lie to protect a woman. Old-style version of the rate for the job. I haven't put that idea to him yet. I didn't feel the time was ripe. Perhaps it is now."

"Waiting for the time to be ripe," complained the other. "That's what you always say. Means missing the 'bus as often as not."

"There's always a risk," Bobby agreed. "Colonel Godwinsson's own method, by the way. I'm told he says nothing till he is sure, and then comes down like a ton of bricks. A concentrated offensive when your preparations are complete, but not before. The Montgomery plan."

"What do you think of him personally?"

"Of Colonel Godwinsson? I think he is the most dignified, impressive personality I have ever met. His standing in the community is the highest possible from every point of view. He would probably have played a much more prominent part in the world, but for the old tradition he seems to take quite seriously of his family's rightful claim to the throne. But, then, his retired manner of life has in one way given him even greater influence. No possible suggestion of self-seeking, and it's not every one you can say that of to-day. In an odd way, too, his family tradition makes him very democratic—inclined to favour labour claims. The ancient royal idea. All are equal before the king, and his duty to protect all impartially."

The senior colleague was looking very impressed. He was a man who had risen from the ranks and had not yet fully freed himself from the most insidious fault of the police in all countries—respect for persons and position. Now he suggested a trifle uncomfortably:

"Sort of bloke we have to handle with kid gloves?"

"Or he might raise a stink," Bobby agreed; "that would ruin all our chances."

"Oh, well," said the colleague resignedly, "kid gloves for the colonel. That's understood. What about this son of his? Gurth, you called him. New name to me—is it German?"

"Good old Saxon from before the Norman Conquest," Bobby explained. "Chief thing we know is that he was deep in love with Lady Geraldine. Witness his letter we found in her handbag. Then there's his umbrella. Highly suspicious, but no proof. You can't judge a man from the umbrella he loses. He has his explanation pat."

"Looks like," said the other, "as though he may have followed the lady to this love-nest of hers and killed her there in a fit of jealousy—and possibly Joey Parsons afterwards to cover up. Fits O.K. Only was the love-nest all her own, or was there some one else? Could it have been Gurth all the time?"

"It could," Bobby said. "It has to be considered."

"What about the other lad? Leofric, isn't it?"

"Well, Mona Leigh is in love with him—more so than he is with her, according to Gurth. I'm inclined to accept that. He seems rather a weak character—the Godwinsson strain rather run to seed. The general idea one gathers is that he comes very easily under the influence of others and finds it difficult to get free again—a sort of mingled loyalty and obstinacy. Weak characters often show it. Then we know he was picked up after the Wharton robbery and that an attempt was made to kidnap him by Cy King and his pals. Why? What they wanted with him isn't clear. Probably they thought he might know something about the Blackamoor pendant and the Charlemagne jewel supposedly not returned with the rest of the Wharton stuff. And he is reported as having been seen near Angel Alley shortly before the murder there."

"And what," demanded the senior colleague, "does all that add up to?"

"Very little," Bobby confessed. "But if we can fit it in with what else we know, or think we know, it may prove helpful."

"What about Miss Mona Leigh, apart from her being in love with Leofric Godwinsson?"

"Well, she seems a very determined young woman who knows what she wants and means to get it. An example of Bernard Shaw's theory of woman as the eternal huntress. Like the Canadian Mounties, she always gets her man."

"My old woman got me all right," agreed the senior colleague, "but she gave me a hell of a chase first. Are we to accept her Putney Bridge yarn? Bit melodramatic—send the shivers up your back and play for sympathy? That it, do you think?"

"Well," Bobby said thoughtfully, "there's no telling. No outside confirmation. But there is the way she seemed to get more and more scared, remembering. As if she hadn't quite understood at the time but now it was beginning to register. She may have been acting. All women act by nature—born to the job. She denies she was jealous, but of course she was, and, on her own story, Lady Geraldine thought so. There may have been good reason for Mona's jealousy. She may have followed Lady Geraldine on her own. If she did she may have taken the opportunity to rid herself of her rival. Quite easy, if Lady Geraldine took too much to drink and dozed off, to put a cushion over her face and hold it there as long as necessary. No telling what a jealous woman won't do. Jealousy—temporary insanity. But fully responsible."

"In my opinion," said the senior colleague, speaking with authority, "no woman is ever completely sane."

Bobby let this profound aphorism pass unchallenged. Later, when he repeated it to Olive, she gave it a grave and thoughtful assent, pointing out that only a degree of insanity could possibly account for any woman getting married. At the moment, however, Bobby contented himself with remarking that so far they had been talking of the jealousy motive only. But there was the stolen—and now returned—jewellery to be remembered. That, and no emotional entanglement, might be where the solution lay.

"We haven't been able to get proof," he said, "but I think we are safe in following up the idea that Lady Geraldine was working in with a gang of expert jewel thieves. It was her job to give them information—such items as where it was kept, when it was going to be worn, when it was going to be taken out of banks and safe deposits and so on. We always felt something of that sort was going on. And now, on the evidence of the rooms where her body was found, there was some sort of emotional tie-up as well."

"Gurth Godwinsson?" asked the senior colleague.

"We've been into that as far as we can," Bobby said.

"Cy King?" suggested the senior colleague. "He seems the sort of elemental male brute that does occasionally attract some women—God knows why."

"I know," Bobby agreed. "Of Human Bondage," he quoted. "And that doesn't always mean the man going under to a woman. Just as often the other way round."

"Joey Parsons? Where does he come in?"

"Which of him?" asked Bobby. "He turns up as all sorts of different people, and we can't be perfectly sure it's always the same. He was certainly also the Kilburn householder, for there we have his wife's identification. For the rest, there's only the evidence of the photograph—and that taken after death. Was he also the fanatical parson who preached hell fire and bullied subscriptions out of Lady Geraldine, and was he as well the jolly business man who took an interest in the boys' club? Probable, but not certain. Nor is there anything that we know of to connect him with the Room of the Seven Lusts. All we can be sure of is that he is dead—or one of him."

CHAPTER XXXI

TIM STOKES TELLS

It was the next morning when Bobby, immediately after breakfast, went across to the garage where he kept his car, that one of the men employed there came forward to meet him.

"There's a bloke waiting for you, sir," he said. "Don't know what's the matter with him—all in a twitter like. He wanted to wait inside your car. I told him to go to hell. I said, didn't he know where you lived? Like a lump of jelly, he was, and I let him sit on the footboard. He's there now on the off side, where no one can't see him."

Bobby nodded, went towards the car, and was not greatly surprised when, as he approached it, he saw ex-Sergeant Stokes peeping at him over the bonnet.

"What's this mean?" Bobby demanded sharply. "What do you think you are doing here?"

Stokes emerged cautiously.

"I've been warned," he said, and wiped a perspiring forehead. "After this," he said earnestly, "I'll get a good, steady, respectable job. I know where there's one going. Attendant at the—" and he named a night club in a Soho side street, a club Bobby was not quite sure could be classed under the heading 'respectable', even in these tolerant days, when psycho-analysis has shown us that the Ten Commandments are merely rather mischievous repressions of our natural instincts.

"Well, Stokes, that's your affair," Bobby said. "But what are you dodging about here for?"

"It's Cy King," Stokes muttered, and looked nervously all round, as if half expecting to see him lurking and sidling in the background. "I've been warned," he repeated.

"I've warned you myself," Bobby told him. "To keep away from Cy King. But I don't think a night club like that one in Soho is the place to do it. Your affair. Do you mean Cy King has been talking to you again? I rather want to talk to him myself."

"No, not him; a youngster name of Eddy Heron heard him talking about me."

"Eddy Heron?" Bobby repeated. "Oh, yes, I know—that's the boy who wanted to get locked up safe out of the way, only our chaps smacked his behind and let him go instead. What about him?"

"It's what he heard Cy King saying—called me a copper's nark trying to get back to be a cop again. Not much chance of that," he added, glancing hopefully at Bobby.

"None at all," Bobby told him, and Stokes hardly looked disappointed, so well had he known what the answer would be.

"Cy's been saying more than that," Stokes went on. "He's been saying it was me did in Joey Parsons."

"Well, did you?" Bobby asked.

"Me? I never," Stokes cried. "Mr Owen, sir, you can't be thinking that. I know I was in with Joey a bit more intimate than I said, but I hadn't seen him or had anything to do with him for a week or more before he was put out. I was keeping out of his way. He got the idea I was nosing after that Lady Geraldine Rafe. I don't deny I wanted to know for sure where she came in—a swell like her. And where they met, because I knew they must have a rendezvous on their own. Joey said the boss had noticed it and if I didn't get out and keep out I was liable to find myself in the river with my throat cut. So I wasn't sorry when I heard Joey had got his; and that's why I went along to the hospital where I met you, Mr Owen, if you remember, so as to make sure. Because I thought it was evens Joey was the boss himself, though he always let on he didn't do more than run errands. And now there's Cy King saying the same about me going in the river," and once again he looked nervously around as though still half expecting to see Cy King there, waiting for him.

"You had better report to the D.D.I.," Bobby told him without much sympathy. "They'll give you all possible protection—and that's a lot more than you deserve."

"You can be very hard, Mr Owen," Stokes said with a kind of mournful reproach. "Cy's been saying it might be a good idea to fix me with Joey's murder, and then the busies wouldn't want to go messing other people about."

"You've nothing to be afraid of," Bobby told him. "If you are innocent, that is. Any information given us will be tested on its merits. I doubt if it will come from Cy King, though. I shall be very surprised if he comes any nearer us than he can help. He knows we have plenty of questions we want to ask him. Why should he think you shot Joey Parsons?—that is, supposing you didn't."

"Oh, Mr Owen, sir," Stokes wailed, "you can't think that."

"Why not?" Bobby asked. "For one thing, how is it you knew so soon what had happened, and how did you know two shots had been fired? That grazed ear-tip hadn't been noticed by any one else. You pointed it out immediately, though the light in that mortuary place was none too good. Any explanation?"

Looking sulkier than ever and with considerable reluctance, Stokes offered one. It seemed, according to him, that the dead man had asked him to come to Angel Alley just to have a drink together. No harm in having a drink, Stokes said defiantly, and Bobby agreed. But on his arrival he was told that two shots had been heard at No. 4, and the voice of one crying out aloud. So the rest of Angel Alley had decided it was best to hear, see, and know nothing, and had retired indoors.

"Is all that why Cy King thinks it was you?" Bobby asked. "Anyhow, you were on the spot, weren't you?"

"Only after the shooting, as I can prove," Stokes declared. "Cy don't think it either, not him. And me innocent as the driven snow. What's put him on me so cruel like is the Wharton jewellery job. I had a drop too much one night, and I let on I knew more than I do. Swanking I was. All I knew really was that Joey was in it. Cy got the idea the Wharton stuff was in Joey's own special hide-out all the boys knew he had, though they didn't know where, and didn't ask, neither. One of 'em put it up to Cy that maybe it was me did in Lady Geraldine, so as to get the stuff, and then did in Joey, too, to cover up. Spoke in malice that was, out of spite, because of having it in for me. But Cy never believed it. Not him. Nor no one else, neither. They couldn't."

"Well, it's an idea, all the same," Bobby remarked. "I've considered it myself." Stokes gave a kind of inarticulate groan of protest. Unheeding this, Bobby went on: "Does Cy think that after all that it was you sent the jewellery back?"

"Because of it's being too hot," Stokes answered. "That's what he says. And to put in a claim for the reward afterwards, and some of it still missing he's saying most like I've got put away, and me that never saw a shine of it, or handled it neither."

Bobby recognized again the rumour he himself had started, to the effect that all the stolen jewellery had not been returned. He had listened very carefully and very thoughtfully to all Stokes had been saying, and was still in much doubt. Cy King's theory was one he had himself considered and had certainly not abandoned. Was it the correct theory, and was Stokes simply trying to forestall an accusation he knew would shortly be made? A cunning move, if it were so, this attempt to create a presumption of innocence by a show of frankness.

"All I can say," he told Stokes again, "is to repeat that any information we receive is always tested on its merits. And I think if I were in your place I should go at once to see Mr Ulyett—he is back on duty now—and make a full statement, telling the truth and telling all you know."

"But I don't know anything," Stokes protested. "What's the use of me saying what I think? All I know for certain is what I've told you, Mr Owen, and not a thing more. I guessed it was her ladyship was the pipe-line. But I wasn't sure. I knew Joey was in it, but I didn't know how much. I don't mind owning up I got a few quid now and then for a bit of help in an accidental sort of way. Joey would pass the word to meet him, and he would say the boss—he always said the boss—wanted to know about police routine and such like, where they were planning a job. Or it might be helping to rehearse or prospect. Careful they were; everything had to go like clockwork. But never more than that with me, and

I never knew their plans, or wanted to. If I knew the time—and I generally didn't—then I took care to be as far away as I could and be able to prove it. And now Cy King trying to make out I was in the thick of it from the start."

"I shouldn't be greatly surprised if he wasn't right," Bobby said. "Or are you doing the same thing now? Do you know there's a fresh job on, and are you trying to establish an alibi? Is that it?"

Stokes hesitated, so much so that Bobby began to wonder if this more or less chance shot of his had hit the mark.

"Mr Owen," Stokes said at last, and now even more nervously than before, "there's another thing, but—well, it's this way. If Cy got to know, I would be for it, if it was the last thing he did. Quick and sure. That's why I wasn't having any when the bloke here tried to push me off, telling me to go round where you lived. 'Get to hell out of here,' he said, and cost me half a crown to let me stay on."

"Ah, yes," Bobby said; "he told me the rest, but forgot the half crown—slipped his memory. Well, get on with it if you've anything else to say. I can't wait here all day, talking to you."

"Watched I am," Stokes repeated; "and so's where you live, and if I was seen near, Cy would know it in an hour, and I would be dead in two."

"Rubbish," Bobby said, though by no means with conviction, for he knew his Cy King.

"It's that young Eddy Heron told me, for he's to drive the car."

"What car?" Bobby asked impatiently.

"The car Cy King and Miss Leigh are going in to Colonel God-winsson's this morning."

CHAPTER XXXII
MUMPS

Bobby allowed no sign to escape him of the surprise and even dismay he felt at this statement Stokes had just made. He found himself wondering if he had been entirely mistaken in the view he had taken of Mona's character and actions, and once again he thought of her story of Putney Bridge and his earlier doubt of its truth. That earlier episode, too, when he thought he had rescued her from Cy King's brutality. Had that been all a sham, staged to instil into his mind a conviction of her innocence? He remembered how differently she seemed to impress different people. His first idea of her had been of a young, quiet, and gentle girl. Others who knew her better had since described her as 'knowing what she wanted and meaning to get it.' Was it possible the 'it' had not been merely, or even chiefly, the man she loved, but that she had a darker, more desperate aim? Bobby saw that Stokes was looking at him in a slightly puzzled way, as if wondering why he was silent. Bobby said:

"You mean you think Mona Leigh works in with Cy King?"

"Well, looks like it, doesn't it?" Stokes asked, apparently slightly surprised by the question. "Pretty plain, I should say. Same as her ladyship pal. Both in it together. If she isn't, why is she going to Colonel Godwinsson's place with him?"

"How do you know she is?" Bobby demanded.

"Eddy Heron told me. He heard Cy talking on the 'phone."

"You can't believe a word that young scoundrel says," commented Bobby.

"Well," Stokes answered, "he says he wants to run straight now and stand in with the cops, after the way they treated him decent and friendly. He says he's fed up with his pals you can't trust and it's different with cops. Know where you are."

"How does he mean they treated him?" Bobby asked.

"It was when he tried to get sent down so as to be out of trouble's way, put safe for a while," Stokes explained. "They upended him and smacked him good and hard, and then they gave him a good feed and a talking to—told him he was too young to have a record, and if he liked they would find him a job. Hard work and low pay. Only Cy King heard, and got hold of him for fear he knew too much and talked. So now all he wants is to get away from Cy and a chance to get the job he was promised."

"One way to bring about reformation," Bobby remarked. "I am sure every modern psychologist would strongly disapprove."

"He means it," Stokes said. "I wouldn't mind myself seeing a kid like that keeping straight. It pays," and Bobby guessed Stokes was thinking regretfully of that good job he had once held as station sergeant and then thrown away—chiefly on dog-racing tracks. Stokes added: "It's him asked me to tell you so you could help if you would."

"Wait here," Bobby said, and went across to the garage office, where he asked if he might use the telephone.

First he rang up the hotel where Mona had taken a room for the time, and in reply was informed that Miss Leigh was not there. She had just gone out. A car had called for her, and she had left in it. She had not said when she would be back, and no one had noticed either the car or its driver. No reason why any one should notice either the one or the other, declared the thin, distant voice, its tone somewhat resentful. Perfectly ordinary proceeding in every way, wasn't it? The hotel wasn't the Gestapo—this last with a distinct suggestion that Bobby was himself trying to emulate that somewhat unpopular institution.

So next Bobby rang up the Yard to explain that some fresh information had just reached him. It might or might not be important, but he thought it seemed worth following up, and he was motoring to Ing Wain, Colonel Godwinsson's place. Finally he rang up the county police to ask that an experienced man, as senior as possible, should be sent to Ing Wain, as there was a chance of developments there. The request was received without enthusiasm. Bobby was asked what developments, and his reply that he had no idea was again received without enthusiasm. Even when he went on to explain that a man named Cy King was concerned; and that Cy King was certainly dangerous, probably desperate, and possibly intending to meet accomplices, the county people remained unimpressed. They had only dimly heard of Cy King as one of those gangsters who, thanks be, usually confine their activities to the big towns and leave country police districts in peace. And they were quite certain that at Ing Wain Colonel Godwinsson was fully capable of dealing with any number of Cy Kings. Bobby tried to explain there might be more to it than that, but he could not, and indeed dared not, be more explicit. One could not, and one should not bring vague accusations against a man of Colonel Godwinsson's high and unblemished character without considerably more to go on. What he did say left the county police even less impressed. They remarked that they had work of their own to do. The batch of orders, counter orders, directives and counter directives that had come in this morning had not even yet been sorted out. And they were desperately short-handed. Scotland Yard might be able to spare men for hypothetical trips here or there, but they found it difficult. However they would, of course, do their best to get hold of some one as soon as possible and dispatch him to Ing Wain. In the meantime they would ring up the village constable and warn him to be on the alert. Bobby, grateful for small mercies, thanked them profusely, said how much he appreciated their help, and rang off; not without reflecting that the word 'appreciate' has two meanings—to estimate correctly as well as to esteem highly. See the *Concise Oxford Dictionary*.

Then he went back to his car and the waiting Stokes.

"I think we had better pay a visit to Colonel Godwinsson's place," he remarked. "Just to see if anything is happening there. Jump in."

"Me?" exclaimed Stokes, startled. "I don't—"

"Jump in," Bobby repeated, cutting short his protests. "You're coming, too. Get a move on."

The dismayed Stokes, in whose programme this visit to Ing Wain had no place, still tried to protest. Bobby, in no mood for half-measures, took him by the scruff of the neck and pushed him into the seat next the driver's.

"You sit there," he commanded. "I'm not having you slip out behind when I stop for traffic lights, and I'm not leaving you here to ring up Cy and tell him what I'm doing."

"I never would," Stokes protested. Bobby started the car. Stokes wailed: "It's abduction, that's what it is. Kidnapping."

"Shut up," Bobby snapped and added: "I'm not letting you out of my sight just yet—not till I know more. I don't trust you in the least. Your story may be true, and it may be faked. It sounds fishy enough, goodness knows. What can Cy King possibly want with a man like Colonel Godwinsson?"

"Maybe," answered Stokes, "maybe because Colonel Godwinsson is the boss Joey Parsons used to talk about."

"Rubbish," said Bobby, but uneasily. "A man in his position."

"Best cover going," Stokes retorted. "Look at Lady Geraldine. Never thought of suspecting a tip-top society dame, did you? Not you," said Stokes viciously. "Run in a bloke like me soon as look at him, but quite different when it's ladyships and colonels. I know. I've been a cop myself."

"There must be reasonable ground for suspicion," Bobby answered, though defensively, for there was just a touch of truth in Stokes's complaint. "People like Colonel Godwinsson, and with a record like his, seldom get mixed up with gangs of criminals. There must be a good case before any action can be taken."

"Look at the facts," Stokes retorted. "I've seen him myself talking to Joey Parsons, though I didn't know then who he was. There's things Joey said I couldn't make sense of at the time. But now I can put them together. Look at the way his colonelship is all mixed up with her ladyship that's had hers, and with Miss Mona Leigh, too—Lady Geraldine's guardian he was, and now the Leigh girl coming to Ing Wain with Cy King. What I say is that very likely Joey Parsons was sort of deputy chief and go-between. But now he's been outed and there's got to be some one to take his place, so the colonel has thought of Cy King, and Miss Leigh is taking Cy along to talk it over with him."

"You've got your imagination in good working order," Bobby remarked, in part amused, in part not amused at all.

"Imagination?" Stokes repeated indignantly. "It's facts. Facts is what I go on. Facts. There's that love-nest over the grocer's. The way it was done up. Shows it was an old 'un. Old 'uns need stimulating. Young 'uns just go to it, and no need for funny work round the walls."

"Well, I don't know but that the psychologists mightn't agree with you there," Bobby admitted. "Psychology is not an exact science, though, and human nature is very much of a variable."

He was driving fast; as fast as permitted his respect for the law and for the crowded condition of the roads—especially the latter. They reached the village, and Bobby drew up before the small cottage that served both as official and private residence for the local constable. A woman came to the door and looked disappointed when she saw Bobby.

"I thought it was Dr Lake," she said.

"Is any one ill?" Bobby asked.

"Mumps," answered the woman gloomily. "First it was Tommy—that's our boy. Now it's Dad; and just rung up to say there's suspicious characters near the colonel's and to keep a look out. Which can't be, when it's mumps."

"Have you reported it?" Bobby asked. "I'm a policeman, and I'm on police business."

"I've rung up the skipper," the woman answered, using the expression often applied by country police to their sergeant. "He's promised to send a relief as soon as he can, but they're that short-handed."

Bobby gave her his official card.

"If a relief turns up," he said, "tell him to report to me at Ing Wain at once. Ring up your skipper again and tell him I'm here and ask him to get in touch with his chief for instructions. I'm going on to Ing Wain now."

Leaving a slightly bewildered, more than slightly doubtful woman still examining his card, he drove on. He found the entrance gate at Ing Wain standing wide open.

"No sign of any car," Bobby remarked as they drove up the long, curved drive towards the house.

"No," agreed Stokes, "but there's Pitcher Barnes."

Bobby had seen him, too, strolling formidably to and fro, like a sentry on duty, before that clump of rhododendron bushes through which, and then over the orchard wall, Cy King had escaped on a previous occasion.

They had reached the house now. Bobby stopped the car before the front entrance and locked it. Almost at the same moment, with a crash of breaking glass, a man dived through a window on the ground floor and fled as fast as his feet could carry him towards those rhododendron bushes and the waiting Pitcher Barnes. Fast and faster still he ran; and as fast Bobby followed; while from the house, through the broken window, sounded the shrill cry of a woman, lamenting in terror and in grief.

CHAPTER XXXIII

AMONG THE RHODODENDRONS

THE DISTANCE from the house to that great stretch or clump of rhododendrons was not more than two or three hundred yards, though a little farther from where Bobby had halted his car before the front door than from that shattered window through which the newcomer on the scene had made his sudden and dramatic appearance. He had, too, a good start—a flying start, in fact—and though Bobby ran at his best speed he could see there was small hope of overtaking him. Probably, Bobby told himself as he ran, a car or motor-cycle would be in waiting once more on the road beyond the orchard.

From behind there followed him the loud crying of a woman's voice. By the car Stokes stood hesitating, wanting very much to disappear, but too afraid of Bobby to dare to do so. In front of the rhododendrons Pitcher Barnes stood and gaped as Bobby and the other runner fled towards him. He was directly in the path they were taking. He could see Bobby, and recognized him. Bobby, losing all hope of overtaking the fugitive, slackened speed for an instant to shout to Barnes to stop him. The thin, shrill crying from the house continued and reached him, carried by a strong wind that was blowing. Pitcher, his dull, slow-moving mind urged by Bobby's command, moved forward.

"What's up?" he called, and Bobby was near enough to hear him. "What you been doing, Cy King?"

Cy probably misunderstood his gesture, misinterpreted his intention. Pitcher was standing right in Cy's way. Bobby saw something flash in the sunlight, saw Cy's arm swing forward, saw Pitcher's arm go out in ready, trained defence to take the coming blow but too late, saw him go reeling back and then sit slowly on the ground.

"He knifed me," he said loudly and with surprise. "A pal didn't ought."

The momentary scuffle, the slight delay, a loss of timing and footing as Cy delivered his thrust and swerved to avoid Pitcher's defence, enabled Bobby to draw nearly even. Cy vanished into the tangle of the rhododendrons, running through them half bent so that he was not visible, but alert and fierce, his knife poised ready in his hand for thrust or throw. Bobby made no attempt to follow immediately on his track. Instead he plunged straight through the bushes to the orchard wall, and then paused and turned, facing the rhododendrons, between them and the wall.

"The game's up, Cy," he called. "Better come quietly. It's always easier in the long run. What about it?"

From somewhere among the bushes a voice called:

"Come and get me."

"Nothing doing," Bobby answered. "You can't stop in there for ever, you know, and I'm in no hurry." He took out a cigarette and lighted it. "I can afford to wait," he said. "You can't. Time on my side, as every one used to say in the war." To this there came no answer. Bobby had not much expected one. He thought how lucky it was that Cy always professed such faith in the knife alone, the silent knife that never missed, and such contempt for the gun, so noisy and so apt to miss. But now there came a flash, a sharp report, and the whine of a bullet passing over his head much too near for comfort. Another followed, again too high. Evidently this time Cy had departed from his usual practice and provided himself with a gun. Bobby—he could always move quickly when he wanted to, and this time he wanted very much indeed—hurled himself into the midst of the nearest bush. Another bullet came whining, searching, but again well overhead. Cy was making the usual mistake of the novice and firing too high. Bobby began to crawl slowly, carefully, cautiously, in the direction whence the shots seemed to come. Fortunately, the strong wind blowing kept the rhododendron bushes in continual motion, so that no unusual or unexpected movement of the foliage should betray him. Cy called:

"Put your hands up. Stand up. Walk off towards the house. You'll be all right then."

Bobby made no answer. He had no intention of betraying his position by speaking. Cy called again:

"Mr Owen, you hear me? I don't want any trouble. I didn't want any. It was that old geezer started it. All I meant was a friendly talk. See? Then he tried to hold me. I didn't want, not him at his age. But I had to dot him one to get away. Hear him cursing when I made my get away?"

Bobby took no notice, only crawled with caution a foot or two, a yard or two, nearer. It was not a man's voice he had heard, but a woman's, nor had it been raised in cursing, but in terror and in grief. Something other than 'dotting him one' had happened. Still more carefully, even more cautiously, every least movement guarded and slow, he extracted his handkerchief. From the nearest bush he cut with his pen-knife a strong twig or branch and trimmed it. He could find no stone where he lay, but he dug out a stiff hard lump of earth he thought would serve as well. Arranging his handkerchief on the end of the trimmed branch he had secured, he let it appear, but only just appear, as far away from where he lay as he could reach, where he thought a gleam of white, as it might be a peering face, would be visible through the drooping rhododendron leaves. Instantly two shots rang out, one, either lucky or well aimed, piercing the centre of the half-exposed handkerchief. Bobby, making his voice loud and shrill, cried out. Cy, his smoking pistol still in hand, ready to fire again, jumped up and ran towards where Bobby crouched. Bobby, half lifting himself, flung the clod of earth he had ready. He flung it with all his force, with desperation, with despair indeed, for he knew on how small a chance his hope of life depended. Almost at the same instant Cy saw him and swung his pistol up to fire. But by the tiniest fraction of a second the clod hit him first, hit him full in the face, and his shot again went wide. The impact of the clod of earth, breaking into fragments as it struck, staggered him for an instant. Bobby, with one great leap clearing the intervening bush, was on him before he could recover, and seized his pistol wrist, twisting it upwards, so that again his next shot, the last in the magazine, went harmlessly astray. Agile as a cat, Cy. Bobby slightly over-balanced from that great leap of his, twisted himself free and dived once more into the shelter of the rhododendron bushes. Bobby was left breathless and disappointed, but at least in possession of the small automatic Cy had used so ineffectively. It was only a point two two, though deadly enough at close quarters. Harmless now that its magazine was empty. Bobby put it in his pocket. He had no idea of letting Cy get possession of it again. Quite possibly Cy had another clip, and Bobby had no wish to serve as target a second time. He called:

"Well, Cy, had enough? Coming quietly now? There'll be some of our chaps here soon."

Cy replied by a string of lurid curses, showing himself as he did so behind the barrier of a great belt of rhododendron bushes.

"You come along," he said. "I'll get you yet. Why can't you leave a bloke alone? You come along where I am if you want me so bad."

"No hurry," Bobby told him. "You are a good deal handier with that knife of yours than you are with guns. A child with guns."

"They ain't no good," Cy agreed. He had been stooping before, but now he straightened himself, confident that the tangled bush between them gave sufficient protection against any sudden rush or leap Bobby might attempt. "O.K.," he said. He showed a knife, gleaming thin and deadly in his hand. "Now then," he said, "you keep away. See? Or you'll get this little sticker of mine in your ribs, same as Pitcher Barnes, same as that old geezer in the house."

"You mean you have murdered Colonel Godwinsson?" Bobby asked.

"It wasn't murder," Cy protested sullenly. Murder is a word none like. Not even the trained and skilled professional Nazi killer cares to use it. "Not murder," he repeated. "I had to. Self-defence. The old fool tried to hold me. Said he would hand me over to the cops. I had to out him. Self-defence. It's him that's the murderer, it's him did in those two—poor old Joey and his girl." He paused, expecting comment. None came. He went on: "Never thought of that, Mr Clever, oh so Clever. Something for you to chew on."

"What makes you think that?" Bobby asked. "Or do you?"

"Plain enough," Cy said. "Any one with half an eye could see that much. Hard up for coin, and that's the way he worked it, with her ladyship to help and Joey to do the dirty work. And then he outed them both to keep the lot for himself."

"What you would have done, no doubt," Bobby remarked. "Colonel Godwinsson has quite a good income."

"A bloke can always do with more," Cy pronounced with authority.

They were watching each other warily as thus they talked across the sprawling, intervening rhododendron bush. Bobby's eyes never left Cy's hand that held the knife. They were alert and watchful for the least sign of movement that hand might make, for well Bobby knew how swiftly, with what deadly accuracy of aim, Cy could send that weapon of his flashing through the air. And Cy watched Bobby with equal intensity of gaze, for well he knew on his side that if Bobby could once get within arm's length, then he himself, agile as he might be, would have small chance. Little desire had he to feel the weight of Bobby's fist, or of Bobby's grip upon his shoulder. Cy began to move. He could not afford to wait. Help for Bobby might come at any moment. He dared not risk a throw till he was sure. Carefully, never taking his eyes from Bobby, alert for any opportunity to use with clear certainty of aim, his skill in knife-throwing, he began slowly to edge away. As cautiously, as carefully, Bobby followed, alert for any opportunity to rush and close, but well aware that Cy was a thousand times more formidable with his familiar knife than with the automatic pistol he so little understood. There were stories that Cy could at twenty paces hit infallibly every time the exact centre of a playing-card. Bobby took off his coat and wrapped it round his left arm to use as a shield. His intention was to wait till Cy—as he must do, for he could not wait, and there was his only hope of escape—made his rush towards the orchard wall, which he must scale to get away. Towards it, he was slowly sidling his way, always careful to keep bushes between himself and Bobby, as guard and protection against any sudden rush.

He was doing this with a skill and care Bobby could not but admire. It seemed as though he had some uncanny power of perception that enabled him to pick his way without looking, for he never relaxed his watchfulness, never removed his intent gaze from Bobby, and yet managed always to keep the denser growths between them. Once or twice, indeed, he moved away from his objective, the orchard wall, so as to be appreciably farther from it, but always with the effect of finding a clear, protected passage through the bushes that brought him nearer again. His manoeu-vres had been so successful that now they were both quite close to the wall—not more than twelve or fifteen feet away—though Cy had managed so well that his own path thereto was fairly clear, while Bobby, though as near in distance, was cut off from it by a dense tangle of bush. That the moment had come was ev-ident; and Bobby, watching as those watch whose life depends on watching, saw Cy's right hand flash back. In the same instant Bobby dropped, but with his shielded arm held up, ready to take the knife. It did not come. Cy did not mean to throw till he was sure, and at the critical moment his attention had been distract-ed. He was cursing softly to himself. Bobby heard him mutter:

"Some one there." And when on this Bobby himself ventured a quick glance towards the house, he saw indeed that there was some one standing at the broken window through which Cy had dived a few moments before.

It was a woman. Bobby could see that much in the one swift look that was all he had dared allow himself, though he had not been able to identify her. She was running towards Stokes, who was still standing by Bobby's car, unable to decide what to do. Cy seemed to recognize her. He said as if puzzled: "What's she up to?" Then he said in a last appeal: "Mr Owen, you leave me alone and I'll leave you alone. What do you say?" Bobby said nothing. "I've a car waiting. Two minutes start. That's all I want. And if you try to stop me, Mr Owen, then your number's up. See? I've never thrown a knife yet, but I've got my man."

Again, and now more openly, he moved nearer the orchard wall. Evidently he had made up his mind that he dared wait no longer. Bobby followed, but still cautiously. He knew that last boast of Cy's was fully justified and he must take it at face value. Edging ever nearer the wall, with that slow, furtive movement of his, sideways and formidable, reminiscent of the panther prepar-ing to spring that Bobby had seen once before, Cy was now quite close to it. Bobby was nearer, too, and the bush dividing them was thinner and narrower. Cy's hand flew back. Like a leaping silver flame the knife flashed across the space between, and only be-cause Bobby had been so on the alert, watching so carefully with the experienced boxer's sixth sense of when the blow is coming and of its direction, had he time to leap to one side and avoid it.

The knife flew by, not three inches from his throat. In the instant when Bobby leaped sideways, and so for the moment lost balance to leap forward, Cy hurled himself upon the wall. He had only hoped the thrown knife would end the pursuit, he had been sure it would give him the momentary start he needed; that was, indeed, all he felt he needed. Was not Eddy Heron waiting there in a car, engine running, ready to tread on the accelerator and be off at thirty, forty, fifty miles an hour? One clear minute, that was all he needed. And he had gained it when Bobby had had to swerve to avoid the flying death passing so near.

Now, with all the wild, fierce energy that uttermost need can call from the strange and hidden reserves all men possess, he was already tumbling over the orchard wall, Bobby's grasping hand just missing his foot. He dropped, tumbled to the ground, and was on his feet again instantly, fleeing through the trees. He had gained perhaps another thirty or forty seconds, and his heart sang within him, for he thought he was safe.

His feet seemed hardly to touch the ground as he sped between the orchard trees straight towards the spot where he knew the wall could be most easily climbed, where a convenient foothold he had arranged, made it possible to reach the top of the wall in two swift movements. He would gain another minute there, he thought, for he knew exactly where to place hand and foot while his pursuer would have to fumble.

Time enough and to spare for him to leap into the waiting car, for Eddy to send it roaring down the road to safety and a sure escape. There was yet another car waiting at an appointed trysting place. To this they would transfer, and so proceed comfortably and calmly to London, while police cars were buzzing ineffectively, helplessly, hither and thither.

So he was safe, he thought, but when that calculated last leap of his brought him triumphantly to the top of the outer wall of the orchard, there was no car waiting there, no sign of it or of Eddy Heron either. Nothing to right or left but the empty road, and as

Cy stared incredulously, Bobby's hand grasped him by one leg and jerked him to the ground.

"Well, that's that," Bobby said. "The game's up this time, Cy," and Cy made no answer, but lay where he had fallen, glaring up with a kind of vicious, dull despair.

CHAPTER XXXIV

DESERTED HOUSE

HOLDING CY KING in a grip that was more secure than comfortable, Bobby made his way towards the gate that admitted from the orchard to the Ing Wain grounds and so on to the house. He noticed with relief as they went that Pitcher Barnes was no longer where he had last seen him, seated on the ground and coughing his surprise at receiving such treatment 'from a pal'. Bobby hoped this meant that Pitcher's wound had not been serious and that he had been able to seek assistance, possibly in the house.

But the house seemed deserted. Nor was Tim Stokes visible. The front door stood open, but when he rang the bell, hammered on the knocker, shouted at the top of his voice, there was no response. He could hear an odd, intermittent, dull kind of thumping and knocking, but it was difficult to tell from what direction it came or to guess its origin. Bobby, embarrassed by the necessity of keeping secure hold of a prisoner he had reason to know was as slippery as any eel, could not investigate. He shouted, but still got no answer. He dragged his captive across the hall, down a short corridor, and pushed open the door of the library—the room in which, on an earlier occasion, he had talked with Colonel Godwinsson. It was silent and empty. A shattered window, an overturned chair or two, the telephone overthrown and broken as though it had been trodden upon in a struggle—all this was evidence enough that whatever had happened, had happened here. Bobby said:

"It was here you knifed the colonel? Or was it somewhere else?"

"I never did," Cy protested. "It was all him. He didn't get no more than a scratch. Let me loose, guv., and I'll help you look for him. You can trust me." When Bobby took no notice of this impudent proposal, Cy said: "You're hurting my arm cruel, twisting it the way you are. You didn't ought."

"Why did you want to kill him?" Bobby asked. "Was there something he knew?"

"There you go again," Cy complained. "All I came for was a friendly talk. How was I to know he would go off the deep end the way he did? I put it to him straight, friendly like, as it was him done in Joey and Joey's girl. He said O.K., it was him all right, and would I take a thousand quid to keep mum? I said not for untold gold I wouldn't. No, I said. I said I would go straight to Mr Owen and help him all I could. Then he went all crazy. Jumped at me, said he would croak me same as he done the other two. Scared I was, proper scared. Him lit up the way he was, my life wasn't worth a moment's purchase. Only for to keep him off, I showed him my knife. Self-defence. Blessed if he didn't run straight on it, same as he meant it. S'elp me God, Mr Owen, that's gospel truth, that is. He meant it, he wanted it. Clean off his head. So then I reckoned all I could do was to make a get-away fast as I knew how. What would you have done in my place, Mr. Owen?"

"Taken care not to be in it," Bobby answered.

"There was me, and him with my knife run in him, and you know yourself," Cy went on, "how cops twist things against a bloke. Believe me or not, I never meant anything like that. But there it was, me innocent as the babe unborn, but appearances looking bad. No sense staying on when what was done was done and couldn't be helped. So I beat it fast as I knew how, and how was I to know," he asked reproachfully, "that you were there, ready to run a poor bloke down like—like," said Cy indignantly, "like a bloody bloodhound?"

"I suppose about the only word of truth in all that," Bobby remarked as he closed the door of the empty library and drew his captive back down the corridor to the entrance hall, "is the part about the thousand pounds. Which means, I imagine, that you were trying a spot of blackmail. Probably Colonel Godwinsson threatened to give you in charge, and you couldn't face that, so you knifed him and ran for it. Does that mean you are yourself the murderer of Joey Parsons and of Lady Geraldine?"

"Me?" demanded Cy, his voice rising almost to a scream. "Me? I never had nothing to do with it, only for thinking when I heard Joey had been outed, and it wasn't none of his pals and no one knew why, only most like it was about his girl, as how there ought to be a chance of getting hold of the Wharton stuff we all knew he had hidden somewhere. Angel Alley, like as not, and I might as well have it as the next man. Only then there was you again, at Angel Alley, always interfering, always busy. I only wish," he went on, and confirmed his wish with an oath or two, "I hadn't ever had nothing to do with it. Never had so much as a smell of the stuff, and look where it's got me. Me as innocent as can be, and you trying to pin a murder on me, and twisting my arm something cruel. It's hurting most awful."

"I expect it'll hurt worse presently," was the unsympathetic reply Bobby gave him.

They had reached the hall again now, and once more Bobby shouted, and once more he got no answer. The utter silence was, however, now broken again by a repetition of that strange, muffled thumping Bobby had heard before and that seemed to come from the direction of the library, though there was no one there.

Uncertain what to do, almost as much the captive of his prisoner as was his prisoner of himself, embarrassed, feeling even slightly ridiculous—'frustrated' is the fashionable word of the moment Bobby stood there in the hall. He wondered if there were cellars in which Cy could be locked till help arrived. But he did not know if any existed, or, if they did, how to reach them. Or for that matter if any of them could be securely fastened. He seldom carried handcuffs, and had none with him. If there had been any cord available he would have tried to tie Cy up. A difficult task that would be, though. A job for an expert, for Cy was agile enough to wriggle himself free from any but the most secure fastenings.

It began to look as if he would have to wait there, Cy and he, giving a kind of absurd Siamese-twin act, till help arrived. He supposed help might have been gone for, and that might be why the house seemed deserted. Why Stokes had disappeared, perhaps. What, then, had happened to Colonel Godwinsson? Had he after all been only slightly injured, and had it been possible to take him, or for him to go, in search of medical help, instead of waiting for it here? Or was perhaps his dead body lying somewhere in the house, and had the frightened inmates fled from it in horror and in terror? Impossible to say.

"A-i-ee, I can't bear it, Mr Owen, sir, I can't—my arm," Cy whimpered, and went limp in Bobby's grasp.

Bobby suspected this was largely pretence—at least, as far as fainting went. No doubt Cy's arm was hurting him, but Bobby had no intention of allowing that fact to interfere with the necessity of keeping his prisoner secure. With intense relief he heard sounds outside, and then a cautious and respectful knocking at the front door.

"Don't stand there," Bobby called impatiently. "Come in here, and quick about it."

A figure in uniform appeared, and regarded with considerable astonishment the odd spectacle presented of Bobby standing in the hall, supporting the limp figure of Cy. But now help had come Bobby was not inclined to support it any longer. He let it go thump on the floor, and Cy said: "Oh," rather loudly, for that had been unexpected. Then he said:

"Can I have a drink of water, please?"

"No," said Bobby, who was in no gentle mood.

"You Mr Owen?" asked the newcomer.

"Yes," Bobby answered. "You are the relief man, I suppose? I'm giving this man in charge—attempted murder. Have you handcuffs? Good. Fix this fellow up with them. But take care. He may wriggle free. Stay with him for the moment and watch out. If you let him escape, you'll be for it. Don't let him fool you with drinks of water or anything like that."

"Very good, sir," said the constable, and handcuffed Cy accordingly.

"I'll watch him. Colonel Godwinsson's place, isn't it, sir?"

"Yes," Bobby answered, "but there doesn't seem to be any one in. I've been shouting, but there's no answer."

"There's some one knocking," the constable said, listening to that recurrent muffled sound that had now begun again.

"It may be from upstairs," Bobby said. "I've not been up there yet. I'll have a look down here first, though."

Leaving Cy in the constable's charge, not without a further warning to take good care of a prisoner as cunning as a wagon-load of monkeys—a comparison which brought a faint smile of approval from Cy—Bobby made a quick tour of all the other rooms on the ground floor, including the domestic offices. All were empty. One or two were in dustsheets, as though in the present shortage of domestic help they had been closed for the duration—of the peace this time? Bobby came back to the hall, made sure that Cy was still safely in custody, and ran up the stairs, still calling as he went to know if there was any one at home, still getting no reply, still conscious at intervals of that recurrent rhythmic thumping.

The landing at the head of the stairs was spacious. There was a great window with window-seats and two suits of armour—genuine, not Birmingham—guarding it. Several doors opened from it, and two corridors stretched away to the remoter regions of the vast old house. He opened two doors into empty rooms. In the third were two people. On the bed lay Colonel Godwinsson, very still and pale, his eyes closed. By his side half sat, half lay a woman. Bobby recognized Mrs Godwinsson, whom he had seen in her invalid chair on the lawn during his previous visit. She had apparently collapsed. She opened her eyes when Bobby entered.

"Doctor," she murmured, "doctor ... I got him here ... Jane helped ... and a man ... they went for help ... I couldn't any more." More loudly she said: "Have you come too late?"

Bobby crossed to the bed. He thought at first that it was indeed too late. Collar and tie had been removed and the shirt undone, so that apparently some attempt at first aid had been made. A clean handkerchief had been placed in position, Bobby lifted it and saw a small incised wound. It had bled only very slightly, and Bobby thought that was no good sign. He thought there was little to be done till a doctor and further help arrived. With a wound of this nature, and probably interior bleeding, he did not dare try to administer any stimulant. He wiped the colonel's lips with a little brandy from the flask he carried and he felt the feet. They were very cold though they rested on a hot-water bottle. He said to Mrs Godwinsson:

"You have sent for a doctor—for help?"

"Jane went," she answered. "With a man. He was there. Aren't you a doctor? I thought you were. Jane had to go because we couldn't use the 'phone. It's broken. There's a man in the library. He's making a noise."

"I've been in there, in the library," Bobby said. "There's no one there."

"Yes, there is," Mrs Godwinsson insisted, "only you can't see him."

CHAPTER XXXV
GURTH'S STORY

Bobby made no attempt to ask for an explanation of this cryptic saying. Mrs Godwinsson was in no state to be questioned. She had sunk again into that kind of comatose condition in which he had found her. The mental shock of what had happened, the physical effort of getting the dying man upstairs, had plainly been too much for her. Bobby saw that she was fairly comfortable where she half lay, half sat. He found a cushion to put behind her back and another for her head to rest on. He took a coat, too, from a wardrobe to throw over her as a precaution against any risk of chill in the present lowered physical condition of her body, and then hurried downstairs again.

There Cy, handcuffed as he might be, was under careful watch, and could hardly move a muscle without being told gruffly not to try that on. His guardian had no intention of 'being for it', as Bobby had warned him, and in a tone that made the words sound ten times more formidable, he would be if he let his prisoner escape. To him Bobby said hurriedly:

"Colonel Godwinsson and his wife are upstairs. He has been stabbed. I think he is dying. He's unconscious. We can't do anything till a doctor comes. Mrs Godwinsson said there was a man in the library, but you couldn't see him. I don't know what she meant."

"It was him did that knocking," the constable said. "Hiding he must have been. Now he'll have done a bunk."

"It was all the old fool's own doing," Cy said. "Ran right on the knife same as he meant it, and me thinking no harm."

The sound of that distant, muffled knocking became audible again.

"Lummy," said the constable.

"Innocent," said Cy. "That's me."

"Come on," Bobby said to the policeman. "Bring him along—and watch him."

He hurried the constable and the handcuffed and sullen Cy, still muttering about his 'innocence', down the corridor to the library. As he did so he said that if they couldn't find any one, the constable had better cycle back to the village and use the 'phone to report to his superiors and to make sure that help was really on the way.

"It was only to do my finger nails I had the knife out," Cy said. "How could I tell he was going to chuck himself right on it?"

They came to the library door. Bobby threw it open.

"No one," said the constable. "Done a bunk all right. Look at that window."

"That was Cy leaving in a hurry," Bobby said.

"Well, there's no knocking now," said the constable.

As he spoke it began again. Bobby shouted. There was no reply, though he thought the knocking increased in energy. It seemed to him to come from behind one of the book-lined walls, the one to the right of where they stood in the doorway. He went nearer and listened. The knocking was louder now. On one shelf the books, a series of heavy tomes of eighteenth-century sermons, seemed in disorder, and one had even fallen to the floor. He swept them in an armful to a chair conveniently near. With the books went a thick, felt pad that had been behind them, so that now a voice came through quite clearly.

"For God's sake, let me out, quick," it was calling, and Bobby, in some bewilderment, said:

"Who are you? Where are you?"

But now he could see that behind where the books and the felt pad had been was a small panel in the wall, pierced with tiny eye-holes. Through them some one was peering, and from behind it came the voice, shouting again:

"Don't waste time. Get me out of here. The door's locked. I'm locked in. Hurry up."

"How do I let you out?" Bobby asked. "And who are you?"

"I'm Gurth—Gurth Godwinsson," the voice answered. "My father's been murdered. I saw it. I couldn't do anything. I'm locked in. Get the key. Don't stand gaping there. Where is he? My father, I mean. Is he there?"

"He is upstairs in his room," Bobby answered. "Mrs Godwinsson is with him. I am afraid he is badly hurt. Help has been sent for. There is nothing much we can do till it comes. Where is the door? Is it behind these shelves?"

"There's a knob in the woodwork at the top on the right," Gurth told him. "Get a chair or something to stand on, and you'll see it. Press it down hard till it catches. It's stiff. When it catches the shelves swing out, if you pull."

Bobby followed the instructions given. But when the central portion of the shelves swung out in obedience to the pull he gave them, release did not seem much further forward. True, a careful look showed the outline of a door, though so cunningly and well fitted into the wall as not to be immediately visible. There was a tiny keyhole, too, close inspection revealed, but there seemed no way of getting the door open.

"Hurry up," Gurth called impatiently. "I can't stop here for ever."

"I can't move it," Bobby said. "It must be locked. Where can I find a key?"

"Dad must have it," Gurth told him. "It'll be in his pocket. Or in a drawer of the writing-table. Look there first."

Bobby did so. There was blood on the leather-covered surface, but only a little. He opened the drawers in succession. There was no key, but in one drawer pushed away at the back was a pistol of that same somewhat rare, now obsolete make, from which, in the opinion of the experts, had come the bullets causing the death of the man found in Angel Alley, whatever his right name might be. Bobby looked at it thoughtfully and gravely, and then with precaution put it in his pocket. Gurth was calling impatiently to know if the key had been found. Bobby said:

"It doesn't seem to be here. I'll go and look upstairs. I'll be back as soon as I can. Tell me first. Did you see what happened."

"I saw it all. I heard it all," Gurth said. "Dad told me a man was coming to try to blackmail him. Dad wouldn't say what about, but he wanted me to be a witness, and I saw it all—everything."

"And me all innocent and unbeknowing," Cy exclaimed indignantly. "A dirty trick," he pronounced.

"Let Mr Godwinsson see him," Bobby said to the constable, who promptly pushed Cy into Gurth's line of vision.

"That's the man," Gurth cried at once. "Thank God you've got him. I tried to get out—when I saw Dad jump up, I mean, and try to collar him. The door wouldn't open. I tried all I knew, but I couldn't budge it. I must have shaken it, and shaken the shelves behind, because the books fell down and blocked my view. Dad had fixed them so I could see, but after they fell down, I couldn't. I hadn't any idea he had locked the door."

"I'll be back as soon as I can," Bobby said again. "I think I can hear a car at last," he added with relief.

He hurried to the entrance hall. It was a doctor summoned over the 'phone from the village. Bobby explained briefly and took him upstairs. There he shook his head gravely over the colonel's condition and said that he wasn't in a fit state to be moved. He did not say, but Bobby felt sure he thought, that the end was not far off. What was immediately needed, Bobby helped him to do. It was agreed then that the constable should drive back to the village in the doctor's car, taking with him that perpetual embarrassment, Cy King, for safe disposal. First, though, he must summon over the village 'phone the fresh help needed, and then report to his superiors. Efforts Bobby made to find the key of the secret chamber remained entirely unsuccessful, and as soon as he could Bobby returned to say so to the imprisoned Gurth.

"I'm afraid you'll have to wait till we can get a locksmith," he said. "There were keys in Colonel Godwinsson's pocket, but none small enough to fit this lock. It must be quite tiny—keyhole's not much bigger than a pin point. Of course, it may turn up somewhere. There hasn't been time for a real search."

"How is my father?" Gurth asked.

"The doctor's doing what he can and he's sent for more help—a nurse and so on," Bobby answered. "But he isn't being very optimistic at present. I am afraid you must be prepared for the worst, though of course one can't tell for certain. There is always hope. Just now there is nothing to do but wait. The county police will be here before long, and I've asked them to bring a locksmith in case the key doesn't turn up. Will you tell me a little more fully what you saw and heard and why any one should think they had a chance of blackmailing Colonel Godwinsson? Did it seem to be something Cy King thought he knew about your father? Or was it about you? Or your brother, Leofric?"

Gurth hesitated. When he spoke at last it was with restraint and caution. He said:

"It was all so sudden."

"Take your time," Bobby said. "This place where you are— what is it? Some sort of secret room? Is it properly ventilated?"

"There are air-holes somewhere, up near the ceiling," Gurth explained. "It's the old priest's hole. Been here for centuries. Some one, years ago, had the idea of fixing it up as a kind of strong room. That's when the lock was fitted. Every one knows about it, of course."

"You could see all right through that kind of Judas arrangement?" Bobby asked.

"Oh, yes, till the books toppled over when I started hammering at the door to try to get out," Gurth answered.

"Yes, I see," Bobby said. "How did it begin? Did Colonel Godwinsson say what the blackmailing idea was founded on, or who was affected? He himself, that is, or you or your brother? Of course, you understand you needn't answer if you don't wish to, and that I shall be asking Cy King for his side of it presently."

"Dad said he was being accused of having murdered Gerry. Well, you know ... I laughed."

"Yes," Bobby said. "What else?"

"I told Dad to let me handle him," Gurth said. "I wanted to kick him out and then tell old Tommy Layton—he's the Chief Constable here. He's a very decent old boy, old friend of Dad's and all that. Same school tie. But Dad said he wanted to hear what the fellow had to say, and he asked me to wait in this place. Now I can't get out. He fixed the books so I could see and hear what was going on. So I could all right till the books toppled over."

"Yes. Go on," Bobby said.

"Dad brought in that fellow you've got," Gurth said. "He said a lot I couldn't make head or tail of. He said a lot of rather filthy things, quite ridiculous, about Dad and Gerry and about the rooms where he said Dad used to meet her.

I would have wrung his neck for half what he said, but Dad listened quite coolly. I suppose it sounded too silly to get angry about. Dad was the cleanest-living man possible. Then he accused Dad of having murdered her. It didn't sound real. I started by being angry, but it began to sound such perfect, utter nonsense I got to feeling more like laughing. And what do you think was the reason why Dad was supposed to have murdered Gerry?"

"What was it?" Bobby asked.

"Jealousy. Being jealous of some one he called Joey. And then, by way of piling it on, he said Dad had murdered Joey, too. But if Dad would put down a thousand quid, then, he would keep quiet. If not, then he would go straight to Scotland Yard. I can't imagine why Dad listened for so long. I suppose he wanted to see what was coming next."

"Possibly," Bobby agreed. "Was your name mentioned or that of your brother, Leofric?"

"There was something," Gurth admitted reluctantly. "I couldn't get it exactly. I think it was something about it being through us two that the chap said he had got on to Dad's being in it. I can't be sure. It was like listening to a madman."

"Colonel Godwinsson didn't say anything?"

"He just sat there, listening—at least, he did till the chap brought that out about the thousand quid to keep quiet."

"What did he say then?"

"He asked the chap if he was serious, and anyhow he was taking a big risk, wasn't he? Talking that way to a man he thought was a double murderer, and why shouldn't a double murderer be a triple murderer, too? So now he was going to wring the chap's neck and bury his body down in one of the cellars out of the way where no one would ever look for it. Of course, he was only meaning to give the chap the scare of his life."

"Yes," said Bobby. "Go on."

"I had to laugh," Gurth repeated. "It was funny to see the chap's face. It was rather silly of Dad, though. It wasn't safe with a scoundrel like that. You see, he thought Dad meant it."

"Yes," said Bobby again. "Go on."

"I saw the chap bring out a knife, and Dad jumped up. I tried to get out then, but I couldn't. The door was locked. I didn't see it all, because I was trying to get the door open and it wouldn't, and then those books fell over and blocked it so I couldn't any more. Look at my hands. Can you see them? They are bleeding a bit still where I banged at the door. It was no good. I couldn't do a thing. I just had to watch. I saw Dad had hold of the chap, and I saw his knife go in and out and Dad fell across the writing-table."

"There is blood on it," Bobby said. "A little. Not much."

"I couldn't see the rest," Gurth went on. "I told you. I couldn't do anything at all. I had to watch my father being killed and there was nothing I could do. My God! What made him lock the door so I couldn't get out to help him?"

"I think that was why," Bobby said. "I think he wished you to know, but not to be able to interfere."

"You aren't going to pretend," Gurth said, "you aren't going to pretend you think there could be even a word of truth in all that mad, fantastic tale?"

"Sometimes," Bobby said, "the truth is both mad and fantastic, too."

CHAPTER XXXVI
CONCLUSION

WHILE BOBBY HAD been talking to the imprisoned Gurth, various sounds had proclaimed the arrival in full measure of the help that had been sent for. Now the door of the library opened and there came in two people. One was a locksmith, who set to work at once on the door of Gurth's prison. The other was a nurse, who seemed a little excited.

"It's Colonel Godwinsson," she said. "We thought he was dead, but now he isn't, and he says he must see you at once—I mean, you are Mr Owen, the police gentleman, aren't you?" Bobby said he was, and hurried upstairs. On the landing he was met by the doctor, looking almost as flushed and excited as the nurse.

He was dead, he said angrily, for he was a man of science, and resented it bitterly when the established and accepted dogmas of science seemed flouted by mere brute fact. "I'll swear he was. Every sign of it. And now he's sitting up. Giving orders. Told me to go. As if he had the right. Absurd." He paused and gave what was meant for a contemptuous laugh, but Bobby noticed that all the same he had obeyed. "Something he wants to say to you."

Bobby went into the room. The nurse and the doctor followed, the doctor still muttering crossly that when a man died he was dead and ought to stay so. Mrs Godwinsson had been taken to another room. Colonel Godwinsson was sitting upright in bed. He was most strangely pale, but his eyes blazed with such an inner light as Bobby had never seen before. He had always had an impressive air, a kind of poise and absolute assurance that had made him seem almost majestical in this our present world of tumult and confusion. And now there was about him, too, a hint of something far off and remote, as if he had returned from some distant land with new authority. His voice was strong and clear as he said to Bobby: "You have arrested a man. You are to understand that he is innocent. What he did, I did through him. He had a knife in his hand, and I forced him to use it against me."

"Everything you say will be put in evidence," Bobby told him. "How exactly did it happen?"

"It was his hand and his knife," the colonel repeated, "but my action and my will. While we talked, I was willing him to kill me. It had become necessary. None of the House of Godwinsson has ever committed suicide, and I could not be the first. We die fighting. But it was necessary for me to die, for I could see that you had guessed the truth, and I knew that you were sure to drag it out, sooner or later. But though he felt my will, he was afraid. A man willing to kill, but only in the dark; ready to stab, but only in the back. At last I had to use threats. I had to use force to make him use his knife."

"If there is time," Bobby said, "I will put what you say in writing for you to sign." He had his note-book out and was taking the colonel's words down in shorthand, though indeed his stenography was more than a little rusty. He said: "Luckily there are witnesses." He turned to the doctor and nurse standing near. "Please listen very carefully," he said, "and try to remember the exact words. It may be very important." He turned back to the colonel. "Colonel Godwinsson," he said, "I think you know you are a dying man."

"I have died already," the colonel answered in the same strong, resonant voice so that every syllable was clear, spoken with emphasis and decision. "Ask the doctor. He knows. But I came back because there were things I had to say."

The doctor looked more angry than ever, and was evidently about to utter a protest, but hesitated, not quite knowing how to phrase it. Bobby motioned to him to be silent and said: "Tell me this, for there is justice to be done—justice to a child. Why did you kill your eldest son, Harold Godwinsson?"

"You knew that?" the colonel asked. "You knew it was my son I killed? How did you know?"

"When he was dying, his last words were 'Don't do that, Dad',," Bobby answered. "Strange words, I remembered them. I wondered what they meant. I began presently to think I knew."

"I thought there must be something like that," the colonel said slowly. "Ever since I saw his photograph lying on the hall porter's desk at the club. I knew it was a sign." He paused and said more slowly still: "Till that moment I thought it would all remain hidden and none would ever know how the House of Godwinsson had ended. But when I saw that photograph lying there—the photograph of my eldest son whom I had killed—then I knew my deed pursued me and that some day all the story would be told." He smiled faintly, indulgently, as if at some hopeless, rather pathetic childish effort he only dimly remembered. "I tried to put you off by showing you an old photograph of myself as his. I hoped it would make you suppose Harold was like the rest of the men of our family—tall and fair, 'goodly in form and face', as the old chronicle says of us. But Harold took after his mother's side. He was like her father, very like. Not like me, no trace of Godwinsson in him. In body or in mind. His mother went off with him to America. That was how it began."

Bobby wondered if rather it had not begun with the old man's almost insane family pride, that was apparently the chief cause of his first wife's leaving him. But that was immaterial. He remarked instead:

"It was that photograph convinced me when you showed it me. It was clearly of a much earlier date than you said. It ought to have been taken somewhere about the nineteen twenties if it had been of your son, Harold. It showed a group of young men. They nearly all had on straw boaters, and none of them were wearing Oxford bags as they used to be called. Several had small union jacks in their button-holes or portraits of popular generals. But in the twenties boaters were out of fashion, and so was patriotism. No self-respecting young man at that time would have dreamed of sporting a union jack. Moustaches, too. I looked up a volume of *Punch* while the Boer War was on. The whole set-up of that photograph was there, just as it was entirely different from the set-up twenty years later. And again you told me Harold had never been in this country owing to a clause in his mother's will. But that photograph's background showed this house, so either he had been here, or else the photograph was of some one else. If so, then clearly you wanted me to believe that he was tall and fair and handsome like your other sons, and that made it equally clear he was none of those things. The man known as Joey Parsons was none of them either, so was he perhaps Harold Godwinsson? Why did you kill him?"

"His identity, yes," Colonel Godwinsson said. "You reasoned that out well enough. But why should you think I killed him? Why shouldn't it have been one of his associates?"

"Why should you try to hide the killer of your son unless you were that killer yourself?" Bobby retorted. "None of his associates had any motive, but in your library there was a treatise on the *'patria potestas'* as the old Romans used to call it. And that treatise had been read. I remembered your claim to ancient and royal descent. If Harold Godwinsson, your eldest son, had become a common criminal—for he was, I think, the head and chief of the gang who got hold of the Wharton jewels I think you found at Angel Alley where Cy King looked for them too late, and that then you returned. And if he had made himself known to his younger brother, Leofric, and was trying to entice him to become an active member of the gang; if you knew he had already succeeded in enlisting your ward, Lady Geraldine; if you knew that he had murdered her—did you?"

"He told me he had, he boasted of it," the colonel answered. "He said she had become a nuisance. She was trying to make him marry her, and he said he couldn't. He didn't say why. Only that it was impossible. But she was threatening that unless he did, and unless he cut loose from his gang and went abroad with her, she would tell the police. He laughed about it. He said she was weakening, her conscience was troubling her. But it meant he had to get rid of her. He boasted of what he had been doing. He had a plan of your flat, he said, and he was going to burgle it, just to show his friends you were nothing to be afraid of. He said he had worked for the Gestapo. He said he was going to get hold of Leofric in spite of all Mona Leigh could do. He said he would very likely have to get rid of her, too, if she went on meddling. He had let her off once, but never again. He had been a fool to do it that once."

"He told you Miss Leigh was working to save Leofric from him?" Bobby asked.

"That's what he said. Apparently she knew Leofric was going to meet him at Angel Alley. Leofric told her something, and she guessed the rest, and that it had to do with the Wharton jewels. It was at the room at Angel Alley where I found them in an old tin box. She is in love with Leofric, I think. I don't know about him. You can ask her. She is coming here to-day. Her uncle rang up to say so. He is bringing her. They want to see me. They'll be too late."

This, Bobby supposed, cleared up the story Stokes had told, and the apparent confirmation it had received when Mona's hotel stated that a car had called for her and she had left in it. Evidently the car had been that of her uncle and solicitor. Bobby said:

"Harold admitted he worked in France for the Germans?"

"You hadn't known that?"

"It seemed likely," Bobby answered. "No proof, though. But the details sent you of his supposed execution were so detailed, so thorough, so carefully official, that they had either to be true—or else faked by the German authorities themselves. All strictly official on the highest plane and backed up by private letters from an old friend. But if Joey Parsons were in fact Harold Godwinsson, then all that was official faking and could only be because the Germans meant to make use of him. I expect when they arrested him they gave him the choice of being shot out of hand as a spy or of working for them. Very likely talked him into believing it didn't mean more than making himself useful in establishing good relations with us when England surrendered. Only England didn't surrender, and once they had him compromised, the rest was easy."

"The rest was easy," Colonel Godwinsson repeated. "Yes, perhaps it was. There was the boys' club, too. Harold boasted that that was where he picked up his best recruits. He kept on laughing and saying he was telling me all about it because there was nothing I could do without bringing everlasting shame on the House of Godwinsson. So I shot him. It was a surprise to us both," he added simply.

"As soon as I can get this written out," Bobby said, looking at the shorthand notes he had taken and hoping they would prove readable, "I will get you to sign it."

"Yes. What was that you said about a child?" the colonel asked suddenly. "Harold wasn't married."

"There's a wife and two children—boy and girl. All perfectly legal and in order, as far as I know. On one side of him, your son seems to have been a good husband and father, fond of his family and his home. Perhaps in time he would have settled down with them. It's possible. Hostages given it may be, not only to fortune, but to Heaven, too."

"Who is she—the wife, I mean? You said there was a boy? The estates are entailed on male issue."

"The eldest child is a boy," Bobby answered. "I think your son met her when she was a waitress in a cafe at Southend. A working-class family. Good stock. Parents dead, I understand; but she has one brother, a foreman road-cleaner for the borough council and a sergeant in the Tower Hamlets during the war. Fine record. Means he is both capable and responsible."

"The child will be heir, then," the colonel said. "Don't let him grow up in dreams and die in truth—like me."

He closed his eyes, sighed heavily, and lay back. The doctor bent over him. He said:

"He is dead; but, then, so he was before."

"I don't think he will return a second time," Bobby said.

"But what," asked Olive, looking very puzzled, after Bobby had finished telling her on his return home how these things had fallen out—"what is going to happen now?"

It was Bobby's turn to look puzzled.

"As far as I can see," he said presently, "nothing very much. So far as the public and the records are concerned, the two murders will have to be regarded as unsolved. Colonel Godwinsson can't be tried for killing his son, because he is dead. And his son can't be tried for murdering Lady Geraldine, because he is dead, too. I imagine the verdict at the adjourned inquests will be murder with insufficient evidence to say by whom. Mona Leigh will get her Leofric, and very likely she'll make a man of him. If she had been more frank with us, it would have saved a lot. But she wasn't going to say anything to get her man into trouble. Probably she never knew for certain how far he was involved in the Wharton jewel robbery. Not very deeply, I think, or Harold Godwinsson wouldn't have been trying to get him into the job of disposing of the loot. It's pretty clear that's why Leofric was hanging about the Angel Alley area. For that matter, Harold hinted as much to their father. It will be an equal shock to Harold's widow to learn the truth about her husband and to know that her son is heir to probably the oldest family name in England—not to mention substantial landed estates. I expect the child will be made a ward in Chancery. I don't know. Possibly with the two uncles, Gurth Godwinsson and the foreman road-sweeper, as joint guardians. There may be a try on to squeeze the road-sweeper uncle out, but if he has any sense—and I think he has lots—he won't stand for that. He has both the right and the duty to look after his sister and the two kids. I must have a talk with Eddy Heron. We owe him something, both for the information he gave and for his not having waited where Cy King told him to. Even if he did get it all wrong about Mona Leigh. If he hadn't cleared off with the car, Cy would have got away again. Quite possibly Eddy will turn over a new leaf. The smacking our chaps gave him, quite indefensibly, seems to have impressed him a lot, taught him that even cops can be human. He has earned his chance, and he shall have it. Odd if he turns into a cop himself. He is due for the Army soon, and if he comes out with a good record, and if the Army has bucked up his physique, as it does sometimes, we might take him on. Cy King will get off much too easily. We can have him for resisting arrest, for attempted blackmail, conspiracy perhaps. You can often work that in. But nothing that will get him anything like the term he deserves—which ought to be life and a bit over. At least," Bobby added, but without hope, "unless the Public Prosecutor boys can think up something else. Not likely. That outfit can only think up things to show there isn't sufficient evidence to convict any one of anything."

THE END

Lightning Source UK Ltd.
Milton Keynes UK
UKOW04f1403260716

279281UK00001B/9/P